TORTURED

Jason and Azazel, Book Three
V. J. Chambers

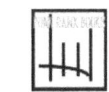

Punk Rawk Books

TORTURED
© 2009 by V. J. Chambers
www.vjchambers.com

Punk Rawk Books

ISBN: 978-0-9841206-3-5
Printed in the United States of America

10 9 8 7 6 5 4 3 2 1

TORTURED

Jason and Azazel, Book Three
V.J. CHAMBERS

PART ONE

But, now, uncertain of the length
Of this, that is between,
It goads me, like the Goblin Bee—
That will not state—its sting.

—Emily Dickinson, "If you were coming in the Fall"

CHAPTER ONE

April 17, 1990

Professor Weem commented on my paper to the entire class today. He said it was the best discussion of ancient religions he'd seen in all his years as a teacher. All of the girls in class hate me even more than they did before. Everyone has a crush on Professor Weem. Even though I'm learning more here than I ever imagined, sometimes I just want to go home.

Above me, the stained glass windows loomed in the darkness, fractured pictures, casting multi-colored bits of light over the wooden pews. Back when the Sol Solis School was first built, and it was a monastery, and this building was the church. Now we used it for assemblies and performances. I was lying back on one of the pews. My boyfriend Jason was kissing me.

I tried to pay attention to the softness of his lips, to the hard curves of his muscular chest against my body. But I couldn't help but stare up at the stained glass.

It was late at night. Jason and I had snuck out of our dormitories to meet each other here. Jason could pick locks and get us into pretty much any building on campus. Except the library, of course. Jason could have picked the lock without any problem. But the library was always guarded. It was frustrating, because the whole reason we'd come to the Sol Solis School was to get into that library.

Jason brushed a stray hair out of my face. He looked deep

into my eyes. "Azazel?" he whispered.

"What?" I said, shifting uncomfortably on the wooden pew.

"Are you okay?" he asked.

I nodded. "Fine," I said, attempting to smile.

He kissed me again, closing his eyes. I tried to close mine, but they fluttered open again. I looked back up at the stained glass above me. We were making out in a church. A church. And we'd planned to come here to do more than make out. I eyed the stained glass suspiciously, feeling ill at ease.

As if in response to my thought, Jason eased his hand under my shirt, his fingers cold against my skin. I jumped.

Jason pulled away. He sat up. "You aren't into this, are you?" he asked.

I sat up too. "I'm into it," I said. And I was. Hadn't I been wanting to be with Jason for months?

"So, then how come you're so tense?" he asked.

"I'm not tense," I said.

Jason sighed. "Hey," he said, "I thought we promised to be honest with each other."

Jason had been brutally honest with me. He'd shared with me his darkest secret, something he'd never admitted to anyone. Something he'd barely admitted to himself. His mentor, Anton, had come to him one night, telling him that he'd found out things about Jason. That Jason wasn't the Rising Sun, or the messiah of the world, but actually a thing of evil. Anton had tried to kill Jason but Jason had killed him first. Jason had told himself over and over that it wasn't

8

really his fault. That it was the fault of the Sons themselves, who'd made Anton believe in things like the Rising Sun or things of great evil power. But Jason had finally told me about it. He'd been honest. I owed it to him to be honest too. Still, this hardly compared. This wasn't some dark secret that I had. This was just something I was too uncomfortable to talk about.

Jason folded his arms over his chest.

I shot one more look up at the stained glass windows. "Well," I said, "we *are* in a church."

"It's not a church anymore," said Jason. "Besides, what are you afraid of? The wrath of God raining down on us or something?"

"No. Not exactly. But, you know, weird things do happen to us, Jason. Especially when we kiss."

Like driving a group of men absolutely insane. Or Jason coming back from the dead.

Jason laughed. "Yeah, okay, point," he said. "But I think we're okay here. No one comes in here at night. And it's been so long." He reached for me again.

I ducked out of his grasp, chewing on my lip.

"What?" he said. "What is it?"

I shook my head. "Nothing," I said.

Jason sighed. "Don't do that, Azazel. It's something. It's something or you wouldn't be trying to get away from me when I want to touch you."

"I'm not trying to get away from you!" I said. Honestly, I didn't know what was wrong with me. I wanted Jason. I did.

I loved him more than life itself. And we hadn't been able to do more than hold hands since escaping from Shiloh two months ago. We'd been living with a group of monks in Rome most recently. Now we were attending the Sol Solis School, the same boarding school my younger brother Chance attended.

It was just that in the past couple months, everything had gotten so serious between Jason and me. Everything had been so focused on what we were trying to figure out. I'd almost forgotten about this part of our relationship. "Shouldn't we be focusing on how to get into that library?" I asked Jason.

"The library?" he said. "We are. We're trying to figure something out. But we've only been at school here for two weeks."

"I know that," I said. "But it's why we're here, isn't it?" Jason and I were trying to find some ancient documents on the history of the Rising Sun. We wanted to know why we'd been able to do the weird things we'd done when we were kissing. We wanted to know if we had supernatural powers.

Jason had been brought up to believe he was the Rising Sun, a savior of sorts for the human race. It was prophesied that he would unite the world under a global government and usher in an era of peace and prosperity. My Satanist family had groomed me as the Vessel of Azazel (a Jewish demon). My purpose had been to destroy Jason and stop him from uniting the world. Jason and I had fallen in love. I hadn't killed him. Ever since then, all kinds of very strange things had happened to us. We'd been chased by one organization or another across the United States. Finally, we'd taken refuge here in Italy. But we had questions and it seemed that no one had any answers. We were hoping that the answers were here.

"It's not why we're here tonight," Jason said, gesturing at the walls of the old church. "We're here tonight to—"

"I know," I said, cutting him off. I took a deep breath and leaned in to kiss him.

His arms went around me, pulling me tight against him. His lips parted mine with his tongue. His fingers lightly stroked my back, the nape of my neck.

I pulled away again. "What if we tried to distract the guys who are guarding the library?" I said.

"You're really fixated on this library thing," said Jason.

"I'm not fixated," I said. "I'm determined. We're here for a reason, and I think we should do our best to try and make sure we follow it through."

"How do you propose we distract them?" Jason asked. "Treat them like dogs and throw them a big juicy steak?"

"No," I said. "One of us could pretend to be hurt. Or we could say that someone had been hurt."

"They'd just radio someone else to take care of it," said Jason. "You know all of the guards carry around walkie-talkies."

The Sol Solis School had pretty heavy security, and not just because children of the most wealthy and influential people in the world attended it. The Sol Solis School was an institution sponsored by the Sons of the Rising Sun, a secret society. They housed their secrets in that library. They didn't want to let anyone in. Especially not Jason or me, if they knew who we were.

"I could flash them," I said.

"Great," said Jason. "You're offering to show your breasts to complete strangers, but you won't even let me hold you."

I looked away.

Jason touched my arm. "What's going on?" He sounded concerned. "Is everything okay? Are you mad at me?"

"No," I said. What was going on? Why was I being like this? "We haven't been together like that since Bradenton."

"That's true," said Jason.

"Since before Lilith," I said. Immediately, I felt as if a weight had been lifted from my chest. That was it! That was why I was upset.

"Lilith?" Jason reached for my chin and turned my face so that I was facing him. "Is this about Lilith?"

I nodded.

"You don't still think that something happened between me and Lilith, do you?"

I shook my head.

"Are you sure? Because I told you about this. Nothing happened. She tried to get me to do something, but I didn't. You know that, right?"

"It's not about that."

"So then what is it about?"

I looked down at the wooden pew between us. At the

whirls in the wood grain. "She said things," I said.

"Like what?" Jason wanted to know.

Now that I'd started to talk about it, I really didn't want to. "Never mind."

"Not never mind. Tell me what you're talking about."

How could I even put this? "She said things about being ... pleased."

Jason looked confused. "Pleased? When?"

"I overheard that conversation you were having. You remember. When she tried to seduce you."

Jason furrowed his brow in confusion. "I don't remember anything about ..." He paused for a second, a different expression taking over his face. "Oh," he said.

I inspected my fingernails, feeling my face heat up. I was glad it was dark, and Jason couldn't see that I was blushing.

"I didn't believe anything she had to say," said Jason. "I know that we're ... that you're ... she was just trying to make me think that you were cheating on me with Jude."

"Right," I said. "That's all she was doing. So it doesn't matter what she said."

"Well, it wasn't true anyway," said Jason. He looked at me. "Was it?"

I hesitated. I didn't know how to talk about this. I'd never known how to talk about this. "Look, let's just forget it," I said. "I don't want to talk about it anymore."

"Oh," said Jason. "So it is true?"

Flustered, I stood up, folding my arms and shrugging. "What's true?"

Jason floundered. "Well, she said that you weren't ... satisfied."

I shook my head quickly. "No," I said. "I am. I'm totally satisfied. I love you, and everything we do is amazing. I'm very, very satisfied."

"Yeah," said Jason, "but I don't think that's what she meant."

"Let's just drop it," I said.

"You brought it up."

"I don't know why I did."

Jason stood up too. He touched my shoulder. "I told you before," he said softly, "I don't know what I'm doing."

"Yes you do," I said. "You're wonderful. Besides, it's not your fault, anyway. It's like she said, she had to show ..." I couldn't continue. My face was on fire. "This is just too embarrassing."

"Hey," Jason said, "you don't have to be embarrassed. It's me. Besides, we said no more secrets. If you're thinking about this, I want to know."

"I just worry that what she said is true. That if I can't do that, then you'll think that I don't appreciate you. And I don't want you to think—"

"No," he said, "this isn't about me. This is about you."

"I know," I said. "There's got to be something wrong with me, right? I mean, shouldn't it have happened already?"

"Well," said Jason, "and keep in mind that I haven't spent a large part of my life listening to locker room talk or having many friends that were my own age. From what I understand, though, it's, like, harder for girls to ..." He laughed. "Okay, well, I'm embarrassed too."

I giggled nervously.

"There's nothing wrong with you," said Jason, "but I think I must be doing something wrong."

"No," I said, "no, I don't think so. I mean, everything's working okay for you."

"But it's not working for you."

"It's fine."

"So, then why are we talking about this?"

"I just wanted to make sure that you knew I appreciated you, that's all. And I wanted to tell you that I was ... I don't know ... that something was wrong with me, and I didn't know if you—"

"Stop it, Azazel. There's nothing wrong with you."

I plopped back down on the pew.

Jason sat down next to me. "Look," he said, "if you told me what to do, you know I would do anything you wanted. I want you to be happy. I want—"

"I don't know what you should do!" I interrupted him. "I don't know how to do it. And that's what Lilith said. She said she had to show guys what to do. And I *don't know* what to do."

Jason absorbed this for a few seconds. "Okay," he said finally. "So, we'll figure it out then. We'll just try stuff."

I bit my lip. "You think that will work?"

He grinned. "It's sex, Azazel. Cavemen could do it. It

can't be that hard to figure out."

I tried to smile.

Jason kissed me again. I tried to just let myself melt into him, to concentrate on nothing but his lips. Eventually, however, I pulled away. "I'm just not really in the mood," I muttered.

Jason didn't say anything for a while. Finally, he said, "Okay."

"You're mad."

"I'm not mad," said Jason. He kissed my forehead. "We've got time," he whispered. "We've got our whole lives."

* * *

My roommate Palomino was crying in the bathroom when I got back to my dorm. Palomino was the daughter of an American senator. She was also my brother Chance's girlfriend. As was the plight of the children of the incredibly rich, she'd been stuck with a totally weird first name. She was cool, though, despite the fact that she was actually dating my dork of a baby brother. Chance was fifteen, and so was Palomino. They'd met when Chance lived with my grandmother in New Jersey. Chance and Palomino had claimed they were "just friends" for months before finally admitting they were girlfriend and boyfriend.

When Jason and I had first realized that the information we were looking for about the Sons and the Rising Sun prophecies were all housed in the Sol Solis School, we didn't have any idea how we were going to get in. The monks we were staying with—the Order of Reddimus—didn't have any connection with the Sons. The Sons themselves had broken off from the Order of Reddimus back in the Renaissance, but that was hundreds of years ago. The organizations no longer had any ties.

Chance and Palomino had really helped us out. Since they both attended the school, they knew the ins and outs of it. They told us which of the people who worked in admissions were total space cadets and would let two seniors into the school two months before graduation. They told us how to make sure we got assigned to room with them. Chance and Jason shared a dorm across campus. I roomed with Palomino.

The only thing the Order of Reddimus really had been helpful with was money. The Catholic Church was willing to throw tons of money at us, considering we were working to overthrow the Sons. The Church hated the Sons. They were their biggest enemy on earth.

Our tuition was paid for, and we didn't have to live with strangers. Plus, this was a good school. I was ridiculously behind on my studies, considering this was the third high school I'd attended during my senior year. Jason was a freaking genius, so he wasn't having any trouble. Palomino and Jason were both helping me study, so I was glad of the assistance.

I knocked tentatively on the door of the bathroom, which was a heavy old door, made of dark oak, and engraved with ornate decorations. "Palomino," I called. "Are you okay?"

Only the muffled sound of sobs came through the door. I looked around at our dorm room. For a high school dorm, it was a pretty nice room. Quite big. Unlike most dorm rooms, rooms in our building—Bianchi Hall—didn't have rooms that looked like cookie cutter images of each other. Each room had a little bit of character. Our room had two large windows on the far wall and a small sort of L-shaped alcove where our closet was. Like all dorms in Bianchi, our bathroom was off our dorm room.

Some students' parents paid enough for private rooms, but Palomino's apparently wanted her to learn what it was like to live with another person. They said it was a social skill. As for me—the Catholic Church was being generous, but not that generous.

I tried the door handle. It was unlocked. "Can I come in?" I asked.

Palomino didn't answer.

When I entered the bathroom, I saw her sitting on the green tile floor, her head between her knees. Her shoulders were shaking from the force of her sobs.

I knelt down next to her, concerned. "What's wrong?" I asked.

She still didn't answer. I put my hand on her back and patted it gently. "Mina," I said softly, using her nickname. "Talk to me. Is it Chance? Was my brother a total dickhead to you?"

"I broke up with Chance," she said, hiccupping and raising her face to look at me. Her eyes were puffy and red, but she was still a really pretty girl. Her long white-blonde hair cascaded over her shoulders. My brother was a lucky guy. Well. He had been, anyway.

"What?" I said. "Why'd you break up?"

"I just don't want to see him anymore," she said, rubbing her eyes with the heels of hands.

"What did he do?" I asked.

"Nothing," said Palomino.

Really? "Okay," I said. "So why'd you break up with him?"

"It's not him, it's me," she said, standing up and going to the sink.

"Um," I said, getting up behind her, "that line might work when you're dumping your boyfriend, but it doesn't work when you're explaining it to your friends."

Palomino surveyed herself in the mirror, making a face at her reflection. "I'm fine," she said. "I don't want to talk about it."

"Come on," I said. "You're upset. Anyone can see that."

She shrugged and splashed water on her face.

I came closer, leaning on one side of the sink. "Look," I said, "I know my brother is not always the politest or even nicest guy ever. I grew up with him, remember? But I know he likes you. He really, really likes you—"

"He won't, though," said Palomino. "He won't when he finds out. This way, it's a clean break. I did it first." She swept out of the bathroom, collapsing on her bed in the bedroom.

I followed her. "Finds out what?" I asked, sitting down on my bed, which was opposite hers.

Palomino pulled a pillow over her head.

I sat back. "I can't imagine that anything you did would make him like you less," I said. "You're a really awesome girlfriend."

She pulled her head out from underneath the pillow. "I'm an idiot."

"No," I said, "you're not."

"It was my idea," she said. "I told him it would be okay. In health class at my old high school, they said it would be okay. You're not supposed to be able to when you're on your period."

I furrowed my brow, a niggling suspicion running through me. "Palomino," I said, "did you and Chance have sex?"

She looked at me like I was an idiot. "We've been having sex," she told me. "Since before I came to this school."

Really? "But Chance said you weren't his girlfriend," I said. "Back when you were hanging out in New Jersey. He said you guys weren't dating. You were having sex then?" This was kind of blowing my mind. Chance was my younger brother after all.

"I knew I was coming here for spring semester," she said. "I didn't want to get attached."

"So you were just randomly having sex with my brother?" I demanded.

Palomino rolled her eyes. "Azazel, you're such a prude.

You wouldn't understand. Never mind." She buried her face in her pillow.

The furrow in my brow deepened. I lay back on my bed, staring at the ceiling. "I'm not a prude," I said. Of course, I had just skipped out on my chance to have sex with my boyfriend. My first chance in months. Was I a prude?

"You've only had sex with Jason, right?" said Palomino.

"How many people have you had sex with?" I asked.

"Three," she said.

"Really?" I said. Palomino was fifteen. How did you fit three boyfriends into fifteen years? When had she started having sex? When she was twelve? "It doesn't make me a prude, because I've only had sex with one guy."

"Whatever," said Palomino, "and I'm sure you guys are always super careful. You probably make him wear two condoms."

"Just one," I said. "And I don't *make* him do it. We've just always ..." Truthfully, Jason and I never talked about the condoms. He always had them. I sat back up and fixed Palomino with my gaze. "What are you saying? Are you saying you haven't been careful?"

Palomino didn't look up from her pillow. Her voice was muffled. "I'm pregnant, Azazel."

* * *

Jason was scrubbing at the blood on his hands. He stood over the sink, the water rushing over them from the faucet. I stood in the doorway, watching him.

"Where did the blood come from?" I asked him.

He turned off the faucet, flinging his wet hands once, so that water spattered against the sink. It was pink with blood.

He came to me, holding his hands out to touch me.

I backed away. "Where did the blood come from, Jason?" I asked.

Jason advanced on me.

I backed into the closed door behind me. I fumbled for the doorknob behind my back.

Jason was coming for me, blood dripping from his hands and fingers, dripping onto the floor, red like roses. The blood was all over his hands. All over his arms. Smeared on his white t-shirt.

"I don't like it when you come home covered in all this blood," I whispered, still trying to turn the doorknob behind me.

It was locked.

Jason stopped in front of me. He put his hands on my cheeks.

I pushed him away. "I don't want the blood on me," I said.

"But it's your blood," said Jason.

"No, it's not," I said.

"It is," said Jason. "Come here and see our beautiful baby."

"What?" I said. "What are you talking about?"

I looked down at myself. I was naked from the waist down. My thighs were covered in smears of deep red blood. And now, suddenly, I could feel it. It felt like something had clawed its way out of my uterus. There was nothing between my legs but tatters of skin. I collapsed onto the bathroom floor, cold green tile against my skin.

Behind the shower curtain, something screamed.

Jason smiled at me. He pulled aside the curtain of the shower with a presentational flair, like he was a showman at a circus. "Isn't he beautiful?" he said.

Behind the shower curtain, a long black worm-like shape slithered over the lip of the bathtub. Its sharp teeth glinted in the lights. Pieces of my flesh still clung to it. Wherever it slid, it left a trail of blood.

I backed away, backed into the door again, shaking my head, muttering, "No. No."

"He's our baby," said Jason.

"No," I said.

"Yes," said Jason.

"No," I said. I stumbled to my feet. "It has to die," I said, lunging for the worm-shaped thing, ready to strangle it.

"Stop!" cried Jason.

* * *

And I woke up.

It was dark in the dorm room and quiet. Quiet the way it is in the morning before the sun comes up. Still. Peaceful.

But my heart was beating out of my chest.

Goddamn dreams.

I'd been having bad dreams—nightmares—ever since Jason and I escaped my crazy Satanist family in Bramford, WV last fall. Recently, however, they'd started to get much,

much worse. I had one nearly every night. Sometimes more than one. They never made much sense. Sometimes they had a basis in things that had happened. For instance, this one was clearly an amalgamation of Palomino's news and the time Jason had come home in Bradenton covered in blood. And maybe it had something to do with the fact that I wasn't quite sure if Jason and I weren't ... evil.

Jason's own mother had tried to get me to kill him. She'd had visions. Visions in which Jason did horrible things.

What if my dreams were like visions? What if ...

I tried to calm down. Monitor my breathing so that my heart would slow down. It wouldn't help anything to think like that. People didn't have visions of the future.

At least I didn't think so.

Sometimes, though, Jason was so violent. I tried not to think about it, because nothing had happened in quite some time. But I'd watched Jason shoot his own mother in the head.

He'd been protecting me.

He'd never talked about it.

The things that I thought about when I woke up from the dreams were sometimes worse than the dreams themselves. I didn't like the dreams, and I didn't like thinking about whether or not Jason was too violent. I didn't like thinking about it at all.

There was only one thing that worked to keep it all at bay, and I'd been so caught up in listening to Palomino tell me about being pregnant that I hadn't bothered with it before bed. Not like I usually did.

It was dark. It was quiet. And my bed was warm. I didn't particularly want to get up.

But I wanted to turn my brain off, and I only knew one way to do that. I climbed out of bed and knelt beside it. Feeling under my mattress, my fingers brushed the cold metal of my gun. It was good to know it was there, but it wasn't what I was looking for.

Instead, I slid out a glass bottle of vodka.

It was easy to buy liquor in Italy, even though I wasn't technically old enough to purchase it. The drinking age was so much lower in Europe. I never had problems. And it wasn't like I was buying it to party. It was like medicine.

I gulped the burning liquid down my throat, feeling the oblivion rush into my temples.

* * *

I had a headache. I always had a headache. Drinking as much liquor as I did every night before bed (or in last night's case, in the middle of the night) tended to make me pretty much constantly hung over. I sat in my morning class, bleary-eyed, barely listening to Professor Moretti's lecture on Post-Colonialism. I'd been through various approaches to education my senior year of high school. The first had been honors classes in the West Virginia public school system. Then general classes in the Florida public school system. Finally, here I was, finishing out my high school career in a posh English language private school in Europe. The approaches all had some things in common, but here at the

25

Sol Solis School, the emphasis was on lecture. I came to class. Professors talked at me. I took notes. Later there was a test. It was the most challenging program I'd ever taken part in.

In my pocket, my phone vibrated.

Looking around to make sure Professor Moretti wasn't looking, I eased the phone out of my pocket and eyed the text message Jason had sent me.

"whats up w/c and p?" it said.

Careful not to look down at the phone too much, I quickly texted back: "what did chance say to you?"

I made a show of scribbling down something on my notebook paper, waiting until my phone vibrated again before looking at it.

"p broke up w/ him? she say why?"

I chewed on my lip, considering. Jason and I had made a pact not to keep secrets from each other, but this wasn't my secret. Last night, Palomino had made it clear to me that she didn't want Chance to know. She was convinced that Chance would leave her if he found out. Apparently, she'd been sort of seeing a guy before Chance had transferred in the early spring. She hadn't had sex with the guy, but Chance didn't believe that. Palomino was sure that Chance would blame the baby on someone else. I told her my brother wasn't like that.

At any rate, I didn't think Palomino wanted her business blabbed to anyone, not even Jason. I trusted Jason, but since he was living with Chance, it would be really hard for him not to want to tell his own roommate. Still, I didn't think

Palomino should keep this to herself for too long.

Conflicted, my fingers hovered over the keys of my phone.

"Ms. Smith," said Professor Moretti.

I didn't look up at first. My name was Jones. But we were undercover at the Sol Solis School and we weren't using our real names. I was going by Amy Smith. My head snapped up.

Professor Moretti was standing right next to my desk. He could see that I was texting.

I blushed and shoved the phone back into my pocket. "Sorry," I mumbled.

Professor Moretti looked concerned. "Ms. Smith," he said kindly, "you really need to heed your studies. Your grades can't afford distractions like this." He was referring to the D I'd gotten on my last test. I couldn't help that I wasn't studying so much. What with nightmares, hangovers, and trying to figure out a way into the library, I was distracted. School didn't seem so important anymore.

I looked down at my desk, ashamed.

Professor Moretti moved on. "The next chapter of *Things Fall Apart* for tomorrow, then," he addressed the class.

Around me, students began to gather their belongings. Stuff their notebooks into book bags. Stand up. A low buzz of chatter started to fill the classroom. The class was over. I didn't move for a few seconds. The noise was making my head pound.

Slowly, I stood up and began picking up my own stuff.

Jason appeared beside my desk, his book bag already slung over his shoulder. "Sorry," he said.

I shook my head. "I should have kept my eye out for Moretti."

"No," said Jason, "it was my fault. And I shouldn't distract you in class, anyway."

Way to rub it in. Jason had, of course, gotten an A on the test. "Right," I said. "Your stupid girlfriend needs to concentrate, or she'll flunk out of school."

He kissed my forehead. "Don't be silly," he said, taking my hand as we left the classroom and spilled into the hallway with the other students. "I just already know this stuff. When people think you're the messiah, they stuff your head full of all kinds of useless knowledge."

I elbowed him. "Shh. Don't say that stuff so loud. Someone might hear."

He tickled my ribs. "Paranoid Azazel," he teased.

"Don't say my name either," I hissed.

"You're in a bad mood," he said. "Did you drink last night again?"

"No," I said. "I forgot. I had a dream that we had a monster for a baby, and it ate its way out of my body."

Jason made a face. "Eew," he said.

I shrugged. "So then I downed half a bottle of vodka at like four in the morning."

We made our way out of Rossi Hall and into the bright, spring day. Outside, other students like us walked in groups of two or three across the sprawling campus. They wound through old brick buildings that had been standing for hundreds of years. Jason and I were heading towards the dining hall for lunch. We usually met up with Palomino and Chance. I wondered how that was going to work out today.

Jason shook his head. "I don't think it's good for you to drink so much."

"And the nightmares? Are they good for me?"

"I just worry about you. You know that."

I did know. I squeezed his hand. "I'm okay."

We walked without speaking for a few moments.

"You don't ever have bad dreams?" I asked him. "After everything you've seen?"

He shrugged. "Used to," he said. "A long time ago. After the sorority house. But not so much anymore."

The Sons had assigned Jason and a man named Hallam, who we used to live with in Florida, to kill a house full of sorority girls. They'd told them the girls were running a prostitution ring, but that had probably been a lie. No one really knew, because they were dead. Jason hadn't done any of the actual killing, but the night had scarred him deeply.

"So, you think it'll get better?" I asked.

"Maybe we should take you to a doctor. Like a psychiatrist or something."

I snorted.

"I didn't mean that you were crazy or anything," he added hastily.

"We both need loads of therapy," I told him. "And we won't be getting it any time soon. Let's just find a way into

29

this library and figure out what we need to know."

Jason stopped walking, looking thoughtful. I stopped too.

"Then what?" he said.

"What do you mean?"

"What if we find out that I actually am the Rising Sun? What if we find out that collectively we're going to bring about the end of the world? What do we do then?"

I didn't say anything. After a few seconds, I started walking again. I didn't look back to see if Jason was catching up.

I spotted Palomino standing in front of the dining hall, hugging herself. Chance was nowhere to be seen. I half-waved at her, and she waved back. As I walked over to her, Jason fell into my stride next to me. Out of habit, I reached for his hand, and he took mine.

"Hey Mina," I said.

"Hey," she said.

"Why'd you break up with Chance?" said Jason.

I elbowed him again. Did he have no tact?

Palomino swung around to face Jason, her eyes welling up with tears.

I dropped Jason's hand and touched her shoulder. "You okay?"

She shook her head. "I couldn't make it through my last class. I started crying, and I had to leave. Everyone saw."

"Wait," said Jason. "Are you upset about breaking up with Chance? Because he's out of his mind, okay? He was freaked out when I got back to the dorm last night. What's going on with you two?"

"Jason," I said.

"No," he said. "Look, if you both still like each other, and you're both sad that you aren't together, you should get back together."

"Chance is a jealous dick," said Palomino. She turned on her heel and stalked into the dining hall.

Jason went after her, and I followed Jason. "Is this about that guy you were seeing? What was his name, Skylar or something?"

Skylar. Another rich kid doomed to a weird name.

"Because," Jason continued, "Chance is really sorry he said anything. And he totally trusts you."

Palomino whirled. "I don't want to talk about it, okay?" She thrust the door open to the dining hall.

Jason stopped and looked at me. "You should back me up here," he said. "He's your brother."

"It's complicated," I said.

Jason rolled his eyes. "Whatever," he said. "It's always complicated with girls."

A line to the serving area had already formed. Jason and I got in line behind Palomino. We got through the line quickly and sat down at our regular table. Jason and I looked at Chance's usual seat. It was empty.

"Where's Chance?" I asked Jason. It didn't seem fair that he had to find another seat.

Jason shrugged. "Don't know." He turned to Palomino. "You know," he said, "Azazel and I had some issues with jealousy. She thought I was sleeping with her best friend."

I glared at him. "And you thought I was sleeping with a gay guy."

"He wasn't actually gay," Jason pointed out. To Palomino, "He was actually my brother, and he tried to kill me."

He *did* kill Jason. At least, he put a bullet in Jason's skull. Jason stopped breathing His heart stopped beating. Until I kissed him.

My life was too weird.

"Anyway," said Jason, "the point is that we worked through that. We talked about how we felt. And we're still together."

Palomino sighed. "I don't want to talk about this, okay?"

"Why not?" said Jason. "What did Chance do?"

She glared at him. "Did Chance put you up to this?"

"No," said Jason, but he didn't meet her eyes.

"I don't want to talk to him," she said. "It's over. Just tell him it's over."

"Mina," I said, "are you sure you shouldn't just talk to Chance about—"

She shot me a murderous look. I shut my mouth. I'd promised not to say anything. But this was huge. My younger brother had fathered a *child*. And his girlfriend wouldn't tell him. How was I supposed to keep this to myself?

To distract myself, I looked around the dining hall. It was a big, open room with high ceilings. Long tables lined the room. I spotted the Weem twins, Faruza and Fairie (more hapless victims of rich people's wacky ideas of names), sauntering across the dining hall. I didn't feel sorry for the Weem twins, despite their names, however. They were awful gossips who were always rude to me. They picked on pretty much everyone except people who had the right last names. People who were related to members of the Council of the Sons.

Since their uncle, Edgar Weem, had stepped down from his post at the Council, the Weem twins had gotten even meaner. They seemed to resent the fact that their uncle had been demoted, as if it threatened their social status. They walked by our table, casting withering glances in our direction. I seethed, imagining how satisfying it would be to let them know that Jason was actually their cousin, since Edgar Weem was his father.

Faruza stopped next to our table, holding her tray and looking down at us. "So, Mina," she said. "I heard about the nervous breakdown in class today. I'm so sorry." She sounded about as sorry as Hitler was for killing Jews.

Palomina glowered at her. "Thanks, Faruza," she said. "You're always so concerned and kind."

Faruza smirked. "So is it true that you found out your skuzzy adopted boyfriend gave you herpes? Because I hear that's what you get when you date Jersey trash."

"Chance isn't even from New Jersey," I said. I couldn't help it. The Weem twins just pissed me off so much.

Faruza turned to me as if she'd noticed me for the first

time. "Was I talking to you?" she asked.

"I don't know," I said. "I think you were leaving, actually, weren't you?"

"Because God knows where you and your boyfriend came from. You're probably charity cases. At least, he's definitely performing some kind of charity by dating something that looks like you."

Jason's jaw twitched. "Don't talk to her like that," he said.

"Ooh," said Faruza, "I guess I struck a nerve."

Faruza's boyfriend, George Churchill (victim of being named after his super rich grandfather), slid in behind her, one arm snaking around her waist. "Hey babe," he said. "You gonna waste your whole lunch here?"

She smiled up at him. "Just catching up," she said.

"Actually," said Jason, "she was insulting my girlfriend."

George shot me a look. "She'd be kind of hard to compliment, wouldn't she?"

Jason stood up, knocking over his chair. "You should really reconsider that statement."

I watched his fist, clenching and unclenching at his side.

CHAPTER TWO

April 19, 1990

Professor Weem stopped me after class and had me stay after. We talked for nearly an hour about ancient religions and mythology. I couldn't believe it, because he really talked to me like I was an equal, not a student. It was neat. If the other girls in class found out, they'd be so jealous. Me, hanging out with dreamy Mr. Weem.

I stood up next to Jason. "Don't," I whispered in his ear. "Don't attract attention."

"What did you say to me?" asked George, an arrogant smile playing on his lips.

Jason looked at me, and I could see the unchecked fury in his eyes. He turned to George. "I don't like it when people insult my girlfriend," he said evenly. "And you don't want to make me mad."

George laughed. "Is that a threat?"

I grabbed Jason's hand, squeezed it.

He looked back at me. He was struggling, and I could tell.

Jason ripped his hand away from me and tore out of the dining hall. When the door slammed behind him, it got quiet in the room.

Everyone looked up with startled expressions on their faces.

The silence hung in the air for several seconds, and then conversation returned.

George started laughing. "What the hell was that?" he asked Faruza.

"Hey," I said. "He's serious. Don't make him mad, okay?"

* * *

When Jason and I were in Rome, things were easier. Things were nicer. Things were idyllic. Sometimes, I wish we could have stayed. We spent our days roaming around the city, doing tourist things. We went to the Coliseum. We ate gelato in the narrow streets. It was warm, springtime in the Mediterranean. I liked it there.

We were staying in a cloister with the Order of Reddimus, monks who had taken us in when we'd gone on the run from the Sons. In particular, we spent time with Brother Mancini, who'd been Sutherland's contact in the Reddimus Order. (Sutherland was a creepy man who'd tried to rape and kill me, but he also had connections, so we'd been forced to deal with him.) Brother Mancini gave us advice about where to go and what to see in Rome. When we ate in the cloister, we took our meals with him, instead of in the larger dining hall where most of the monks ate. He was a friendly man, a little pudgy, but he spoke very good English, unlike some of the other monks there.

Jason and I had separate rooms, and we couldn't see each other in the evening at all. Still, we made the most of our days together. We wandered through the streets of Rome, holding hands. It was more romantic than the movies.

But we had to leave.

According to Sutherland, Rome was considered sanctuary by the Sons. Sanctuary was any holy place of any kind, like a church or a cemetery or Stonehenge. The Sons wouldn't commit acts of violence in a place of sanctuary. Since Rome was the Holy City, the whole city was off-limits for the Sons. Sutherland had told us we'd be safe there.

But the Sons weren't playing by the rules anymore. They'd shot up a church in Shiloh, Georgia the fall before. They were desperate to get at Jason and me.

One day, Jason and I came back to the cloister after one of our idyllic afternoons on the streets of Rome. Brother Mancini was waiting for us. He looked worried. He told us that we needed to talk about something important and that it couldn't wait.

Concerned, Jason and I went with him to a small meeting room in the cloister. It contained only a simple table and several chairs. We all sat down together.

"What is it?" Jason asked, sitting on the edge of his chair. "What's going on?"

It was bad news. I could tell.

"We've discovered some information about the Sons," said Brother Mancini. "I'm afraid it's not good."

"I knew it," I muttered.

"Azazel, your great uncle, Ian Hoyt, has taken Edgar Weem's place on the Council," said Brother Mancini.

"We know that," said Jason. "Sutherland told us."

"It seems," said Brother Mancini, "that Hoyt has taken over to a certain degree. He's declared himself the head of the Council and is currently making decisions for the Sons at large."

"That's bad?" I asked.

"On the face of it, not exactly," said Brother Mancini. "It's the decisions he's making that aren't very good. He's decided that the Sons no longer officially think you're the Rising Son, Jason."

"But that's good," said Jason. "Right?"

"He's decided that they should kill you," said Mancini.

"Oh," said Jason.

"Furthermore, nearly half of the council doesn't agree with him. I'm sure you remember the summit in 2002, when the Council made the official decision that you were the Rising Son?"

"Yeah," said Jason. "I remember that."

"Those Council members feel their evaluation was thorough. They don't agree with Hoyt. But Hoyt is having none of it. They must either agree with him or leave the Sons. Of course, he can't really let them *leave*. They know too much."

"You mean Hoyt's going to kill them?" I asked.

Brother Mancini nodded. "Unofficially, of course. He couldn't admit to a policy of killing former Council members. But those who don't agree with Hoyt and don't want to die will escape."

"Escape?" said Jason. "And go where?"

"Here," said Brother Mancini. "The long and the short of it is that there are going to be about ten or fifteen former

Council members seeking sanctuary here with us. We're not sure if it would be a good idea if you remained here while they did. We don't want Hoyt to figure out where you are, and we can't be sure that they won't be in communication with him."

"Wait," I said. "If they're about to be killed by Hoyt, then they wouldn't kill Jason on his order, would they?"

"Probably not," said Brother Mancini, "but we can't be sure that Hoyt won't have planted a rat among them. Someone who is secretly loyal to him. Even if none of them try to kill you, we aren't sure it would be a good idea for them to see you."

"Why not?" I asked.

"If they're disagreeing with Hoyt, it's because they think Jason is the Rising Sun. They might fawn over you."

I had a quick flashback. Jason and I were leaving Michaela Weem's house in Shiloh. There were members of the Sons everywhere. As we walked by them, they dropped to their knees and whispered, "He's the one." Fawning, indeed.

"That might suck," I said.

Jason looked thoughtful. "Why are they coming here?" he asked. "Why would they seek sanctuary with you? Aren't you the enemies of the Sons?"

"The enemies," said Brother Mancini, "and the origins."

"Origins?"

"Did you think the Sons simply materialized out of thin air?" asked Brother Mancini.

"I didn't think they came from the Church," I said.

"Actually," said Jason, "it makes sense. The Brothers, the celibacy ... They're like monks."

Brother Mancini nodded. "The Order of Reddimus is an old order," he said. "We were founded sometime in the fifth century, in order to spread the gospel throughout Europe."

"The gospel?" I said.

"Christianity," said Brother Mancini. "During the fifth century, very little of Europe was actually Christianized. Only the Mediterranean—Greece and Rome—and even their hold was tenuous. The leaders at the time knew that if they could bring the barbaric countries in the north to Christianity, then they could expand the empire."

"So they wanted to convert people because they wanted to control more land?"

"In essence," said Brother Mancini. "I'm certain there were some devout men in the lot, who truly were concerned with the souls of the Celts, but for the most part, they wanted to expand their power.

"They created the Order of Reddimus, a special group of missionary monks, whose sole purpose was to go to the furthest reaches of the unknown world and witness to the people there. The monks were instructed to make it as easy as possible for these barbarians to come to know Christ. They were taught to find out the religion of the place, learn its lore, and attempt to mix the pagan ideas with the Christian, to ensure a smooth transition between the two."

"You're kidding," said Jason. "I've always know that

certain Catholic saints have a great similarity to pagan gods, and that pagan traditions were adopted by early Catholics. But you're saying that this kind of thing was Church policy?!"

Brother Mancini smiled. "In the fifth century, it absolutely was. The Order has ancient records indicating the same. We, however, can't and won't share these records with the world. You can imagine what kind of negative impact such an admission would have on the faithful."

I raised my eyebrows. "You think it's better to lie to the public than to tell them the truth?"

"No," said Brother Mancini, "but I think that the most important thing for the world is a united Mother Church. I think that certain transgressions are overlookable in the service of that idea."

"But," I said, "there are a whole bunch of people who aren't even Catholic."

"But there are many people who are," countered Brother Mancini.

I chewed on my lip, but I didn't say anything. I didn't want to offend Brother Mancini. We owed him a lot for letting us stay here.

"Do all of the members of the Reddimus Order believe in Catholic doctrine to the letter? Of course not," Brother Mancini continued. "Not all of this order's members even believe in Christ, per se. We've all been exposed to too many ideas in other religions that are similar and that seem to resonate just as deeply for us. But we are devoted to the

Church, and the Church is loyal to us."

"Yeah," said Jason, "because if they aren't, you could go public with the whole history of your order, which would look bad."

Brother Mancini chuckled. "You are so cynical for one so young, Jason."

Jason shrugged. "I'm not cynical," he said. "I'm realistic."

"Call it what you'd like."

"So," I said, "the Sons will seek refuge with you guys because they were originally an offshoot of the Reddimus Order?"

"Exactly," said Brother Mancini. "Long ago, our Order pledged that we would welcome our wayward brethren back to the fold if they so chose. We think it's likely that, since they will be in fear for their life, they will choose us."

"We have to leave, don't we?" said Jason.

"We aren't going to just send you out into the street," said Brother Mancini. "That wouldn't be very charitable. But for your own safety and comfort, we don't think it would be wise if you remained here."

I looked across the table at Jason. He shrugged at me, looking defeated. This was the story of our lives. Whenever we found someplace that we could stay and be happy, whenever things seemed to have calmed down, we had to leave. People were always chasing us. People were always trying to do us harm. I wanted to reach for him, but Jason and I had decided to chill out our displays of affection in front of the monks. It just seemed improper.

"I understand," said Jason. He stood up.

I wasn't just going to take it, however. I addressed Brother Mancini. "So, you have any ideas where we can go?" I asked him.

"There might be one way that the two of you could free yourselves from the Sons once and for all," he said.

Jason sat back down. "How would that be?" he said. "They either think I'm the messiah or they want to kill me."

"If," said Brother Mancini, "you could prove to everyone that you weren't the Rising Sun, then Hoyt and his followers might not see you as a threat any longer. And those who believed in you might see reason and stop trying to worship you."

"You don't think he's the Rising Sun?" I asked. I wasn't sure anymore. We'd seen things. Done things. I was confused.

"Of course not," said Brother Mancini. "This Rising Sun business was never part of the original Reddimus doctrine. Certainly, there were vague hints here and there, but it never was such an all-encompassing idea. And furthermore, it's only been popular among the Sons recently. I'd say within the last hundred years."

The last hundred years was recently, huh? Weird to think that way.

"But things have happened," Jason said. "Azazel and I have been able to do things."

"He died," I said.

"You both know that there's no conclusive evidence that

43

the gunshot wound Jason sustained was serious," said Brother Mancini.

That was true, as far as it went. It was possible that Jason hadn't been hurt as seriously by the gunshot as we'd thought. Still, I remembered the way he'd lain motionless in my arms. He hadn't been breathing.

"What about what happened in Shiloh with the Brothers?" I asked. "They all went crazy."

"Maybe Weem did it," said Brother Mancini. "Maybe he placed something in their minds through hypnotism. He triggered it with a text message."

I raised my eyebrows again. "That sounds farfetched."

"And the fact that the two of you are mystical beings doesn't?"

When he put it that way ...

"I'm not saying I don't believe in miracles," said Brother Mancini. "I do. But both of the things you're talking about happened in Shiloh. There are biblical prophecies that point to a place called Shiloh being quite powerful. Maybe it wasn't you. Maybe you were just in the right place at the right time."

The right place at the right time? I narrowed my eyes. It couldn't be that simple. "But there are so many Shilohs, all over the south. There are two in Georgia alone." The idea was too confusing to even formulate.

Brother Mancini just smiled. "It's only a thought," he said.

And that was how we ended up at the Sol Solis School.

Brother Mancini thought that there might be some ancient records in the library at the school. He hoped these would help us prove that Jason wasn't the Rising Sun. Usually, I hoped that too. I didn't want to believe that some ancient power controlled Jason's destiny. Controlled mine.

But other times ... Other times, I half-wished that we'd find out we did have magical powers. Maybe we could zap all our enemies. Rearrange everything to our liking. Would that be so bad, really? And in my darkest moments, I sometimes wondered if it wouldn't be really, really nice to rule the world.

* * *

"Someone's coming," I whispered to Jason.

He was kneeling outside the back door to the library, lock-picking tools in the keyhole. He was biting his tongue in concentration. "Damn it," Jason muttered, pulling the tools out of the lock. "Is it guards?"

I peered back around the corner of the building at the dark landscape of the campus at night. Between the bushes that hugged the building, I could make out the uniform of the Sol Solis security guards.

"Yeah."

Jason stood up, grabbing my hand. "Are they coming this way?"

"I don't know," I said.

"Damn it, damn it," he said. He shot one look towards the corner of the building, the same way the guard was coming. Then he turned to look down the stretch of the building on the other side. "Let's go," he said, tugging me with him as he broke into a sprint.

Seconds later, we rounded the other side of the building, panting a little. Jason flattened himself against the other side, stealing a look back at the spot where we'd been.

"Is he there?"

"He's rounding the corner," Jason told me.

"He didn't see us?"

"I don't think so." I breathed a sigh of relief.

"He's still coming," Jason said, pulling me forward again.

We ran along the side of the building, towards the front.

"There are always guards out front!" I said. Stationary guards. They stood in front of the entrance twenty-four/seven.

Jason took a wild look around as we continued to run. "The church," he said, switching direction.

The old church, our assembly hall, was directly perpendicular to us. I quickened my pace to keep up with Jason.

"We'll go in the side door," he said to me.

The side door of the church was shadowed by several large trees, making it difficult to see, especially at night. Jason should be able to crouch there and pick the lock without the guards seeing.

We arrived at the door and stopped again. My breath came in deep gasps, but I positioned myself behind one of the large trees so I could see if one of the guards was coming.

I couldn't see anyone now, just the walls of the library, dark red brick in the darkness. Behind me, I heard Jason's lock picks scraping against the metal of the doorknob. He'd picked this lock before.

"So far, so good," I told him.

"This'll just take a second," Jason said.

I watched. Nothing moved.

I turned back to Jason to see how he was progressing. He was still digging inside the lock.

I turned back. Still nothing.

Wait.

The guard was starting to round the corner.

"Jason!" I hissed.

"One second," he said, jiggling the long metal tool in the lock.

The guard was in full view now, but he was looking around at the side of the library building.

"I can see him!"

"Got it," Jason said, and the door swung open.

I raced through the door, and Jason shut it behind me. We were back inside the church. Memories of the last time we'd been in here—last night—flooded through me. I looked up at the stained glass, remembering the way I'd felt it was glaring down at me, watching me and Jason.

"I told you we wouldn't be able to get into the library," Jason said, throwing himself into one of the pews.

"We have to try, though," I said.

"Do we?" asked Jason. "Just because Brother Mancini

told us to? Is that why we have to?"

I sat down next to him. "I thought you wanted to find out. I thought you wanted to prove you were normal once and for all."

Jason snorted. "I'm not normal," he said. "I'll never be normal. I've come to terms with that."

I rubbed his leg. All Jason had ever wanted was a normal life.

He sighed. "No, you're right. I do want to find out. I want to get into that library. But I don't know how we're going to do it."

The wing of the library we wanted to enter was under heavy security. It housed the ancient documents that the Sons used for research. No one could get in without express written consent from the Council. Sometimes a professor from Sol Solis might obtain permission for one of his classes, but even that was rare, and it wasn't likely to happen this late in the year. We figured our best chance was to break in after hours, but even our best chance wasn't working out very well.

I lay my head on Jason's shoulder, feeling frustrated. "I don't know either."

He reached around to stroke my cheek, shifting so that he faced me and I was looking up into his eyes. "We'll figure something out. We always do."

I touched his forehead. His chin. Then I brought my lips up to meet his. For a second I felt the weight of the church bearing down on me like it had last night, but I ignored it, and it fell away. My hands moved on Jason's chest, and he pulled me into his arms.

* * *

"That didn't work," said Jason, stroking my hair as I lay on his bare shoulder. "Did it?" We lay between the pews in the old church, moonlight bathing us through the stained glass windows.

I played with the few tiny hairs on his chest. "It worked," I said. "I mean, it happened."

"That's not what I meant," Jason said. "I meant that you didn't ..."

"Do we have to talk about this?" I asked.

Jason's hand scampered across my thigh and darted between my legs. "No," he whispered. "No talking is required."

And so we were quiet.

For a long time. Jason's fingers were the only thing that moved.

"Is this okay?" Jason finally whispered.

"Uh huh," I said.

"Do you like this?"

"Uh huh." Even though, truthfully, whatever he was doing didn't really feel like anything. I could feel him touching me. It didn't hurt. But it didn't ... It didn't feel the way I thought it should.

Jason moved his hand. "You've got to be honest with me Azazel."

"I am being honest," I said.

He raised his eyebrows.

I sighed, burying my face in his soft skin. "Sorry," I murmured.

"Did you like that?" he asked.

I hesitated, then shook my head against him.

He didn't say anything for a minute. "I wish you would have told me," he said.

"I didn't hate it," I said. "I don't know."

"So, what do you want me to do?" Jason asked.

"I don't know!" I said. "Can we just drop it? It's not important. You don't have to try."

Jason sat up, dislodging me from where I lay on his shoulder. "Hey!" I protested.

He put his arms around his knees and studied his kneecaps. "Azazel," he said, "I want you to enjoy it when we make love."

I sat up next to him, touching his arm. "I do enjoy it," I said.

He turned to me. "Not as much as you could. Not as much as I do."

"I love you, Jason," I said. "I love being with you. It's okay."

"It's not," he said.

"Jason ..."

He turned away from me and started yanking on his pants. After a couple seconds, I started wriggling back into my clothes too. "You know," I said, "it's my body. I should be able to decide whether or not it's okay if I don't have an orgasm."

He sighed heavily. "You already told me it wasn't okay. And then you said tonight that you don't want me to try anymore. Am I that bad at what I was doing?"

What? Why couldn't he understand? He wasn't bad at it. I didn't know what bad at it was. I didn't know what good at it was. But the way I'd felt when he was touching me before—spotlighted, like I needed to do something to prove to him he was pleasing me—well, I didn't like that feeling at all. "You're not bad at anything," I said.

"Right," he muttered. He shrugged into his shirt and started buttoning it, not looking at me.

"Jason, it's okay," I said. How was this fair anyway? I was the one who wasn't having orgasms. Why was I comforting him?

"We should probably get back to our dorms," he said.

So he was done talking to me, then? Okay. "I guess so," I said. "Are we going out the side door?"

He nodded.

We paused at the door, peering out the window to make sure the coast was clear. Outside, the campus of the Sol Solis School stood motionless, dark, and quiet. We didn't see any guards, just rolling grass and trees. Carefully, we stole out of the assembly building and into the night air.

Jason started forward ahead of me, but a movement caught my eye, and I grabbed him. "Wait," I whispered.

He turned to me. "What?"

I pointed.

We looked. Beside the dining hall, which was far in the distance, a small dark figure was walking. It looked like he was walking right towards us.

Jason pulled me behind the large tree.

"Is that a guard?" I asked him.

"Why isn't he wearing his uniform, then?" Jason asked me.

I swallowed. There was only one group of people that we knew of that followed us around in the dark and showed up wearing all black.

Jason ducked back in front of the tree. "He's gone," he reported.

"Gone where?" I asked.

"I don't know," he said, taking my hand, "but let's get back inside and fast."

I nodded, squeezing his fingers with mine. "Jason," I said, "you don't think it's the ..."

"The Sons?" he said. He gave me a dark look. " Just let them try to kill me. I might like a challenge."

CHAPTER THREE

April 20, 1990

Professor Weem shared some interesting things with me about the Rising Sun prophecy. It's no secret that he's on the side of the Rising Sun being a person, not a metaphor or anything else. He takes the prophecy really, really seriously. I was floored and flattered that he wanted to talk to me about it. I've been spending time with him nearly every day.

I thought Palomino would be asleep by the time I got back to my room. But when I snuck back in after Jason picked the lock on the front door for me, she was sitting on her bed pouring over her biology textbook. She didn't look up when I came in. I collapsed on my bed, not in a particularly good mood. I kept thinking about the way Jason had pulled away from me after we had sex.

I'd originally thought of this whole issue as my problem, but now it was affecting Jason too. And it was stupid, because there was absolutely nothing wrong with him. He was perfect. How could he think that there was something wrong with him? There was something wrong with me.

"Mina?" I said.

"Huh?" She didn't look up from her book.

"When you have sex, do you, you know ... like ..."

"What?"

"Have orgasms?"

She slammed her book. "Why are you asking me this?"

I sat up on my bed. "I just wondered."

"Yeah. I mean, not always, but yeah."

"Did you always?"

"Not right at first, I guess. But since then. Do you think that's why I got pregnant? Because I read this thing online that said that the female orgasm is designed by nature to like spasm the sperm deeper — "

"Eew!" I cut her off. "That's my brother's sperm we're talking about."

She rolled her eyes. "Maybe if I was just one of those frigid chicks who just lays there, none of this ever would have happened."

"Frigid?" I said. What did that mean?

"You know, like a prude," she said.

"That's what you called me last night," I said. And I wasn't. I'd gotten busy tonight. I'd wanted to. I liked having sex with Jason. That wasn't the problem.

"I have hormone issues. You can't blame me for stuff I say."

"I wasn't blaming you." I was worried. Was I frigid? Was there something seriously wrong with me? "So ... how did you have these orgasms?"

"I don't know, they just happened," she said. "Why are you bothering me with this? I have a biology exam tomorrow, and I'm pregnant, and I'm alone. Spare me another lecture on how much of a slut I am."

"I didn't say that about you," I said, confused. "Besides, you don't have to be alone. Just talk to Chance."

"I'm not talking to Chance. And that is totally what you said last night. With the whole I-was-just-randomly-hooking-up-with-Chance comment."

"Okay, I kind of remember saying that," I said, "but I never called you a slut or implied that you were one."

"Whatever."

Why was she attacking me? None of her problems were my fault.

"They just happened?" I asked.

"What?"

"The orgasms."

"Yeah, they just happened."

"So ... um ... what did they feel like?"

"Oh my God," she said, "you've never had an orgasm, have you? I knew that Jason guy was too good to be true, with his big dark eyes and his 'we talked through it' stuff. Pretty and sensitive? And willing to defend your honor? Maybe, but only if he sucks in bed."

That was uncalled for. I stood up and went into the bathroom. "He doesn't suck in bed," I told her. "He's amazing."

"Sure he is," she said.

I got out my toothbrush and ran it under the sink. Palomino appeared in the doorway. "Why can't you just admit he's flawed, Azazel?"

Flawed? Jason? Well, there was the fact that I'd watched him kill more people than I could count on one hand. But that didn't matter, did it? Not when I'd killed for him too.

Held a gun to the head of a girl who'd once been my best friend and pulled the trigger. Watched her brains spray everywhere, her skull shatter. Neither Jason nor I was perfect. "He's flawed," I said flatly. I popped my toothbrush into my mouth.

"So he can't get you off?"

I didn't answer.

"You're going to have to show him how to do it."

"I don't know how," I said, but my voice was muffled by the toothbrush in my mouth.

"What?"

I spit into the sink and glared at her. "I don't know how."

She laughed and went back into the bedroom.

I rinsed out my mouth. "You're in really nice mood," I called after her.

"Hormones," she shot back, "or did you forget I'm pregnant?"

"If you hate being pregnant so much," I said, "then why don't you just get an abortion?"

She reappeared in the doorway, a horrified expression on her face. "I can't believe you'd say that. Abortion is murder."

"Okay," I said.

"Don't tell me you think it's okay."

"I ..." If I were pregnant, there was no way that I could bring a child into the world Jason and I inhabited. Better for the fetus to be terminated in my womb than to live only to get shot in the head by the Sons. "The Sons are so freaking

Catholic," I muttered.

"Azazel, are you telling me you'd have an abortion?"

"My life is too screwed up as it is," I said. "I don't have anything to give a kid." I pushed past her, through the bathroom doorway, and lay back down on my bed. "I'm going to sleep." I changed into my pajamas and crawled under the covers.

"God," said Palomino, "what am I going to do?"

"Tell Chance," I said, switching off my bedside lamp.

"I'm not telling anyone," she insisted.

"Sooner or later, people are going to figure it out."

"Maybe not, if I wear the right clothes."

"Jesus." Was she crazy? Did she really think she could keep this a secret?

"And you can't tell anyone either. Promise me you won't."

"Mina—"

"Promise!"

"Fine," I said. I closed my eyes and burrowed into the softness of my pillow. It was late. I just wanted to go to sleep.

For several minutes, it was quiet. I heard Palomino climb back on her bed and open up her biology book. "Azazel?" she said.

"Hmmm?"

"If you don't know how, you're going to have to figure it out. You're the only one who can."

"Figure out what?"

"You know what. It's your body. You can't be afraid of your own body."

I wasn't afraid of my body. Not exactly. My thoughts were getting sluggish as sleep crept up on me. I would worry about how to have orgasms in the morning. I drifted. My last thought was that I'd forgotten to drink before bed tonight again. But I was tired. Maybe I wouldn't dream ...

* * *

I dreamed. In my dream, I was in a cheap hotel, lying on the stained bedspread, completely naked. I could feel the air from a chugging ceiling fan, which was badly fastened to the cracked ceiling.

My arms and feet were tied to the bedposts. I struggled, but I couldn't pull away. I looked around the room, panicking. At the foot of the bed stood two figures. They were wearing long black hooded robes. They were holding a bell. I wasn't close to the bell, but I could see that it had an engraving of the sun rising over the ocean. I couldn't see their faces.

They were speaking to each other.

"If we do this," said one, a female voice, "do you think it means we're evil?"

"Evil?" said the other male. "It's just what comes naturally."

"Naturally to you," she said.

"Naturally to everyone," he countered. "Everyone wants her. Everyone wants to take her violently. Look at her skin. So soft, so vulnerable. Imagine how it will sound when she screams."

The female giggled. "I like it when they scream."

"I know you do, my sweet," said the male.

I thrashed against the ropes on the bed. It was clear that something very bad was going to happen to me here. I was going to have to do something about it. If only I had a gun.

Magically, the way it sometimes happens in dreams, I looked over on the bedside table and a gun was there. I reached for it, but, of course, I couldn't even brush it with my fingertips.

"I'm not vulnerable," I told the black-robed people. "I'm tough. I can take care of myself."

"No," said the female. "You're weak and scared. And flawed. We're the strong ones."

"If you touch me, I'll kill you," I said.

The black-robed people laughed. "You won't kill us," they said together.

"I can hear you now," said the male. "No, don't. Not like this."

Not like this. That was what I'd said, a long time ago, to Jason in hotel when his hands were ripping at my clothes—

And the male in the robe lowered his hood. It was Jason. He climbed over the foot of the bed to lie on top of me, laughing. "Not like this," he said again, mocking me.

I shook my head. "No," I said. "No, don't be Jason."

Jason was opening his robe over top of me. He wasn't wearing anything under it. "You know you want it," he said to me, his face hideously close to mine, twisted into a grotesque leer. "You love me."

"No," I said. "No."

The female lowered her hood. "Of course we love Jason," she said.

She was me.

I glanced from Jason's grinning face to my own. She (me) looked at me, laughter in her eyes. "We love Jason, because he taught us to kill."

"You're mine," Jason whispered to me, his hands on my body, twisting and pinching me. It hurt.

"No," I said again, but it was barely a whisper.

She (me) was pushing Jason off of me. "No, no," she said. "You don't know how to do it. I'm the only one who knows how to do it." She shoved Jason off, onto the floor.

He climbed back up, a wounded look in his eyes. "Am I that bad at it?"

She (me) brandished the bell and pushed my legs apart. "I'm the only one who knows how to do it," she said, cackling.

Everything went black.

* * *

I woke up breathless and sweaty, spasms racking my pelvis and thighs. I gasped, opening my eyes.

Sunlight was pouring through the windows of my dorm room. I leapt out of bed, tumbled into the bathroom, and threw up in the toilet.

There was nothing in my stomach for me to vomit. Instead, my empty stomach heaved and twisted on itself, bile rising in my throat. I spit, wiped my mouth with my hand, and collapsed on the floor next to the toilet.

"You okay?" called Palomino from the bedroom. "I thought I was the one who was supposed to have morning sickness."

"I had a nightmare," I told her, getting up off the floor. I crawled back into the bedroom and back towards my bed. Once there, I felt under the mattress for the bottle of vodka I had there.

"Was it a gross nightmare?" Palomino asked.

"Yeah," I said, taking a long swig of vodka and gagging at the taste.

"Jesus, Azazel!" exclaimed Palomino.

"I just ..."

I just couldn't face the dream. You didn't have to be Carl Jung to figure out what it meant. But I didn't want to think about it. Not Jason's violence. Not my violence. Not the fact I couldn't have orgasms. Okay, so I was bothered. Fine. Did it mean I had to have those horrible nightmares?

"I just need this," I said, taking another long draught.

"I think doing that is just going to make you throw up more," said Palomino, looking concerned. She'd never seen me drink in the morning. She'd never seen me drink so much. I kind of felt guilty about that ...

... but then the easy swimming sensation of liquor took over my thoughts, and I didn't feel guilty about anything.

"I don't throw up," I told her. "Not anymore."

"Azazel—"

"Whatever," I said to her. "Shut up about it, or I'm calling Chance and telling him he's about to be a dad."

"Don't you dare!" she said, sitting up straight in her bed.

I shrugged. "Don't worry," I said. "I was joking anyway."

"It wasn't funny," said Palomino.

"I'm taking a shower," I said. "I have class." I took another nip from my vodka bottle. It was almost empty, but that was okay. I had more bottles of vodka underneath my bed. I'd probably be taking one with me in my purse today.

"You're going to class that drunk?" Palomino called after me.

"I'm not drunk," I told her.

* * *

"What do you think about the pole shift theory?" asked George Churchill.

I was in my science class. My drunkenness was fading away, and I didn't like it.

Professor Halverson sighed. "George," he said, "what does this have to do with plate tectonics?"

"I just want to know your stance on it," said George. "I know it's not accepted by the mainstream scientific community, and I want to know why."

I still had most of the small vodka bottle I'd brought with me to class left. I could go to the bathroom and take a few gulps of it. I raised my hand.

Unfortunately, someone else did too, at that exact moment.

Professor Halverson called on her first.

"What's a pole shift?" she asked.

Professor Halverson sat down at his podium heavily. "Okay, okay," he said. "You've succeeded in derailing me from my lecture for a few minutes. But all the information in Chapter Seventeen is on the exam, no matter what."

I lowered my hand. He was going to talk for a while, wasn't he?

"The theory goes that the earth's north and south poles will shift to a completely different location suddenly," continued the professor. "This would cause massive climate changes and disastrous consequences like floods and storms. Essentially it would be apocalyptic."

"Why would that happen?" asked the same girl.

"That's why it's so ridiculous," said Professor Halverson. "People think it will happen in 2012, when the Mayan calendar ends. They think the world will end. But there's no scientific basis for this theory. It's nonsense."

I raised my hand again.

"Ms. Smith, you have a comment?" asked Professor Halverson.

"May I use the restroom?" I asked.

Professor Halverson looked annoyed. "Fine," he said.

* * *

Chase was sitting at our usual table when Jason and I arrived at lunch. I didn't see Palomino anywhere. I considered walking around the dining room, trying to find her, but I was really too drunk to walk in an actual straight line, so I didn't think it would be a good idea. I'd had to lean on Jason just to get to the table to sit down.

"What's wrong with my sister?" Chance demanded when I sat down.

Jason just shook his head.

"I'm fine," I told Chance.

Jason heaved a huge sigh. "Azazel, you stay here, okay. I'm going to get us both some food. You need something in your stomach to soak that liquor up."

"Liquor?" said Chance. "You're drunk?"

"Shh!" I told him. "Someone might hear, and I might get in trouble."

"Just watch her, please?" Jason said to Chance.

"I don't need watching," I told Jason, but he was already walking over to the food line to get our trays. I turned back to my brother. I was feeling a little unsteady. It probably hadn't been a good idea to excuse myself to the bathroom during my last class and kill the bottle of vodka. I wasn't sure how much I'd had to drink this morning, but it was a lot. I tried to smile at Chance. "I'm fine," I said.

"Why are you drunk, Zaza?" asked Chance. Chance was the only person alive who was allowed to call me Zaza. Everyone else who used to call me that was dead. Usually, it just reminded me of them. But with Chance, it didn't feel bad. It felt comforting.

I bit my lip. "I've been having dreams," I said. I picked up the napkin on the table and began twisting it. "Chance, you know, there are things that Jason and I did. Things that I did. You don't know this, but Gordon and Noah aren't off doing some weird job for Grandma Hoyt together in California. Chance, there's no easy way to tell you this. They're—"

"Who says you get to sit at this table?" interrupted a voice.

It was Palomino. She was holding her tray. She was pissed.

"Mina," said Chance, looking both happy to see her and concerned by her anger. "Sit down."

"I'm not sitting with you," she said. "You'll have to move."

"I'm not moving," said Chance.

"I don't have anyone else to sit with," said Palomino.

"Well, neither do I," said Chance.

"Azazel is *my* friend."

"She's my *sister*. Besides, I have to watch her. She's drunk."

"I know. I watched her get wasted the minute she woke up this morning."

Jason returned the table, sliding a tray full of steaming mashed potatoes and gravy in front of me. "Hi Palomino," he said. "Are you and Chance trying to work it out?"

"I want him to leave," Palomino said.

I looked up at Jason. "I can't eat this," I said.

"You have to," he said, sitting down. "It'll make you feel better."

"Smelling it is making me nauseous," I said.

"Eat," Jason said. He turned back to Palomino. "Are you

joining us?"

"Not with him," she said.

Chance hung his head. "You know what? Fine. I'll move."

"No," I said. "I don't want you to move. This is all silly anyway. She just needs to talk to you." I looked at Palomino. "You should just tell him."

Palomino sat down. "Don't even think about it, Azazel," she growled.

"Tell me what?" said Chance.

"Nothing," said Palomino icily.

And then everyone was quiet.

I looked down at my mashed potatoes, which seemed a little blurry. I wondered if the amount of alcohol I'd had to drink was impeding my vision. Could alcohol do that? I picked up my fork and poked at the potatoes. They kind of smelled good, but in a foreign way, like something I liked in a different state of consciousness.

I looked over at Jason, and he gave the potatoes a meaningful look. Ugh. Fine. I took a tentative bite of potatoes. They did taste good. The cafeteria staff at the Sol Solis School used the real thing, not instant potatoes. I chewed and swallowed, then took another bite, bigger this time. As I swallowed that, I felt sanity returning, my drunkenness beginning to fade. I didn't want that. I put down my fork.

"This is stupid," I said. "Palomino's pregnant."

I don't know why I said it. I wasn't thinking clearly.

Drinking tended to fuzz out my brain. I wanted my brain fuzzed out, because I didn't want to face my dreams or myself. But it had the unfortunate side effect of making everything else fuzzy too.

Jason dropped his fork.

Chance choked on his bite of roast beef.

Palomino stood up, her chair squeaking against the floor. "I hate you, Azazel," she said. She stormed off. I was pretty sure she was crying again.

Jason and Chance both gaped at me.

I shrugged. "Well, Chance, don't just stare at me. Go after her," I told him.

I took another bite of mashed potatoes. Maybe it would be better not to be so drunk after all.

For several seconds nothing happened. I shoveled mashed potatoes into my mouth, feeling less and less drunk with every bite. Then Chance stood up. He was shaking.

"Chance ..." I started.

But he walked away without looking at me.

I took another bite of mashed potatoes. A big one.

"How long have you known this?" Jason asked me.

I swallowed my potatoes. "She told me not last night but the night before."

"Why didn't you tell me?"

"I just did," I said.

"No," said Jason, "you just announced it to the entire table, and you said it kind of loud, so who knows who else heard."

67

I flinched. "I didn't realize I said it so loud."

"Well, you did. And you kept things from me. And we promised no more secrets."

"It wasn't my secret," I said. "It was Palomino's. I didn't think I should tell you."

"But you didn't have any problem blurting it out just a second ago."

"I'm drunk," I protested.

"Right," said Jason. "Well, that makes everything better." He stood up. "I'll see you in Calculus." And he walked off too.

I bit my lip. I sure knew how to clear a table, didn't I? I took another bite of mashed potatoes. They really were very good. It would be a shame to let them go to waste.

* * *

"Jason!" I screamed, rushing across the courtyard outside the dining hall. "Stop!"

I'd walked out of the dining hall, using the back door. Most people didn't go out that way, but it was the closest way to get to my next class. I just had to cross a small courtyard. Usually nobody was ever on the courtyard. But today, I'd been greeted by the sight of George Churchill punching my boyfriend in the nose. Jason's head had been whipped to the side. He'd stumbled backwards. But I could see that Jason's fists were clenched, and he was about to use the momentum from George's punch to fuel a punch of his own. I just didn't want Jason to put George in the hospital.

Luckily, at the sound of my voice, Jason looked up to see

me. George looked up too.

My feet pounded against the ground as I raced over to them.

"What did you just call him?" George asked.

Damn it! I'd forgotten that Jason and I were undercover. Jason was going by Jeremy. Jeremy Black. How could I have been so stupid? I ran faster.

In the second that George looked away, Jason balled up his fist and undercut George, hitting him on the chin. George's head snapped back. He cried out.

Jason didn't let that stop him. He followed up his first punch with a second one, this one hitting George's cheekbone. George's head whipped the other way, blood spilling out of his mouth.

I was still running, but closing in on them. I leapt into the air and tackled Jason. We tumbled into the grass, both breathing hard.

Jason pushed me off of him, struggling to get to his feet.

"Jason, no!" I said.

George wiped his mouth with his hand, looking at the blood on it in shock. "Why are you calling him Jason?"

"Shut up," said Jason to George. "You really need to learn to keep your mouth shut."

"You plan on teaching me?" George said, still studying the blood on his hand. It was as if he didn't quite believe that he could bleed.

"Hell yes, I do," said Jason.

"Let it go!" I shrieked. "If you hurt him bad, it will draw

attention to us."

George looked up from his hand. "Don't hurt me," he said. He suddenly looked really afraid. "Are you ... ?" He looked back at the blood on his hand. "I won't say anything. I won't say a word. Just ..." He held up both his hands, palms outward. "I'll back off."

Wait. Did he know who we were? Did he know who Jason was?

Jason clenched and unclenched his fist. "You're not going to say anything?"

"Nothing," said George. "Especially not about what she called you. I wasn't here, okay?" He started to back away. "And I'm sorry about that Palomino girl. I'm sorry I said anything."

"You won't say anything like that anymore," said Jason. It wasn't a question.

George shook his head fervently. "No. Nothing like that." He took a few more steps backward.

"You say anything, and I'll kill you," Jason said. He sounded so serious.

George swallowed. Then he turned and ran.

Jason and I watched him go.

"Maybe I should kill him anyway," Jason muttered.

"Jason," I said in horror.

"He knows who we are. Why did you say my name?"

"I'm sorry," I said. "I just freaked out. You were punching him."

"You should have heard what he said about Palomino,"

Jason said.

"You know," I said, "you can't just go around punching people every time they say something you don't like."

Jason laughed dryly. "You sound like your parents."

I didn't respond. Sure my parents had spouted lots of psychobabble about nonviolence and making constructive decisions, but in the end, they'd engineered a really disturbing ritual, which was supposed to culminate with my getting raped. Jason should know better than to bring them up.

"That guy could use beating up," Jason said.

"It doesn't matter!" I said. "We can't afford exposure, and you know that."

"Whatever," Jason said. He started to walk away.

"Jason!"

He stopped. Looked at me. "I can't talk to you right now."

I started to say something. Then I stopped. I just let him go.

* * *

When I got back to my room after classes that evening, they were all there. Jason, Chance, and Palomino. Palomino was standing by the door, holding her book bag, looking angry. Her face was red and puffy. Jason and Chance were standing next to our beds, both of them staring at the floor with their hands jammed into their pockets.

"How did you guys get in here?" I asked. Guys weren't allowed in the girls' dorms, and vice versa.

"Jason snuck us in," said Chance. "We just got here actually."

"They were here when I got here too," said Palomino. She didn't sound happy.

"Mina," said Chance, "we need to talk."

"No," she said. "There's nothing to talk about. You aren't even supposed to know, but thanks to Azazel, here—"

"Chance is right," Jason cut her off. "You guys need to talk. Azazel shouldn't have blabbed it the way she did, but Chance deserved to know."

"Deserved?" demanded Palomino. "Why?"

"Because it's not just about you," said Chance. "It's about us."

"I don't see how it's about you," said Palomino. "It's my body."

"Of course it's about him," said Jason. "He's part of it. Obviously."

No one said anything.

"Unless I'm not," said Chance finally. "Unless Skylar's a part of it and not me."

"I knew you would say that," Palomino said. She turned to me. "Didn't I say he'd just blame it on Skylar?"

"I don't think he's—" I started.

"How many times do I have to tell you that I never had sex with him?" Palomino said, stomping across the room and throwing her book bag on the bed.

"So it is ... mine," said Chance.

"Of course it's freaking yours!" said Palomino.

Chance made a confused face. "So why did you break up with me?"

"Because I knew you'd break up with me when you found out, and I wanted to beat you to it," she said.

Chance looked confused. "I don't want to break up with you," he said.

"You don't?"

"See?" said Jason. "You guys need to talk." He looked at me. "And I need to talk to Azazel."

We snuck out of the dorm through the fire escape stairs, which no one used. Jason had figured out how to get them open without setting off the alarm. Once outside, we crossed campus to Jason's dorm. One of the fire escape doors was propped open slightly. Jason had left it that way for us. We crept up the steps and into his dorm room.

I'd never seen it before, but I was prepared for the mess, since I'd lived with Chance for most of my life. The boys hadn't spent much time trying to keep it clean. Their clothes were strewn all over the floor and in piles on their desks and chairs. Neither of their beds were made. Instead, their covers were flung on the floor or tangled together in the middle of the bed. I didn't even want to look in their bathroom. I was afraid of the horrors that might greet me there.

Jason led me to his bed, and we sat down on it. He took my hand.

"I'm sorry I yelled your name out in front of George today," I said, figuring we were gearing up for apologies and getting mine out of the way.

"Don't worry about that," he said. "I brought you here, because I was thinking that maybe if we weren't in that old church, things would be easier for you. Like, maybe you'd be more comfortable, and then—"

"Wait," I said. "I thought you wanted to talk."

"Later," he said, leaning over to kiss me. "We can talk later."

I pulled back. "Jason, I think we—"

He cut me off with another kiss. His pulled me close, one of his hands sliding under my shirt. His kisses were insistent, like he was devouring me with his mouth. His hand slid up my rib cage, pushing under my bra.

He shifted, pushing me down on his bed and settling on top of me before claiming my mouth with his again. I felt like I couldn't breathe.

Jason's hands kept moving on me, thrusting my clothes out of the way, so his fingers could assault my bare skin. I tried to break away from his mouth, to tell him to slow down, to give me a chance to think, but he didn't seem to notice that I wasn't into it.

I started to feel a little panicky. I wasn't sure I wanted to be doing this right now. Jason was moving too fast. He was pushing too much. I loved Jason, and I loved being with him, but he was scaring me. There was too much urgency in his hands, in his tongue. It reminded me of ...

Of the hotel room. In Pennsylvania. A hotel room that looked eerily like the one I'd dreamed about last night.

Thoughts of the nightmare immediately quelled any

possible good feelings I might be having. I struggled under Jason, pushing at his shoulders.

He didn't seem to notice, and he didn't stop. It was no good pushing at him anyway, because he was stronger than I was.

I thrashed beneath him. Jason just kept kissing me, his lips crushing mine with his own.

CHAPTER FOUR

April 22, 1990

Jed (that's what Professor Weem wants me to call him) has an idea about bringing the Rising Sun into the world. He says it's about time that it happened. He says that it can be done. It's just a matter of finding the right people to do it. I got in trouble with my dorm mother for being late last night, but I told Jed about it, and he said he'd take care of it.

Jason pulled back, propping himself up on his elbows. "Hey," he said gently. "What's wrong?"

"Get off of me," I told him, pushing at his chest.

He looked hurt, but he did what I asked. As soon as he sat up, I jumped off the bed and crossed to the other side of the room.

"Azazel, what's wrong?" Jason said, following me.

"No," I said, "don't come over here."

He stopped. We stared at each other across the dorm room.

"What did I do?" Jason asked.

"I don't like it like that, and you know it," I said. "It's like that time in the hotel, our first time, when you tried to ..." When he tried to what? When he scared me with his intensity. He scared me so much lately. So much.

"I thought you wanted to," Jason said, staring at the floor.

"No you didn't," I said. "You didn't even stop to see if I wanted to. You just started to do it. And you didn't pay any attention to what I wanted."

"I thought ..."

"You scared me."

He went back to the bed and sat down. "I didn't mean to. I'm sorry."

I advanced on him, trembling with anger. "After everything that's happened to me. After Toby, and Sutherland, and everything, you should know that you can't just try to make me do it, just because you want to."

"Jesus, Azazel. You make it sound like I was trying to rape you or something."

"That's how it felt," I said.

He shook his head. "Don't say things like that. You know I would never hurt you."

"Do I?" I demanded. "Do I know that? How many times have I watched you hurt someone, Jason? How many people have I seen you *kill*? And I'm supposed to believe you'll never do that to me?"

He stood up. "Yes. You are. You are, because I love you, and you love me. And I hate to point it out, Azazel, but if I hadn't killed those people, you'd be dead."

"I can take care of myself now. I don't need you to—"

"Right," said Jason, "you can. And while we're on the subject of how many people I've killed, let's not forget that you've killed people too. Your own brothers. And your best friend."

I shuddered. "I did that because of you, Jason."

"And I did what I did because of you."

"Michaela Weem said that you would turn on me."

"She also said that she thought both of us were evil and needed to die."

"She said that being close to you made me evil!" I returned. "And what if—" I didn't finish. What was I saying here? Was I truly accusing Jason of turning me into something evil? Was I saying that Michaela Weem was right, that Jason was an abomination that was destroying everything he touched? I didn't believe that. I didn't.

I went to Jason and touched his forearm. "I'm sorry," I said softly. "I'm so sorry."

He looked into my eyes. "It is my fault. If I'd never met you, none of this would have happened."

"It's not your fault," I said. "If I'd never met you, I'd only be half-alive. I love you."

"I love you," he said, drawing me into his arms. I buried my face in this chest. He kissed the top of my head. "I'd never hurt you. Please believe me. I'm so sorry I scared you."

I looked up at him. "I know you wouldn't hurt me," I said. "I'm sorry I was scared. I should have trusted you."

He stroked my cheek. "Well," he said, "if we can't make passionate love in my dorm room, at least I can do the other thing I wanted to do, which was ask you to prom."

* * *

Prom. Trust Jason to want to milk any "normal" high school tradition for all it was worth. The Sol Solis School didn't have a prom, per se. They had a formal spring ball, just a few weeks before graduation. They didn't call it prom, they call it the Spring Formal, but since most of the students at the school were American students, we saw it as an analogue to a traditional American prom.

I strolled across campus back to my dorm, shaking my head. I barely registered the familiar buildings as I walked by them. I was caught up in my thoughts.

Jason hadn't had a normal childhood. He'd spent his formative years on the run with a member of the Sons named Anton, who'd taught him to shoot guns. He'd spent his early adolescence living in a community of Brothers, being sent on missions to kill sorority chicks. His idea of adolescence had been culled from Molly Ringwald flicks. He had some romantic notion about prom. He wanted to go, because he'd been sure that he'd never be able to.

Now his life had shaped up in a somewhat normal way. He was attending a school. He had a girlfriend. He wanted us to go to the prom. He wanted the whole nine yards. Wrist corsages. Me in a god awful fancy dress. Him in a tux. If we had parents, he'd want them to take pictures on the front lawn.

I sighed. It wasn't that I didn't want to go to the Spring Formal. I'd told Jason that we'd go. I'd gone to my junior prom with Toby, back in Bramford. I remembered how exciting the entire experience had been. My mom had helped me pick out my dress. We'd made a day of getting ready. Toby had come to pick me up. There were pictures of the two of us somewhere: me in my pink satin strapless number, him in stiff black and white with a bow tie. I remembered the picture on the mantle in my parents' living room. There we were. Toby and I grinning out at my parents' house, a place full of empty grins and pseudo-happiness.

That was the thing, I guess. When I was younger, I believed in all this crap. I wanted the typical high school experience. A handsome boyfriend. A limo. Pretty dresses. Dancing.

But now, all of that stuff just reminded me of the person I used to be. Things had changed so much. And wholesome American adolescent traditions like the prom just reminded me that I was different now. I didn't like to be reminded.

But Jason wanted to go to the prom, and so we would. Whatever he wanted, I'd do. He deserved some semblance of normalcy in our ridiculously abnormal lives.

As if to remind me how abnormal they actually were, I passed the library. The library. That's what Jason and I should be focusing on. Not the prom. Not my lack of orgasms. We needed to get inside that library and find out who the hell we were. After all, that was the reason we'd come to the school.

I paused for a second and stared at it. How were we going to get in? The guards stood at attention at the front door, staring straight ahead, reminding me that we had practically no recourse. We'd tried one night, but that hadn't gone well. What were we going to do?

I started to turn away, but stopped when I saw one of the

side doors of the library open. That was strange. They almost never used the side doors. The authorities wanted one way in and out of the library. The front door.

The door opened, and a figure clad all in black emerged. This far away, I couldn't see his features. He looked up at me and froze. We stood like that for several seconds, staring at each other.

Then he quickly opened the door and disappeared into the library again.

* * *

I met Chance outside my dorm. He'd just snuck down the fire escape steps. He looked a little frazzled.

"Hey," I said. "How are you doing?"

He ran a hand through his hair. "I'm, um, I'm okay," he said. "Mina and I talked. It was good."

I nodded. "That is good."

"Yeah."

He shoved his hands in his pockets and looked at his shoes. Looking at him, I couldn't help but remember the fact he used to stand like that when he was a little kid and had done something wrong. My little brother. Now he was taller than me, with a goatee and broad shoulders. And he was going to be a father. Weird.

"Zaza," he said. "What am I going to do?" He looked up at me, his eyes full of fear.

"Oh God Chance," I said. I opened my arms to him, and he fell into them. I hugged him and patted his back. It reminded me of our parents' funeral. I had comforted

Chance while he cried. I'd been dry-eyed.

He pulled back. "She doesn't want to tell anyone," he said.

"I know," I said. "She's got some silly idea that she's going to be able to hide the fact she's pregnant."

"I don't know who we'd tell anyway. Mina's parents would go through the roof, and Grandma Hoyt would be less than pleased."

I pictured our stern, proper grandmother and grimaced. Chance was right.

"But she's got to see a doctor or something right?" he asked me. "I mean, she can't just let it go."

I shook my head. "No, she needs a doctor. I think." Now that it came down to it, I knew very little about pregnancy. Considering I was the only biological child my mother ever had, I'd never even seen her pregnant. I had no idea what to tell Chance.

"She's just so scared," he said. "But I am too. I'm freaked out. And she's had a few days to adjust to the idea. I've only had a few hours. I want to comfort her, but I don't know what to say or what to do."

"I'm sorry I just blurted it out like that today at lunch," I said.

"No, I'm glad I know. She wasn't going to tell me, and I'm glad I know."

"Well, she's going to have to tell someone sometime, Chance."

"Yeah." He looked so overwhelmed.

"Hey," I said, reaching out to touch him, "you're doing the best you can. She needs you. If you're just there for her, it'll be enough."

"I don't know," he said. "I don't know if it will or not."

In the distance, the clock tower on campus began to toll the hour.

"Damn it," said Chance. "I've got to go. I'm going to miss curfew."

"Me too," I said. "Take care of yourself, Chance."

"You too," he said. He started off, then stopped. "And watch the drinking, huh, Zaza? I don't need to worry about you and Mina too."

"Sure," I said.

But when I got up to my room, I downed half a bottle of vodka. No way was I dealing with one of those dreams tonight. No way.

* * *

I awoke to Jason bending over my bed, shaking me. "Azazel," he was whispering urgently. "Wake up."

Making a face, I sat up in bed. "What are you doing here?" My head was pounding, but I was used to that.

"Shh!" he said.

I rubbed my face with my hand. "What are you doing here?" I whispered.

"Come with me," he said. "I'll explain once we're out of the dorm."

We snuck out the fire escape again. Outside the dorm, there was a cool, night breeze that licked at my skin. I pulled my pajamas close, shivering a little. "Jason," I said, "what are we doing out here?"

He grabbed my hand. "Come on." He pulled me with him as he walked.

"If you're taking me out for some tryst or something, I am so not in the mood for that kind of thing right now."

"Are you drunk again?" he asked.

I glared at him. "I wasn't going to have another one of those dreams. You don't know what they're like."

"I do know what they're like. I've had nightmares before. They're bad. But you've just got to come to terms with whatever it is you're trying to run from."

"What?" I said.

"I think what we've got to do tonight will help you with that," he said.

"What are we doing tonight?" I asked. "Where are we going?"

"The Assembly Hall," he said.

The old church. "You are trying to get me to have sex with you again, aren't you?"

Jason stopped and pulled me close. He kissed my forehead. "Azazel, I'm an eighteen-year-old guy. I'm always trying to have sex with you." He pulled back. "But no, that's not why I snuck you out of your room tonight."

"So why?" I said.

Jason started walking again. "It's not going to be easy for you to hear," he said. "Especially if you're drunk."

"I'm not drunk," I said. "Or even if I am, I'm always

about this drunk, so it's not that big of a deal."

He sighed. He just kept walking. I hurried to catch up. It didn't take long to get to the old church. We went around to the side door. I expected Jason to pick the lock, but it was already open. I shot him a look of confusion. He just pulled me inside.

"I've already been in here tonight," he explained, shutting the door behind us.

I gazed up at the stained glass. Tonight, it seemed as if it were watching me, judging me, telling me that I was unworthy to set foot inside this building. I shivered again, but this time it wasn't from the cold.

Jason was looking at the floor, shifting nervously on his feet. "This isn't going to be easy for you to hear," he said again.

A mounting feeling of dread seemed to pour down on me, through the stained glass windows. "What?" I said again.

"It's Chance," said Jason.

"What happened to Chance?" I asked. Chance was all I had left. My family was all dead, and if something had happened to Chance —

"Nothing happened to him," said Jason. "Not yet, anyway."

What did that mean?

Jason took my hand again. "Come with me." He led me through the back of the old church and down some steps into its basement. The basement was ancient, constructed from old stone. It smelled musty and alive somehow. Jason found a light bulb, hanging on a chain, and turned it on. The light bulb swung violently, casting moving shadows throughout the room. In the corner of the basement, in the shifting light, I saw Chance. He was tied up and gagged. His eyes were closed.

"I knocked him out," said Jason.

I was shocked. I was appalled. "You did *what?*"

"I told you this wasn't going to be easy for you to hear," said Jason.

I went to Chance. Knelt by him. Touched his face. There was a slight sheen of sweat on his forehead. His breathing was labored.

Jason yanked me away from Chance. "Don't go near him," he said.

"Jason, what have you done to my brother?" I demanded, struggling against him.

"Hold still and listen to me," Jason said.

I was angry. I was betrayed. Jason was what everyone said he was. He was evil. He was trying to kill off my entire family. If it weren't for him, they'd all still be alive. Jason had started this whole mess, running into my life out of the woods.

I held still. "I'm listening," I said. This needed to be good.

"I was using Chance's computer to do some homework," said Jason, "and I found something."

"What?" I said.

"You know how you can set AOL Messenger to save your

chat history in a file in your documents?"

"You looked at his chat history?" I asked. "Why would you do that?"

"I don't know," said Jason. "I was just suspicious. It seems like it was too easy. Getting us into the Sol Solis. How did Chance have the ability to get us assigned roommates?"

"Jason, we made seventy zillion phone calls and filled out mounds of paperwork to get into this school," I said. "It wasn't exactly easy."

He shrugged. "Whatever. The point is that I looked at the chat history. And I found out that he's in communication with the Satanists."

"What Satanists are there to even be in communication with?" I asked. "Michaela Weem is dead. You shot her yourself. She's the one who masterminded this whole thing."

"I don't know who it is," said Jason. "They use handles, and I don't know his real name. But he and Chance are planning something. They're planning to kill us both."

I shook my head. "No," I said. "I don't believe that."

"I read it," said Jason. "It was all right there. In black and white."

"No."

"Listen, you've got to face the facts. Your family can't be trusted. You're all alone in this, just like I am. We can't trust anyone except each other."

"Chance didn't know anything about the Satanists," I insisted. "They never told anyone in town until you were eighteen. And I've never told him. So he *still* doesn't know."

I was starting to cry. I didn't believe Jason. I wouldn't. He was wrong. Not my baby brother Chance. No. He was my only link back to the person I used to be. And I loved him.

Jason patted my back, trying to comfort me, but I shook him off. "Don't touch me," I said. "You're lying. You're just saying this stuff because you want me to be alone like you. Fuck! God knows what you're doing to me, Jason. Before I met you, I would never have done the things that I have done. And now ..." The faces of my brothers Noah and Gordon flashed in front of me, just the way they'd looked in their final moments. Stunned. Blood trickling out of the holes in their foreheads. Holes that I'd made.

Jason put a gun in my hand. "I know you're upset," he said. "But we have to stop him."

"No," I said. I looked down at the gun in my hands, wanting to fling it away from me. Instead, I flipped off the safety and pointed it at Jason.

"Jesus, Azazel," said Jason, looking frightened.

I sobbed and let the gun go slack at my side. I went back to Chance, tucking the gun into the waist of my pajama pants. I wiped tears away from my face and sniffled as I untied him.

"Azazel, don't do that!" Jason said.

I pulled the gun out and pointed it at him again. "We're not hurting Chance," I said. "No. That's the line. We're not crossing that line."

"He's trying to kill us," Jason said. "Doesn't that mean

anything to you?"

"He's not trying to kill us! You're wrong! He's my little brother, and he would never do that!" I broke out into fresh sobs as I freed Chance's hands.

"Azazel," said Jason, reaching for me.

I jammed the gun back in his face. "Stay back," I said.

I shook Chance. "Chance, wake up," I said. "Wake up."

"You're crazy," said Jason. "You're crazy, and drunk, and frigid, and I don't know why I waste my time on you."

I turned to him for a second. "That's what you think of me?" I asked, stunned.

"Well, what is it you think of me?" Jason asked. "That I'm a psycho killer? That I'm evil? Which is worse, Zaza? Huh?"

Jason never called me Zaza.

That was weird. I looked around for a second. In fact, everything seemed a little weird. In fact—

But Chance was stirring. I turned to face him. "Chance, are you okay?" I asked, tears streaming down my face.

Chance had a gun. Where had he gotten that gun?

"Thanks for untying me," he said. "I'm glad you've come around. We've been waiting for you to see what a monster Jason is. Now that you see, it shouldn't be too hard. Kill him."

What? We? I shook my head slowly. "It's true?" I asked. "You're working with the Satanists?"

Chance sighed. "Are you going to shoot Jason or am I?" He leveled the gun at Jason.

"No," I said.

Chance's finger tensed on the trigger.

And there wasn't time for thinking, there was only time for action. I whipped my own gun up, quickly aimed, and squeezed three shots into my little brother's torso. His face registered shock, pain, and then ... nothing.

Sobbing, I feel into a heap on the floor, forcing my eyes shut tight.

* * *

And when I opened them, my dorm room was bathed in sunlight. I was tangled in my bed covers. I was still sobbing. And my head was pounding like a brass band was playing in my head.

It had been a dream?

But it had seemed so, so real.

Rubbing at my eyes and trying to calm my sobs, I picked up my phone from my nightstand. I called Chance. It rang and rang and rang for a ridiculously long time, but then he answered.

"Zaza?" he mumbled sleepily. "Why are you calling me at six in the morning?"

I sobbed in relief. "I'm sorry," I said. "I just had a dream. I needed to know you were okay. You're okay, aren't you?"

"I'm not going to be able to go back to sleep," he said.

"I'm sorry."

"Are you crying?"

"No. No, I'm fine," I said. "Try to go back to sleep."

I hung up. I flopped back on my bed. My head throbbed in response to the sudden movement.

Well. Drinking wasn't working anymore. It didn't drown out the dreams. And it just left me with hellish hangovers. Maybe it was a sign. Maybe whatever my subconscious was trying to tell me was too important to be ignored anymore. Maybe I was going to have to face it.

But before I did any of that, I was going to drink a lot of water and take a lot of ibuprofen. Ugh.

CHAPTER FIVE

April 25, 1990

Jed finally revealed his plan to me, and he wants me to be a part of it. Me? Can you believe it? I can't. We're going to start working immediately, probably tonight. And he's worked it so that I can stay out as late as I need to help him. I'm actually getting an independent study credit for this. I'm so excited!

Jed is so, so gorgeous. And the fact that he picked me to help with this plan means that he must think there's something special about me too.

Professor Moretti had asked me to stay after class. I stood at his desk, hugging my books to my chest. He was flipping through a stack of papers to find mine. I wished he'd just say whatever he had to say and let me go. I knew I wasn't doing very well in school. I didn't really care. I probably had a bright future as a professional assassin, and you didn't need a high school education for that.

"Ah, there it is," said Professor Moretti, pulling my paper out of the stack.

"I'll try to do better," I said.

"What?" said Professor Moretti. Then he shook his head. "Oh, no. Amy, that's not why I wanted to talk to you. I found your paper very insightful."

"You did?" I was pleasantly surprised. I was still hung over from drinking before bed last night, but it felt good to have done something well. I didn't feel like I'd done much of anything right in weeks. I barely remembered writing the paper. I did remember that it was about *Things Fall Apart*, the book we'd been reading. Well, the book we'd been assigned to read. I'd cobbled it together from reading a few chapters, class discussions, and a judicious use of SparkNotes.

"You seem to have quite a large amount of empathy for Okonkwo," said Professor Moretti.

"Well, his whole life gets destroyed, doesn't it?" I said. "It's not his fault. It's the fault of the white missionaries. They just come in and totally mess everything up."

Professor Moretti shrugged. "Some critics think that Okonkwo is a classical tragic figure, like Odysseus or Hamlet. His tragic flaw could be seen as his pride or his rashness. Some feel that Okonkwo brings his downfall upon himself."

"I thought you said that my paper was insightful," I said. Why was he pointing this out to me, anyway?

"I think it was. I think that most of my students have difficulty identifying with an African character from the late 1800s. You seem to be able to put yourself in his place quite readily. I think that qualifies as insight into the work."

I nodded slowly. "So was it good or was it bad?"

"The paper is well-written. You shouldn't worry about that. I'm sure I'll give it a high mark."

Then why was I talking to him? "Thanks," I said. "Is there ... anything else?"

"I just find it so interesting that a girl of your age and

your experience would so strongly be able to put yourself in Oknokwo's place."

"I didn't really do that," I said. "It's just obvious. I mean, all Okonkwo can do is react. Everything just goes from bad to worse in that book. I mean, isn't that why it's called *Things Fall Apart*? Because things fall apart in the book?"

"The title is an allusion to Yeats poem. We discussed that in class."

"Yeah," I said. "I've studied 'The Second Coming.'" Three times this year, actually. In every English class I'd been enrolled in during my senior year. "But, I mean, that's Yeats' point too. He thinks that the world's coming to an end. Or that the era of Christianity is coming to an end. And everything's falling apart."

"Do you agree that everything's falling apart?" asked Professor Moretti. "That a rough beast is slouching toward Bethlehem to be born?"

"Of course not," I said.

"Perhaps slouching towards Shiloh?"

I jumped back as if I'd been burned. Shiloh was the place that Jason was born. Did Professor Moretti know? "Shiloh?" I repeated, trying to sound nonchalant and clueless.

"What's happened to you in your life that you understand Okonkwo's plight, Amy?" asked Professor Moretti.

"Nothing," I said. "I don't understand his plight. I don't know. I guess he did have flaws. I mean, maybe he did bring the whole thing on himself."

"Maybe he did," said Professor Moretti. He put my paper down on top of the pile of other students' papers and stood up. "In *Things Fall Apart*, the rough beast that changes the world of the Igbo is the white missionaries. This school is funded by the Sons of the Rising Sun, as I'm sure you're aware of. Do you know much about the Rising Sun legend?"

I swallowed. "Why are you talking to me about this?" I asked.

"Are you late for something, Amy?"

I shook my head. "It's lunch," I said.

He nodded. "That it is. I won't keep you too long. I promise." He smiled. "The Rising Sun?"

"A little bit," I said. "But I don't see how it connects. I mean, the Rising Sun isn't a 'rough beast' is he? He's not evil."

"Our legends tell us he would impose a completely new order on the world," said Professor Moretti. "He would change everything. Is there any way for change to happen without violence and bloodshed and revolution? Aren't there some people who would see that as evil?"

"But it's a legend, right?" I said.

Professor Moretti shrugged again. "There have been reports," he said. "Buzzing in our organization. Signs and wonders. A boy who can drive men insane and rise from the dead. A boy and with him ... a girl."

I swallowed again. Shit. He did know. "But that doesn't fit, does it?" I said. "I mean, the Rising Sun was supposed to act alone, right?"

"You know more than a bit about this legend, don't you?"

"No," I said. "No, I don't know anything. And I really was supposed to meet someone for lunch."

Professor Moretti nodded. "Mr. Black, then? The two of you seem quite close."

Damn it, damn it, damn it. He had to know. First George Churchill. Now this. Jason and I were going to get ourselves killed. Of course, George had seemed scared.

"The reports," I said. "Officially, I thought that the organization didn't think that the boy in those reports was anything special."

"Well," said Moretti, "wouldn't it be odd if things were falling apart in the organization? If the center couldn't hold?"

"So this boy, then," I said, "if you saw him, you might think that he could be, well, dangerous. To things he perceived as threats." I was treading a pretty fine line, here. After all, Professor Moretti did work for the Sons. Directly. And I was all but admitting who I was. Still, if the word about Jason had travelled this far, maybe I could still scare him. Maybe.

Professor Moretti raised his eyebrows. "Noted, Amy. Noted." He smiled. "I wouldn't think he had anything to fear. Not from me. Go to lunch."

* * *

I couldn't find Jason in the cafeteria. I tried calling his cell phone, but he didn't pick up. Instead, I just sent him a text message, telling him we needed to talk as soon as possible. Palomino and Chance were sitting at our regular table. I got some food and sat down with them.

"Where's Jason?" asked Chance.

"I don't know," I said. "I haven't seen him since our last class. He's not answering his phone."

"Are you two fighting?" Chance asked. "Because last night when I got back, he didn't seem like he was in a great mood."

"We're not fighting," I said.

"You can tell us," said Palomino. "We were fighting, you know. It's okay to fight."

"We're not fighting," I said.

"Is it about your drinking?" asked Palomino.

"Yeah, are you drunk right now?" Chance asked.

"I'm not gonna drink anymore," I muttered.

"We're just trying to help," said Chance.

I got up. "I'm not really hungry," I said and walked off. Chance and Mina were calling after me, but I didn't pay attention.

Instead, I left the cafeteria and went for a walk. I had a lot of things to think about. Outside it was warm. The leaves on the trees were green. The grass was growing. It was late spring. I could hear birds calling to each other. Could see insects crawling along the sidewalks. It was a beautiful day. And everything was going to hell in my life. Fast.

I wandered between the ancient buildings of the Sol Solis school, gazing at my feet if I passed anyone. I wanted to be alone with my thoughts. I didn't want to talk to anyone. I didn't even want to smile at anyone.

It was bad that Professor Moretti seemed to know who Jason and I were. Even if he said that we didn't have anything to fear from him. What did that mean, anyway? How had he figured it out? Was it really because of my stupid essay? Was that enough to arouse his suspicions? I guess, despite the fact that Jason and I had changed our names, we still did seem suspicious. We appeared right after the incident in Shiloh. We were together. And Jeremy and Amy were maybe too close to our real names. What was Professor Moretti going to do? Would he tell someone? Would he try to hurt us?

Even if he didn't do anything, I didn't like the idea of his knowing who we were. It meant he had power over us. If we didn't need to get into that library so bad, I would have told Jason that we just needed to leave. Of course, it wasn't like we had anywhere to go. We were fugitives from the Sons and probably from the authorities too. Maybe there were wanted posters up in Georgia, with my picture on it. I was a murderer after all.

That was what the dreams were trying to tell me, weren't they? I was always dreaming about doing horrible things. Clearly, I hadn't worked through my guilt over killing my brothers and Lilith. But hell. Was that the kind of thing you worked through? Did you forgive yourself for stuff like that? Was there even a way to forgive yourself for something so horrible?

Did I even deserve to be forgiven?

Why had I done it?

I'd done it for Jason. I'd done it for me. They were going to kill Jason—Noah and Gordon. They'd captured me. They'd pursued me in their car. They'd forced me to wreck. They weren't exactly nice brothers. But that didn't mean they should be killed, did it?

My parents had always told me that life was about choices, and the best thing you could do was to make the most constructive choices possible. Anything destructive, they'd said, should be avoided at all costs. And I'd destroyed my brothers. And Lilith too. With Lilith, it seemed like a clear case of self-defense, though. She'd had a knife to my throat when I did it.

Still.

Even if I'd been defending myself. Even if I'd been defending Jason. I couldn't accept the fact that I'd done what I'd done. It had been bad enough when I'd had to deal with the fact that Jason killed people to defend me. This was something that I just couldn't deal with. I didn't know how.

The worst part of it was that sometimes I wondered about Jason himself. My family had been convinced he was so evil that he deserved to die. His own mother had prophesied that he'd enslave the human race. His own father thought that Jason was a monster that he'd created. And my brothers had shown me all these interviews with people who said that Jason had killed people. And that while he'd been doing it, he'd been smiling.

Jason said it wasn't true. I believed him.

Didn't I?

I had to believe him, didn't I, because if I didn't, what did I have left? I'd done everything, sacrificed everything for Jason. If I didn't believe in him, what did that mean my life was? A farce? A waste?

Besides, I knew Jason better than I'd ever known someone. Hadn't I held him when he'd cried? Hadn't I slept in the crook of his arms, feeling him hold me, listening to him murmur that he'd do anything to keep me safe? If I'd sacrificed for Jason, he'd sacrificed for me too. Every time he did something to save me, he lost a piece of his innocence, and he didn't have much left. I'd wanted to spare him that. I'd wanted to take care of myself. But if we kept this up, would there be anything left of either of us, or would our souls disappear into calluses? Would we rub them so raw that eventually the only protection we'd have would be not to feel?

In some ways, Professor Moretti was right. I did feel like Okonkwo's life had been stolen from him. And I felt like my life had been stolen from me too.

But the truth was that things were never going to be the way they used to be. I was never going to be normal girl, going to school, just thinking about school dances or what to do with my hair. And if I were honest with myself, I didn't even want to go back to that kind of naivete. Ignorance might be bliss, but knowledge, however painful, was always preferable.

* * *

By the time I got back to my dorm after classes that afternoon, I was starting to get worried about Jason. He hadn't called me back, and he hadn't been in any of the afternoon classes that we had together. I didn't know what had happened, but I hoped Professor Moretti didn't have something to do with it. He'd said that Jason didn't have anything to fear from him, but now, as near as I could tell, Jason was missing. As I made my way up the stairs to my dorm room, I tried calling him one last time. It went to voicemail, as it had all day. Where *was* he?

I burst into my room and flounced on my bed. I was worried.

"Hey," said Palomino.

"Hey," I said.

"Why'd you run off at lunch?" she asked.

"I've got a lot on my mind," I said.

"Like what?" asked Palomino. "Because I'm trying to figure out what I'm going to do with this baby, and I'm not being rude."

I sat up and surveyed her. "That's debatable," I said.

She threw a pillow at me. "Come on," she said. "What's going on? You can tell me."

"I haven't seen Jason since English," I said. "I've been calling him nonstop and he's not answering."

"He's probably hanging out with his brother," she said.

I stood up. "What?"

"I was going to tell you at lunch, but you ran off," she

said. "I met Jason's brother this morning. His name's Jude or something?"

Jude. Crap. I crossed the room to Palomino. "Where did you see him?"

"Outside the dorm this morning," she said. "He asked me if I knew Jason."

"And you said yes?" I was incredulous. "Didn't you ever think there was a *reason* Jason and I are going under assumed names?"

"Jesus. Don't yell at me. He's Jason's brother," she said.

"Who tried to *kill him* the last time we saw him!" I exclaimed.

"Oh wait," she said. "Maybe I do remember something about that."

"So help me, Palomino, if anything happens to Jason because of you —"

"Calm down," said Palomino. "I didn't tell him anything. I just said that I knew who Jason was, but I didn't know where he was."

"You didn't tell him anything? Nothing at all?"

* * *

I called Chance. Jason wasn't in his room. He hadn't been all afternoon. I told Chance to let me know the minute he showed up, or better yet, have Jason call me. I paced, even though Palomino couldn't understand why I was so upset. I wanted to break down and spill everything to her, but Jason and I had decided that it was safer if Mina and Chance were in the dark about most things. The more they knew, the more danger they'd be in, or so we thought.

I wasn't sure what to do. I didn't think Jude was really a match for Jason. Jason had been trained by the Sons, and he was fast and strong and very deadly in a fight. Jude had spent all his time growing up with his crazy mother. Jude hadn't had any training. Of course, that hadn't stopped him from putting a bullet in Jason's skull, just a few months ago. If Jude had a gun, could he have ... ?

I didn't want to think about it, but I couldn't think about anything else.

There was no one to help me.

The last time Jason had disappeared and I couldn't find him, I'd had Hallam, Jason's friend from the Sons. But Hallam had been working with Edgar Weem all along, betraying us. Hallam was out of the picture. Jason had told Hallam that if he saw him again, he'd kill him. And I was pretty sure Jason had been serious.

I asked Palomino where exactly she'd seen Jude and began asking everyone who lived in our dorm if they'd seen him too. They hadn't. And they hadn't seen Jason either.

I thought about trying to call Brother Mancini in Rome, but the Reddimus monks weren't violent people, and I didn't think they'd be able to do anything. Besides, while Brother Mancini and the Church were willing to help us in our struggle with the Sons, I didn't think they were extremely concerned with our welfare.

As the hours ticked by, I began to get more and more desperate. Every call I placed to Jason's phone went straight to voicemail. I didn't know what to do. I could go and look for Jason, but I had no idea where he might be. If Jude had taken him or done something to him, they could be anywhere. I didn't have the first idea about where to look.

But I had to do *something*. Curfew was looming, but I left the dorm anyway, and went to the assembly hall. The old church didn't seem a likely place for Jason and Jude to be, but it was the only place Jason and I went to besides our dorms. And I had dreamed about it the night before. I felt drawn there. The guards there were getting ready to lock up the building, but I told them I really needed to go the bathroom, and it would take me just a second. They let me in. I hid there, hoping that they'd go do some rounds and think that I had left while they weren't looking.

It worked.

Once the guards were gone, the old church was silent and dark. I crept out of the bathroom and did a quick sweep of the sanctuary. No one there. I'd known this would be a bust. There was no reason to come here. There was nothing I could do, except sit by my phone and wait. But if Jude had ...

On impulse, I traced the path from my dream last night, back through the church. Jason and I had never been in the church's basement. As far as I knew, it didn't have one. The basement in my dream had been a figment of my imagination. There was no way that there was a door back here.

But there was. And it looked exactly like my dream.

Had I seen this at some point, out of the corner of my eye

when I was in the church? How could I have dreamed about something I didn't know existed? Swallowing, I eased the door to the basement open.

A flickering light greeted me from the bottom of the steps.

I took a step inside, placing my foot on the first step. I tried to do it carefully, and slowly, but it made a noise.

"Hello?" said a male voice from the basement.

And before I could move, Jason rushed up the first few steps. He was a little sweaty, his dark hair sticking to his forehead. His face was dirty and so were his clothes. He was holding a gun.

"Azazel," he said.

I rushed to him. "You're okay?" I asked, hugging him hard.

He hugged me back. "I'm okay," he said. "How did you find me?"

"I ... I had a dream ..." I pulled back from Jason and surveyed the basement. Jesus. It was exactly the same, even down to the light bulb hanging on the chain. And in the corner, tied up in the same place Chance had been, was Jude. He looked unconscious. He looked like he'd been beaten up pretty badly. I could see that his right eye was red and swollen and that his lip had been bleeding. I turned to Jason. "What happened?"

Jason shrugged, wiping at his sweaty forehead with his dirty shirt. "I ran into Jude," he said.

"That's it?" I asked. "Why is he tied up? What did he try

to do you?"

"Nothing," said Jason. "I didn't give him a chance to do anything."

"Okay, so why is he tied up and beaten up?"

"Well, he did shoot me in the head the last time I saw him, you know. I don't think he's exactly trustworthy."

That was true. But Jude looked like he'd been punched around a little. Okay, a lot. "You hit him?" I asked.

Jason was quiet for several seconds. "Azazel, why don't you go back to your dorm," said Jason.

"What?" I said. "No. What's going on here? You haven't been answering your phone—"

"I've been busy," said Jason.

"You weren't even going to tell me about this?" I asked.

"Of course I was," said Jason.

I looked around the basement again. It was so much like my dream. The whole situation was weirdly like my dream. But instead of my brother tied up, it was Jason's brother.

"Look," said Jason, "it's obvious what has to be done about Jude. And I know that you've been having those dreams. And I didn't want you to have to be part of it. It doesn't bother me so much, so I thought I'd just take care of it, and then let you know after. But you don't have to watch, you know."

I furrowed my brow at him for a moment, not understanding. Then chillingly, his words made definite cold sense. "You're going to kill him," I said.

"He tried to kill me."

"Today? Did he try to kill you today?"

"No. No, today he's just been talking about our Dad."

Dad? Oh. "Edgar Weem is Jude's father too? I thought Michaela Weem thought he was disgusting and evil. Why would she have sex with him again?"

Jason laughed, but he didn't sound amused, not really. "Who knows?" he said. He began to pace, gesturing wildly with the gun. "Apparently, 'Mommy' didn't just have sex with 'Daddy' again, but he used to visit her and little bro, Jude, here. And that's why when the Sons captured Jude, he didn't get in any trouble at all. He just got released into 'Daddy's' custody."

"Jason—"

He wasn't done. "No, near as I can figure from what Jude said, the only reason Michaela was mad was that Edgar broke it off when Jude was about five."

"Jude said that he didn't know who his dad was," I said.

"He didn't. He thought Edgar was one of Michaela's boyfriends. Apparently, she had a few of those."

"It still doesn't make sense," I said. "We know that Michaela was plotting your death from the moment you were conceived. Because she told my parents about the vision she had of me, and—"

"No," said Jason. He stopped pacing, turned, and looked at me. "No, she always hated me. It was just Edgar that she couldn't make up her mind about."

I went to him. Put my hand on his cheek. "Oh, Jason, I'm so—"

He shrugged me off.

" —sorry," I finished. I'd never seen Jason upset about his family. Usually, he seemed to have no interest in them at all. And he certainly hadn't had any qualms about hurting his own mother. She wasn't a very nice person, granted, but ...

Jason shook his head. Squared his shoulders. "You don't have to be sorry," he said. "There's nothing to be sorry about."

I was quiet for several seconds. If Jason couldn't acknowledge that it hurt him that his mother had hated him, had tried to have him killed, then there wasn't much I could say. I looked at Jude, who still hadn't regained consciousness. "You can't kill him," I said quietly. "Not if we don't know why he's here."

"You're saying I should trust him?"

"I'm saying ..." God, I really had no idea.

"Do you remember what Jude said to us when we were leaving the house in Shiloh? He said, 'This isn't over.' That was a threat, Azazel, and I'm pretty sure he was serious."

"But we can't just kill him," I said.

"*We're* not doing anything. *You're* going back to the dorm. *I'm* going to handle this."

Handle this. Like it was a job or something. Like it was an annoyance. An everyday occurrence. I shook my head. "So you're just going to put a bullet in his head? Or were you going to rough him up some more? Are you enjoying beating him up?"

"Enjoying?" Jason looked at me like I was insane. "Do

you even know me at all? I don't want to do this—"

"Then don't," I said.

"You want me to let him go? Just let him go? And what happens when he does whatever he's planning to do to make sure I don't forget I killed his mother? What then?"

"We don't know that he's going to hurt us."

"We can't afford to take the chance," said Jason.

"It's wrong," I said. "Killing people is just wrong."

"Wrong?" Jason shook his head. "Wrong? What happened to 'sometimes there is no right thing?'"

"What?" I said.

"You said that to me, after I shot the Sons in New Jersey. You said that sometimes there was only a choice between two wrong things. Do you remember that?"

Maybe I did remember saying that. And maybe I also remembered that I didn't believe in absolutes like right and wrong. Maybe I remembered that I believed that people had to make productive decisions. And maybe what Jason was doing here was simply that. If we wanted to make sure we stayed alive, we had to eliminate Jude. But ... "This isn't the same," I said. "That was self-defense. They had guns in our faces. They'd already shot a lot of people. Jude hasn't—"

"It's the same," said Jason. "But maybe it's not really about that. Maybe it's about something else. After all, you told me that you let Jude kiss you in Shiloh."

"So that I could get his keys!" I said.

Jason shrugged. "Well, that's what you say, anyhow. I wasn't there. Maybe you kind of have a soft spot for Jude, though. Maybe there's some part of you that—"

"Jason Wodden, there is no part of me that is the least bit interested in Jude romantically."

Jason snorted, staring down at the guns in his hands. "The lady doth protest too much, methinks," he said. He looked at me. "You'll notice that I didn't say anything about a romantic interest. You went there on your own."

"You brought up kissing for God's sake!" I exclaimed. I sighed, crossing my arms over my chest. "I thought we were past this stuff."

"Past it? How can we be past it when you don't even want me to touch you anymore?"

What? Why would he say that? "Of course I do."

"Out of three attempts I've made to make love to you, you've turned me down twice," Jason said. "And then there's the whole orgasm thing."

"Jason, Jesus!" How could he possibly think that any of this stuff was related?

"Maybe you can't come because it's not me you want," he said. "Maybe you want Jude."

My jaw dropped. I was stunned. Completely and utterly flabbergasted. I couldn't speak, because I was floored by the idiocy of what he'd said.

"Guess I hit a nerve," Jason muttered.

I took a deep breath. "You know," I said, "Just because I don't want him dead doesn't mean I want to screw him. I have absolutely no interest in Jude. And I don't particularly ever want to see him again. But I don't think that means you should shoot him. That's all."

"Whatever," said Jason.

"Is that why you want to kill him?" I asked. "Because you're jealous? Which, may I say, you have no reason to be?"

"Stop saying that I *want* to kill him! I *have* to kill him! I don't have a choice!"

"You always have a choice, Jason," I said and started for the steps.

He caught me by the hand and turned me to face him. "Jesus, Azazel, he's my brother," he said, and he sounded agonized. "He's my brother, and he tried to kill me. And my mother tried to kill me, and my father thinks I'm some kind of monster and that I might have to be put down like a rabid dog or something! Everyone thinks I'm psychotic. And now you keep saying that I *want* to kill my own brother. Do you think it too?"

His eyes looked so haunted and earnest.

"Is there something wrong with me?" he whispered. "Are they right? Am I destined only to destroy things?"

"No," I said. "No, Jason, there is nothing wrong with you." Even though, as I said it, I had to admit that I wasn't even sure anymore. I cupped his face in my hands. "It doesn't matter how they feel about you, Jason. I love you."

He put his arms around me and pulled me in close to him. "Eventually, everyone thinks it, though," he said. "Anton. Hallam. They all start thinking that I'm—that I'm evil."

"Jason ..." But hadn't I wondered this? Hadn't I thought this? "There isn't such a thing," I said. "I don't believe ..." And I didn't know what to say. I didn't know how to comfort him, so I just kissed him.

As our lips met, I wished as hard as I could that we had some kind of help. That people supported us. That we didn't have to struggle endlessly against everyone in the world. If only there was someplace where people really just ...cared about us.

He kissed me back hungrily, like he was trying to find comfort in my lips. I opened my mouth to him, letting the sweetness of his tongue into my mouth. I felt like we were drowning in each other, like there was nothing left in the world that either of us had besides each other. And we kissed like that until Jude stirred behind us.

"Could you start hitting me again?" Jude said, his voice raspy. "Because watching you two make out like that is really a lot worse than when you were just beating me up."

Jason and I stepped back from each other.

"Still got it bad for my big brother, huh?" said Jude. "You know, Azazel, they say it's hard for women to leave men who scare them."

"Jude, don't," I said.

"Did you know she told me that once, Jase? She said you scared her," Jude continued. He licked his bruised lips.

"Shut up, Jude," I said. He was making things worse. Maybe he'd been listening to our conversation. Maybe he knew that he was pushing Jason's buttons.

"I don't get it, honestly," said Jude. "I mean the guy's a jealous freak. He's killed as many people as Jack the Ripper. What do you see in him?"

I wrenched the gun in Jason's hands away from him and strode over to Jude. I put the gun in his face. "Shut *up*, Jude," I said.

"Come on," he said. "Why don't you just tell him how you really feel about me?" Jude smiled.

I flipped the safety off the gun. "Listen to me, Jude," I said, my voice flat. "If you say one more thing, I will blow your head off. All that stuff you're saying about Jason ... We're the same, Jason and me. Okay? So, don't push me. Don't push Jason." I looked into Jude's eyes. "Nod if you understand."

Jude didn't move for a second, but then he nodded.

I noticed something, next to Jude on the ground. I knelt to pick it up. It was a leather-bound book. I opened it. Handwritten writing filled the pages. A journal of some kind? I held it up. "Jason, you know what this is?"

Jason shrugged.

"That's mine," Jude said.

"I told you not to talk, didn't I?" I asked him, gesturing with the gun.

Jude pressed his lips together firmly, but he glared at me, clearly angry.

I stood up, putting the safety back on the gun and handing it back to Jason. "We'll gag him," I said. "We'll gag him, and we'll make sure he's tied up really tight. And we'll leave him here until we can talk about what we're going to do. Okay?"

Jason looked down at the gun and then over at Jude. He nodded. "Okay."

* * *

As I was falling asleep that night, I thought about what had happened. I thought about what Jason had said to me, about everyone coming to the conclusion that he was evil. He was right. His mentor Anton, had found out that Jason was a product of Edgar Weem's twisted creation and decided to kill Jason. Hallam, under the direction of Edgar Weem, had been ready to kill Jason if he thought that Jason's violence was getting out of control. Every member of his family had been ready to kill him. Were all of these people wrong? Was there something dark within Jason? And if there were, what should I do?

If I hadn't found Jason tonight, and he'd gone ahead and killed Jude, I would have felt horrified. So much of what Jason had done already horrified me. But tying someone up, beating him bloody, and then putting a bullet in his head? It was something that only monsters did. I didn't think Jason was a monster. I loved him. He was my everything. But I was glad that I'd been able to stop him from killing Jude.

How had I stopped it, anyway? I'd found him. But that had been because of my dream. In my dream, Jason had been about to kill Chance, my little brother. In reality, Jason had been about to kill Jude, his brother. In the dream, I'd threatened to kill Jason. I'd said, "This is the line. We're not crossing it." Then I'd shot Chance anyway, when he'd threatened to hurt Jason.

What did the dream mean? And why did it have such an eerie similarity to reality?

Because I'd put a gun in Jude's face too, just like I'd aimed at Chance in the dream. And when I'd told Jude that if he spoke again, I would shoot him, I'd been serious. I would have killed him. I'd said to Jude, "Jason and I are the same." Were we? If Jason did monstrous things, then so did I.

Suddenly, I flashed on the moments before I'd shot Lilith in the head. I hadn't thought about that in any detail pretty much since I'd done it. But I suddenly remembered the moments of clear, cold thought I'd had before I'd done it. I remembered that I had thought about the conse-quences of the action, the ease of casual violence, the fact that I'd be haunted and disturbed by it. And I'd chosen to do it, anyway. Because, I'd thought, no matter what anyone said about fate or Shiva or the power of Azazel, in the end, it was my responsibility. My choice.

But I'd dreamed last night, and my dream had come very close to true. And Jason and I had done things that had no explanation. If we were what they said we were, then we didn't have choices. Because then we were only fulfilling destiny.

I couldn't have it both ways. I couldn't believe that I had choices and responsibility and also believe that there were mystical forces interfering with our lives. So what would I believe? What was the truth? And how did I decide how to proceed?

One thing was for sure. Jason and I were falling further and further into an abyss. It was like black water closing over our heads. And even if we remembered how to swim, I didn't know which way was up anymore. For all I knew, all our flailing was doing nothing more than dragging us down deeper.

Right before I fell asleep, a note of panic stole into my thoughts as I realized I hadn't had anything to drink. But I shook it away grimly. If the dreams were coming for me, I'd have to face them. And with that thought, I slipped into black and dreamless sleep.

* * *

The next day was Saturday, and we didn't have any classes. In the morning, when I woke up, Jason called me because he wanted to talk about what to do with Jude. I wasn't ready to talk about it. Instead, we decided that we'd check on him periodically throughout the day. I went right after breakfast, and I even brought him some food. Jason and I hadn't talked about whether we were feeding him or not, but I wasn't going to let Jude just die of thirst or starvation down there. That was a crueler way to kill him than simply shooting him. I couldn't believe that I was considering the most merciful way to kill someone.

I untied Jude to let him eat. As he shoved food into his mouth, he asked me, "What are you guys going to do with me?"

I didn't want to talk to Jude, especially because I didn't know if he was going to die soon. I wanted to distance myself from him emotionally. "What do you think we should do?" I said. "We clearly can't trust you."

"Listen, I want that diary back," said Jude.

"Eat," I said.

"You took it from me, and I want it back," said Jude.

"How did you get away from the Sons anyway?" I said. "And why should we trust you? Aren't you just trying to kill Jason?"

Jude guzzled some of the iced tea I'd brought him. "I just want my diary back, okay?"

I left Jude as soon as I could. Jason was going to check on him in the afternoon. I made sure that Jude's bonds were as tight as possible and gagged him again, even though he begged me not to. When I left him, I felt dirty somehow, like I needed to take a shower to scrub off the inhuman part of me. I told myself that being tied up and gagged in a basement was better than dead. Jude should be grateful.

Palomino's mother had sent her some money for a prom dress. She wanted me to come shopping for one with her. Our school wasn't too far from Milan, and I had to admit there was something appealing about going shopping for a prom dress in the fashion capital of the world. Palomino had a car. A good portion of the kids at school had them, but students were forbidden to use their cars except on the weekends. So Palomino and I took off for Milan.

We did our shopping in the square near the Duomo,

which was an awe-inspiring cathedral that looked like something out of a fairy tale. Built of light stone, with at least 50 intricate spires reaching for the heavens, it was impossible to look away from. It simply didn't look real. I wanted to go inside, since it was a major tourist attraction. However, for Palomino, the Duomo was old hat. She'd seen it too many times to count and didn't seem the least bit affected by it. She had to pull me away as I stood staring at it, open mouthed.

Even though Milan is the fashion capital of the world, not all of the stores around the Duomo were priced in the stratosphere. Of course, Palomino wanted to visit those, but when I told her my budget for my prom dress, she took me to a more reasonably-priced store instead. "Actually," she said, "I should get one here too and save the rest of the money my mom gave me. You know, for the baby."

The store had various levels. Prom dresses were on the top floor. After we climbed the steps, I began sifting through the dresses on the racks. "Mina," I said, "seriously, what are you going to do about this? If you do manage to hide the fact you're pregnant from everyone, they're still going to know when you, like, have a baby."

"Yeah," she said. "I know." She held up a hot pink strapless dress with black polka dots. "What do you think of this?"

"Um … it's very *Pretty in Pink*, I guess," I said.

"Yeah, it's ugly," she said, putting it back on the rack. She pulled out a long shimmery green dress with spaghetti straps.

"Pretty," I said.

"You try it on," she said.

"You saw it first," I said.

"Azazel, try on the dress. Let's try to have some fun girl time for once."

Right. Fun girl time. When Jude was sitting in a basement tied up and bloody, and my roommate was pregnant with my little brother's bastard child. Okay. She held the dress out to me.

"What size is it?" I said, sighing.

"Oh, who can understand this ridiculous Italian sizing? It says it's huge, but it's made for dwarves, so don't worry about it and try it on."

I took the dress and went into the dressing room.

It was low cut and bunchy around my waist. I surveyed myself in the mirror. "I don't think so," I said.

"Let me see," said Palomino.

"No, it's bad."

"Show me!"

I emerged from the dressing room. Palomino was waiting for me in a long black dress with a halter top and an empire waist.

"That dress is awesome on you!" I exclaimed.

"Thanks," she said. "I wanted something that would hide my belly."

I rolled my eyes. "Mina, prom is in a week. What kind of belly do you think you're going to have?"

"I already have one!" she exclaimed.

"You do not!"

"Besides," she said. "This dress is cheap. My parents give me money for all kinds of things, like dresses and stuff. If I don't spend it all and save it, and maybe if I sell my car, then, when they find out about the baby and they kick me out on the street, maybe Chance and I can ..."

I hugged her. "You don't really think your parents are going to throw you out, do you?"

She shrugged. "They're going to be really, really mad, Azazel."

"That sucks." My parents would never have done something like that to me. Of course, they'd tried to keep me pure so I could participate in a Satanic ritual. Parents pretty much sucked no matter how you sliced it. "I'm so sorry."

"It's okay," she said. "I'm glad you told Chance. He's been really, really awesome. And I think it's gonna be okay. I really do." She smiled. Then she looked at my dress. "Oh God," she said. "That's awful."

"I told you," I said.

We ducked back into the dressing room and changed out of our dresses. Mina hung hers up on the door and helped me hunt through the racks some more. I tried on at least ten dresses. Some of them were okay. One of them looked really, really nice on the hanger, but didn't look so nice on me. One of them I really liked, but cost way too much money.

And just when I was beginning to despair ever finding a dress at all, Palomino rushed forward with a dress in her hands and gave it to me. "This one," she said.

She was right. That was definitely the dress. As I zipped it up in the dressing room and surveyed myself in the mirror, hardly able to believe how well it fit me, my phone beeped at me. Text message. I dug in my pants on the floor to get it out.

It was from Jason. "Get back here. NOW," it said.

"what's up?" I texted back.

"NOW!!!" was all he replied.

"Mina," I said, "we've got to go back to school."

CHAPTER SIX

April 26, 1990

Jed had a lot of information for us to go through this evening. He says he believes the Rising Sun could be born from the Weem line and that we needed to try to find someone young among his cousins that could possibly bear the child. Then our business would be to prepare that person as best we could. But ...I've been spending a lot of time with Jed, and I have an idea. It's crazy and weird, and I'm afraid to even bring it up to him, because I'm not sure what he'll think about it. But if we go the route that Jed's suggesting, it could take years to really get things rolling. And he says that we're running out of time, because the Rising Son is a key player in 2012.

Jason met us at the entrance to the dorm. He grabbed me by the arm and started to drag me away with him. "Come with me," he said.

I had my dress in a bag draped over my arm, so I shook it in front of his face. "I have a dress I need to put away," I told him.

He took the dress bag from me and shoved it at Palomino. "Take that upstairs for her," he said.

Mina took the dress and stared after us as Jason pulled me along. "Where are you guys going?" she asked.

"Don't worry about it!" Jason called over his shoulder. Once we were out of earshot, he said, "We've got a problem."

"Problem?" I said.

"I'll show you," he said.

We went to the Assembly Hall. It was open and there was a guard at the door. Inside, the drama club was on the stage up front, practicing the spring play.

"Someone's gonna see us," I hissed at Jason as he pulled me towards the basement door.

"No, they won't. They're not paying attention." He thrust open the door to the basement and pushed me inside first. I went down the steps. "Is Jude gone or something?" I asked.

But when I emerged in the basement, Jude was still in the place we'd left him. His head was slumped over, and he wasn't moving. I turned back to Jason. "What?" I asked.

Jason strode over to Jude and lifted his face up by the hair. Jude's eyes were open. They stared dully out at the dark basement. There was a large bloody wound in his forehead. A gunshot, most likely. Jason dropped Jude's head. It thudded back against Jude's body. "He's dead," Jason said.

"I see that," I said.

"You were the last person to see him," said Jason.

"What?"

"After all that stuff last night about not killing him, then you just come in here after breakfast and shoot him?"

"I didn't do it!" I said. "You must have." Although it didn't make sense for Jason to accuse me of killing Jude if he'd actually done it. He wouldn't lie to me, would he?

"You wouldn't lie to me?" Jason said, echoing my

thoughts.

"Of course not."

"I didn't do it either," said Jason.

I let this sink in. If neither Jason nor I had killed Jude, then someone else must have. Someone else knew about Jude.

"Are you sure?" said Jason. "Because you've been drinking a lot, and maybe you blacked out or some-thing—"

"No, I haven't had a drink since before we found him," I said. I paused. "Maybe he did it to himself?"

"Then where's the gun?"

"Oh. Yeah."

"This is not good," said Jason.

"No," I said. "It's not."

We didn't have any idea who would kill Jude. Could it be someone with a grudge against Jude already? Someone who'd followed him here? Someone who didn't care about us at all?

That seemed too good to be true. We were concerned that the body of Jude was less about him and more about us. Maybe it was a message, letting us know that *someone* knew who we were and where we were. Whoever that someone was, he wasn't afraid of putting bullets in people's heads.

Jason and I didn't know what to do. We couldn't leave Jude's body here. It would start ... smelling at some point, and so we were going to have to try to get it out of here. We agreed to meet back at the old church after lights out that night. With trash bags.

* * *

At dinner that night, Jason seemed tense. He moved his food around on his plate with his fork, but didn't actually eat much of it. I squeezed his hand under the table, and tried to tell him with a look that everything was going to be okay. I didn't know if everything was going to be okay or not. But I wished someone would tell me that right now.

Palomino and Chance didn't notice that the two of us weren't our usual selves, due to the fact that Mina chattered constantly, relaying our adventures in Milan, including how awed I'd been with the Duomo, which Palomino found hysterically funny. Chance defended me, saying that he thought it was pretty amazing too.

Then Palomino launched into detailed descriptions of our dresses.

"Wait," said Chance, "aren't we guys not supposed to know about these dresses until prom?"

"You're thinking of bride's dresses," said Palomino. "Grooms aren't supposed to see the bride before the wedding."

"Oh," said Chance.

"Azazel's dress is really pretty," said Palomino.

"So is yours," I said.

"Mine is slimming," said Palomino.

I rolled my eyes. "You're one of the slimmest people I know," I said. "You don't need to be slimmed."

Mina patted her still-flat stomach as if she was actually showing her pregnancy already.

"Is this seat taken?"

We all looked up to see who was talking to us. It was Fairie Weem. We exchanged a look. Why would Fairie Weem want to talk to us? No one said anything. Fairie seemed to take this as an invitation. She sat down.

"Hey," she said brightly.

No one said anything.

"So how are you guys?" she asked.

I looked around. "Where's the rest of them?" I said. "How does this turn into a big joke on us?"

Fairie sighed, chewing on a celery stick. I noticed she only had low calorie foods on her plate. Celery sticks. Lettuce. Cucumbers. Maybe she was anorexic. "Look, I know we gave you guys a hard time at first, but honestly, it was all in good fun."

"You said that I was on heroin and that I had AIDs," said Palomino. "How was that in good fun?"

"I'm sorry," said Fairie, sounding defensive. "Geez. But, you know, I never said anything like about you two. Amy and Jeremy." She beamed at us.

"Did George tell you something?" Jason asked.

Fairie looked completely confused. "What's George got to do with this? Okay, Faruza's only banging him because he's got a really big dick. She might dump him anyway, if you guys—" she gestured at Jason and me "—think he's stupid."

What the hell?

"Look," she said, "a bunch of us are having a get together

tonight. Outside by the rec center. Starts around nine. Don't worry about curfew. It's totally taken care of. It'd be really cool if you showed." She smiled and got up. "Oh, Amy," she said. "You should totally wear that little black tank top you were wearing the other day. It's super cute."

And she swept off.

I felt like I'd just been hit by a bus. "That was weird," I said.

"It *is* a cute tank top," said Palomino.

"They hate us, though," I said.

Palomino shrugged. "Well, I think we should go."

"Are you kidding?" I said. "They'll dump pig's blood or something on us."

Chance chuckled darkly. "I think they'll wait until the prom for that."

"Okay," said Jason. "We'll go."

I turned to look at him, astonished. "What?" I said. "But—" *We have a body to dispose of tonight.*

He gave me a look.

I shrugged. "Guess we're going."

"Cool," said Palomino. "Party." She grinned, then frowned. "Damn it. I can't drink!"

I made a sympathetic face. "I'm totally not wearing that tank top, though," I muttered.

* * *

Jason explained to me that he thought it would be easier for us to sneak out of the party to take care of Jude's body than it would be to sneak out of the dorm. Plus, being at the party meant that we could use the rich kids' curfew pass to our advantage. It made sense, but I was kind of frustrated with him because the clothes I wanted to wear to move a body were not the clothes I wanted to wear to a party. I tried to find a happy medium. Clothes that looked kind of nice but could get messed up, and I wouldn't care. This was really next to impossible, so I ended up in an outfit that I figured I was just going to have to sacrifice.

We showed up at the party around nine, even though Mina protested that it was totally uncool to be on time. Jason and I wanted to get there early enough that we could make an appearance and then sneak off without anyone realizing we weren't still there. We figured this would be easy, since we weren't very popular at the Sol Solis School. We didn't know very many people, anyway. We were wrong.

When we got to the rec center, about ten of the richest kids in the school were already there. They had set up a snack on the picnic tables under the pavilion. The picnic tables were covered in crimson tablecloths and set with real silverware and plates. It looked very elegant and innocent. Faruza and Fairie were there already, fussing over flower arrangements. When they saw us, their identical faces lit up, and they rushed over.

"Hey!" said Faruza.

"Hi!" said Fairie. "You came! I wasn't sure if you would."

Faruza shoved Fairie playfully. "I told you they'd come," she said. She linked arms with me and started to walk me over towards the picnic tables. I shot a terrified glance over my shoulder at Jason, but he was following, being led in a similar way by Fairie. Behind us, Chance and Mina trailed, looking confused.

I felt confused too. This had to be a set up of some kind. People who hated you didn't suddenly just get nice for no reason.

" ... so don't worry," Faruza was saying to me.

"Huh?" I said, trying to concentrate on what she was saying.

"I was saying that all this stuff is just a show for the heads," she said. She meant the headmasters and mistresses of the school. "They usually show up to these things when we throw them and stay for about an hour or two. Once they leave, we break out the booze."

I nodded. "And you don't get in trouble for throwing parties on campus?"

Fairie pulled close with Jason in tow. "Our parents donate a significant amount of money to the school," she said, smiling and winking.

So I guessed that was what it was like to be a really rich kid. And the Weem twins were really rich kids who went to a school full of rich kids. They were the richest of the rich.

Sure enough, within fifteen minutes, the heads of the school showed up. They got snacks and chatted with the students while sitting at the fancy picnic tables. Jason and I didn't have a minute to ourselves. Faruza and Fairie yanked us around, introducing us to people who didn't know us and asking our opinions about all kinds of ridiculous things.

Faruza seemed very concerned over my thoughts on the pattern of the china which we were using. "Next time," she said, "you should totally help me pick it out or something, because I want to make sure you guys like it."

Why did she care if we liked it?

It got worse. "I told George not to come," Faruza told me as we munched on smoked salmon and crackers. "I know that you guys aren't really very fond of him."

"Um, I really thought it was the other way around. I thought you guys didn't like us."

"That's just not true," said Faruza. "I mean, I think at first, I was caving to a lot of peer pressure and stuff, and I really want to apologize for that, because it seriously wasn't cool. We think you and Jeremy are pretty much the most awesome thing that's ever happened to this school."

"Yeah?" I said. "Since when?"

Faruza looked a little troubled for a second, as if she was thinking really hard. "Well," she said, "I want to say since always, but that doesn't make sense, does it? Because I remember that I was, like, really mean to you. I remember that Fairie and I had the idea to invite you to the party last night. We couldn't believe we'd left you out."

"To invite Jeremy and me," I said.

"Yeah."

"But not Chance and Mina?"

"Oh, of course, it's fine if your friends want to come. It's one of the things I admire about you the most. That you're just so nice to everyone, even people like that."

"Chance is my—" I stopped talking. I'd been about to tell her that Chance was my brother, but I couldn't say that out loud.

"No, no!" said Faruza. "I know that you four are all really close. That's awesome. And they should stay, because it's awesome. Seriously." She smiled at me, as if she were afraid we all might just bolt.

Which was annoying, because that was exactly what Jason and I wanted to do.

I searched the crowd for Jason. I could see that he was with Fairie on the other side of the pavilion. He was holding a plate filled with hors d'oeuvres and stuffing them into his mouth as several people chattered at him. How were we going to get out of here?

The night wore on. The heads left. The alcohol came out. This wasn't like a keg party back in Bramford, however, or even a party on the beach in Bradenton. There were fancy cocktails served in crystal martini glasses with glass stirrers. More of the Weem twins' friends started to show up and swarm me. They told me how much they liked my outfit. They complimented my hairstyle (a ponytail—nothing fancy). They wanted to know what stylist was doing my hair and makeup for the prom.

"Um," I said, "I was going to do it myself."

"Wow," they all said, "what a cool idea."

"Yeah. It's so simple."

"And self-sufficient."

"Amy, you're an inspiration."

I felt like I was going to choke. I managed a half-smile. "I need to find my boyfriend," I said.

"Oh!" said Faruza. "We've been hogging you all night, haven't we? I'm so sorry! Let's go find Jeremy." She took my arm and dragged me over to where Jason was standing. He was surrounded by a group of girls and guys. As I approached, I could hear their conversation.

"So, where did you get that shirt?" one of the girls was asking.

"I don't know," said Jason, sounding just as weirded out as I felt.

"God," said one of the guys. "That's so cool. He doesn't even know where his clothes came from."

"Yeah, dude, that's awesome," said another.

Jason spotted me approaching. He reached out for my hand and pulled me close.

"Hi," I said.

"I am so happy to see you," he whispered in my ear.

I nodded. "Me too," I mouthed. Then, more loudly. "Oh God, Jeremy, I left something in my dorm room. Can you come with me to get it?"

"Of course," he said. "Good idea," he whispered. To the crowd of onlookers who had gathered around us, "Excuse us."

The crowd parted to let us out. Jason clasped my hand, and we walked away as fast as we could. It was all I could do not to run.

The rec center was on the opposite side of campus than

the assembly hall. We started walking back in that direction. Within several minutes, we were out of sight of the rec center.

"Okay," said Jason, "that was weird."

"Yeah," I said. "What was that?"

"If it's a prank, they're really putting a lot of effort into it."

They were. And they all seemed so genuine. Why would they waste so much time being nice to us if they just wanted to make fun of us? "Do you think maybe it's not a prank?" I asked.

Jason shot a glance at me. "You mean like they all suddenly think we're really awesome?"

I swallowed. "Why would they think that?"

Jason's jaw twitched. "I think George told them something. When he ran away from me, it seemed like he knew something, didn't he? Like he knew who we were."

"But Faruza said she told George not to come tonight," I said. "And besides, would that make them like us?"

"It might make them afraid of us," said Jason.

Maybe. I considered. "So, then, wouldn't they run from us instead of being all sweet and nice?"

Jason shook his head. "I don't know. I don't know. Maybe it's a prank."

"Maybe," I said. It was strange that thinking it was a prank was a comforting thought. "But if it's a prank, then we just left Chance and Palomino to deal with the brunt of it."

"We'll go back," Jason said.

"But we'll be ...messy," I said, shuddering a little. I didn't want to think about what we were getting ready to do. Not one bit.

Jason had left the garbage bags inside the old church, at the top of the basement steps. It took a little doing to get the door unlocked. Jason had to pick it. We went in through the side like always, while I stood watch and looked for guards. No one seemed to be out tonight. At least not near the old church. I could see the back of the guards who stood at the entrance to the library. Apparently, those guys never left.

The garbage bags were still there. But Jude's body wasn't.

There wasn't a trace of him. No clothes, no blood, no marks from dragging a body on the floor. Nothing.

Jason and I stood inside the small enclave of the basement, the light bulb swinging back and forth crazily, making the shadows dance on the wall, and we didn't move.

"This isn't good," I finally whispered.

"No," said Jason. "It's not."

* * *

Maybe Jude hadn't really been dead, I wondered. But Jason assured me that he had been. He hadn't had a pulse. He'd been fatally wounded. Jude had definitely been dead.

Jude had been killed. We didn't know who had done that. Whoever had done it had known where Jude was, and no one except us knew where Jude was. Then someone had come in and moved his body. It was probably the same someone who had killed him, but we couldn't even be sure of that. It was unnerving. We were worried. Was it the Sons?

Had they killed Jude to silence him? Was it Edgar Weem? Had he had Jude killed to silence him?

Who could have done it and why?

And part of me, no matter how much I told myself it was crazy, couldn't shake the worry that Jason had killed Jude and moved the body and that he was just lying to me about it, because he knew I didn't want him to kill Jude.

I didn't want to go back to the party, but Jason said we had to or it might look suspicious. The only bright side the evening was that my clothes hadn't actually been ruined. We walked back across campus to the rec center, where the pavilion was lit up with Christmas lights and filled with people laughing and drinking. Almost immediately, we were jumped by the Weem twins and their entourage, but Jason and I stayed close this time.

I wanted to find Chance and Palomino, so we wound through the bodies looking for them for nearly a half hour. Finally, we found them on the fringes of everything. Chance was drinking an expensive bottled beer, and Mina was drinking coke. They were sitting alone, just talking to each other.

Jason and I sat down with them. I motioned the crowd who had followed us to go away. Reluctantly, they did.

"You guys okay?" I asked.

Chance and Mina both smiled at us brightly.

"We're great," said Chance.

"Yeah," said Mina. "We're having an awesome time."

"Sorry that we got sidetracked by all those people," said

Jason.

"No problem," said Chance. "I can see why they'd want to talk to you."

"We get to talk to you guys all the time," said Mina. "It would be selfish of us to hog you."

Hog us?

"Um ..." I said, "well, we hang out with you guys because we like you, you know. We want to hang out with you."

Mina beamed. "That's sweet. It's so cool that you said that."

"Yeah," said Chance. "But the two of you have people to see. Don't worry about it, okay?"

Jason and I exchanged a look over their heads. Was it just me, or was everyone suddenly starting to act really, really weird?

* * *

The week continued with increasing weirdness. On Monday, Professor Moretti read my paper on *Things Fall Apart* to the entire class, praising it as the most insightful and comprehensive treatment of the novel he'd ever read. When he was done, the entire class applauded.

At lunch that day, Jason and I were barraged with people who wanted to sit with us. Fifteen people gushed over my outfit. The rest of the week continued the trend. Jason and I were excused from two tests because the teachers thought we'd "already proven our capabilities adequately." The head of the school invited us to a private lunch with him on Wednesday, where he told us how happy he was that we'd chosen his school and how honored the Sol Solis family was to count us as part of their ranks. Confused and a little fed up with this treatment, I'd asked him why. Did everyone know who were were, suddenly? Was that why everyone was behaving differently towards us?

The head had replied that we were special. He knew that we weren't just normal students. And then he'd winked.

Jason had looked positively sick when he saw the wink. He'd leaned forward across the table we shared with the head and asked, "How did you find out who we are?'

The head had looked confused. "I think I always knew," he said. "But I had this idea to have you for a special lunch on Friday of last week, I think. It was late."

Friday again. Faruza had mentioned that same night to me.

It wasn't conclusive evidence that the head knew Jason was the Rising Sun. He never used those words. But we were definitely getting special treatment. And we were getting it from everyone.

Thursday we were back to our crowded lunch table. Faruza and Fairie flanked us on either side, both with plates full of salads.

As Faruza shook red wine vinegar on her salad, she looked at me. I had a plate with pasta salad and a hamburger. "Wow," said Faruza. "Amy, how do you stay so thin eating all of that?"

I looked down at myself. "I'm not that thin," I said. I was kind of average looking. Not really skinny, but not exactly fat either. Faruza and Fairie were both thin enough to be models or Hollywood actresses.

Faruza speared a piece of lettuce with her fork. "You're totally thin," she said. "I really wish I looked like you."

"Aren't you going to put some oil on that salad?" I said. "I thought it was supposed to be oil and vinegar, not just vinegar."

"Oil is fat," spoke up Fairie.

I looked around Jason at Fairie, who looked so earnest. Then I looked back at Faruza, also very serious. If being that thin meant I couldn't have olive oil, I didn't think I cared that much. Also, it was pretty clear that Faruza and Fairie had kind of unhealthy eating habits. Maybe I could use my newfound (and totally weird) celebrity for some kind of good. "If you want to look like me, Faruza," I said, "you should eat a hamburger."

"White bread buns?!" exclaimed Fairie.

"Red meat? Saturated fat?!" said Faruza.

I nodded. "Yeah."

"Hamburgers are good," said Faruza.

"I'll go get some," said Fairie, running off to the lunch line.

Jason laughed quietly to himself. I grinned at him.

When Faruza took a bite of her hamburger, she made a small moaning sound. A satisfied sound. It was thanks enough.

But not for Faruza, apparently. "Gosh, thank you so much for telling me to eat this," she said.

"No problem," I said.

"No, seriously," said Fairie, "you two seem to give so much, and you never get anything back."

Jason arched an eyebrow. "What exactly do we give?"

"So, so much," said Faruza. "Don't be modest."

This whole situation was really, really weird, but it wasn't exactly all bad. I mean, it was kind of nice having people complimenting us all the time.

"There's gotta be something we could do for you," said Fairie.

"We're fine," I said. "Lots of people have been doing lots of nice things for us lately."

Faruza sighed at Fairie. "This is why they're so great," she said. "They recognize the smallest kindnesses."

The two of them looked at us with huge, admiring eyes.

"Please," said Jason. "It's not that big of a deal."

"What is it you guys want?" asked Faruza. "I mean, what is it you really want?"

I want the Sons to stop chasing us, I thought. *I want Jason and me to be normal kids. I want all of this to be over.*

"We have been trying to get into the library," said Jason. "But we haven't had any luck. Can't get around the guards."

"You guys?" said Fairie. "I bet the guards would just let you in if you asked."

"I bet they would," said Faruza. "Let's try this evening. After dinner? You want to?"

I looked at Jason. It couldn't be that easy, could it?

* * *

It was a warm spring evening, still light as Jason, the Weem twins, and I crossed the lawn towards the library. The library loomed ahead of us in its somber glory. It was an old building, with ornate stone architecture decorating its corners. In front, as always, were the guards. They glared out at us. Overall, the library looked just as impenetrable as it always did. I didn't think this was going to work. But the Weem twins were sure that no one could deny us anything we wanted. And for the past week, it had seemed to be true. Even at dinner earlier, one of the cooks had asked Jason and me what we thought about the food. She'd offered to prepare something especially for us if we didn't like what was offered. We'd assured her that everything was fine.

What was going on? I didn't know. It was creepy, but part of me didn't exactly want it to stop. Was that wrong? I didn't know that either.

As we approached, one of the guards called out to us. "What are you kids doing here?"

Great. See, I'd known this wasn't going to work. We should just go back to our dorms. Really.

But Fairie just waved and scampered up to him. "We want to go into the library," she said.

The guard looked us over. He gestured to Jason and me. "You two want to go in?" he asked.

Jason nodded. "Yeah, for weeks now."

"Why haven't you come by?" asked the guard, going to the door and unlocking it with one of his keys.

"You're letting us in?" I asked, shocked.

"Well, we don't just let anyone in," said the guard, "but you two and your friends, well, that's no problem."

Okay, if things hadn't been officially weird before, they most definitely were now. The guard opened the door, a large heavy wooden thing, and we walked inside.

Inside the library, it was dark. There were a few hanging chandeliers, but they did little to shed light in the huge room. The library was exactly that—one enormous room. It was at least three stories high, and every wall was lined with books, all the way to the ceiling. In the center of the huge room were rows and rows of bookshelves, each groaning under the weight of their tomes. The ceiling was covered in an intricate mural painting of mythological creatures. Half-bulls, half-men, chimeras, Poseidon with his trident, mermaids, men carrying flaming swords, dead dragons. In certain places, the plaster was chipped and there were holes in the painting. We all stood inside the entrance for several minutes, simply taking the place in.

"Amy, Jeremy," said a friendly voice.

It was Professor Moretti. "Or," he continued, "should I say Azazel and Jason?"

The Weem sisters both made identically confused faces. "Who?" they asked.

Professor Moretti chuckled. "Don't worry about it, girls," he said. He nodded at a few computers along a desk near the entrance. They looked completely out of place in the ancient room. "You two want to check some email or something while I talk to them?"

"Sure," said Faruza, bouncing over to the computers with her sister in tow.

"You know who we are," said Jason to Moretti.

"The Rising Sun and his consort," said Moretti. "It's an honor." And he *bowed* to us. Deeply.

I took a step backwards, grabbing Jason's hand. Jason squeezed my fingers.

"Um," said Jason, "you don't have to do that. The bowing thing."

Moretti straightened, raising his eyebrows. "It's simply a token of respect," he said. "Respect which you both deserve."

He was our *teacher*. He wasn't supposed to bow to us. He was an authority figure.

"So," said Moretti. "What brings you two to the library?"

"We're looking for information about the Rising Sun," Jason said.

I shot Jason a sharp look. Should we be admitting this? We really should have talked strategy before getting into the library. But I hadn't really believed that we'd actually be able to get in. So it hadn't occurred to me to think about what we'd do after.

"Actually," said Jason, "we kind of think the whole thing's a crock."

Moretti raised his eyebrows even higher. "A crock?"

"Yeah," said Jason. "I don't want to be the Chosen One or whatever, all right? People are always chasing us and trying to kill us, so we have to keep running. It sucks. We thought if we could find some information in this library that proves that I'm not the Rising Sun, then maybe everyone would just leave us alone."

"You can't be serious," said Moretti. "There have been signs. You two experienced them. You can't honestly think that it isn't true."

Jason and I looked at each other. We shrugged.

Moretti sighed. "This is going to be harder than I thought," he muttered. "Come with me."

He started walking back through the stacks of books, without looking back to see if we were following.

"Guess we go after him," Jason said, leading me forward.

In the back of the room, there was a staircase. It was twisting and narrow, built entirely of stone. We followed Moretti down into the bowels of the building. As we descended, the air got mustier. The stone walls on either side of the staircase went from orderly rows of perfectly cut pieces to rougher stones, fit together at crazy angles. There were electric lights fastened to the walls, but their light seemed to get dimmer and dimmer as we made our way down the stairs.

Eventually we emerged into a room about the size of a living room. The ceiling was low, and everything—walls, ceilings, and floor—were all composed of interlocking stones. The room was empty except for a few desks, which had laptop computers on them (of all things). Moretti held up a hand and told us to wait there. He disappeared through a small dark doorway on the other side of the room, and we could hear him calling out something in Italian.

Suddenly, a group of men came rushing through the doorway. They were all dressed entirely in black, many of them carrying guns.

The Sons!

I didn't wait. I didn't think. I just took off back up the stairway as fast as I could.

As my feet pounded against stone, I thought about how many times Jason and I had trusted a teacher. They'd always betrayed us. Why had I thought this would be any different?

CHAPTER SEVEN

April 30, 1990

Oh my God. Oh my God. He kissed me.

Well, at first, I told him what I was thinking. About the fact that he was of the Weem line, and that he could easily be the father of the Rising Sun. And that I could, you know, be the mother. And he laughed at me.

When he realized I was serious, he was mostly just angry. There was no way. He'd taken vows of celibacy, and I was just a kid. But I'm eighteen, and I know what I want.

We argued for a long time. And then suddenly, he just grabbed me by the shoulders. And he said, "Dear God, you know there is a part of me that wants this more than anything." And then. He kissed me.

I think I'm in love with him.

"Azazel!" yelled Jason.

Wait. Why wasn't Jason running with me? Why hadn't I waited for Jason?

I paused on the steps. Turned. Jason was at the bottom of the steps.

"It's the Sons!" I said.

"It's the Brothers," he said.

I made a confused face. What was the difference, really? The Brothers were the branch of the Sons that did all the dirty work. Jason had described them as Freemasons with guns or a cross between Jesuits and James Bond.

"I think it's okay," Jason said. "Come back down."

I hesitated.

"I'll make sure you're okay," said Jason.

I started back down the steps.

When Jason and I reemerged into the stone room, all of the men were on their knees, their heads bowed, including Moretti. I clutched my forehead with one hand. "So they're like worshipping you now?" I asked Jason.

Moretti stood up. "Respecting," he corrected. "Both of you."

This was *weird*. I looked at Moretti. "Can you tell them to get up?"

"Tell them yourself," said Moretti. "They are here to serve you."

I shot a look at Jason. He made a face at me. "Uh," he said. "On your feet."

The black clad men all stood up. They crowded around us, beaming at us expectantly. There were so many of them. They didn't all fit in the room. Some of them were spilling back into the hallway. What were they? What were they doing here?

"These men," said Moretti, as if reading my mind, "are true believers. Defectors from the Sons. They don't agree with Hoyt's edict that you are not the Rising Sun. They refused to be part of a plan to kill you."

Well, that was nice anyway, even if it was creepy. "Thanks for not killing Jason," I said, trying to smile.

"They've been arriving here, once I was sure that the two

of you were who I thought you were," said Moretti. "We're here to assist you in any way we can. We already took care of a problem for you. In the basement of the assembly hall."

"You killed Jude?" asked Jason.

"Indeed," said Moretti. "And disposed of the body."

"You know," I said, "the thing is, we weren't sure if we were going to kill him yet."

"May I speak?" asked one of the Brothers.

Moretti turned to us.

"Uh, sure," said Jason.

"I was there," he said. "In Shiloh, when he shot you. I carried him off that night, while he was screaming that he would stop at nothing to see you dead. If it had been up to me, I would have killed him right then. Trust me when I say that one would have caused you nothing but harm."

I didn't know what to say. I looked at Jason, but he was looking down at the ground. I tried another smile at the Brother. "Well, thanks, then," I said. "We're, um, not really used to having anyone look out for us." *And,* I added silently, *I'm not sure if I really think these guys are doing that exactly.*

Jason looked up. "Yes," he said, nodding. "Thank you all."

The Brothers all smiled, like they'd just been thanked by God himself. I grabbed Jason's hand. I wasn't sure I really liked any of this.

Moretti held up his hand again. "If you all could leave us now. We have things to discuss."

The men scurried out. Moretti folded his arms over his chest. I inched closer to Jason. He let go of my hand and put his arm around my waist. He pulled me against him. I looked up at him. He gazed down at me reassuringly.

"Well," said Moretti, "it would appear that it doesn't exactly matter whether you think you're the Rising Sun or not. They do."

"Yeah," said Jason, "I guess they do. But, you know, I've grown up surrounded by people who thought I was the Rising Sun. Excuse me if that doesn't exactly completely change my mind."

"I thought you might say something like that," said Moretti. "And I could simply say that whatever your beliefs were, you had a responsibility to those men, and also a responsibility to me. Which I think is true. However, I think I can offer you some more convincing evidence. Follow me."

He took off through the doorway.

"You know," Jason called after him, "I've heard all the prophecies already."

Moretti stopped and turned. "Not prophecies exactly, Jason." He gestured around him at the stone walls. "This place used to be your father's study, you know."

* * *

The room seemed a little more comfortable than the big stone room we'd been in before. It was smaller. It had carpets on the floors and a couch along one wall. There were stacks of old books lining the walls. Moretti settled into a chair at a paper-covered desk, and gestured for us to sit down on the couch.

We sat down gingerly.

Moretti chuckled. "You look so much like your mother, Jason. She was brilliant. I still remember some of the essays she wrote for me." He looked at me. "Your essay on *Things Fall Apart* almost reminds me of them."

"Yeah, well, she wasn't my mother," I said. But I had to admit I was a little confused. Michaela Weem had been brilliant? And Moretti had read her essays?

"Your mother attended the Sol Solis School," said Moretti.

Jason shrugged. "Yeah, well, she did say she went to school in Europe. Can we stop calling her my mother? Michaela Weem is fine with me."

"Her name was Aird when I knew her," said Moretti. "She was a bright, eager student. She had so much potential."

"Right," said Jason, "until Edgar Weem got a hold of her."

Moretti shook his head. "I don't think you quite understand, Jason. Ted—Edgar—was a colleague of mine at the time. He taught Philosophy and Mythology. He and I spent a great deal of time together in those days. We were friends."

"You aren't anymore?" I asked. I couldn't help it.

"Ted went on to greater things than I did," Moretti said, shrugging. "The Council. A high position in the Sons. I stayed here. Of course, he couldn't very well have continued working here. Not after the business with Michaela. There were suspicions at that point that something untoward had happened."

"Well, something had, hadn't it?" I asked.

"Michaela told us all about it," Jason said, looking sullen. He turned to me. "Azazel, we don't have to stay here. We can go."

There it was again. Jason wasn't the least bit interested in his family. Why not? "Aren't you slightly curious?" I asked.

He shot a look at Moretti and then brought his eyes back to me. "Maybe," he said. "Maybe a little." He sat back on the couch. "So people thought that my dad was a jerk and didn't want him teaching teenagers anymore?"

"Ted was a very good-looking man back then," said Moretti.

"So what?" I said. The way Michaela had described it, Edgar Weem had raped her, repeatedly, and forced her to do all manner of disgusting things, like drink bull semen. What did being good looking have to do with that?

"Michaela wasn't exactly unwilling to participate in his experiments," said Moretti. "Ted was a very popular professor, quite adored by the female population. I rather suspected it was a point of personal satisfaction for her. She seemed quite taken with him."

"Yeah," I said, "but when we talked to her, she described him as vile, didn't she?"

"She also said I was an abomination," said Jason. "You know I've never really believed a word that came out of her mouth. Go ahead, Professor. What were these experiments? What did my father do and why?"

Moretti smiled. "Well, I don't know all the details. I wasn't involved in them. For obvious reasons, Ted felt they were private. But I do know that when he first started teaching here, I had the opportunity to engage in many conversations with him about the nature of the Rising Sun. It's always been a hotly contested issue within the Sons. For many years, it seems that there were two separate camps of thought. One school of thought held that the idea of the Rising Sun was simply a metaphor—that it referred to a period of time when the world would change significantly. Another school of thought was convinced that the Rising Sun was literally a person. That he would return to us like a dying god out of a myth.

"Now," Moretti continued, getting up and crossing the room to take a book off a shelf, "I had always been firmly in the camp with those who looked at the Rising Sun as a metaphor. I knew that the official position of the Council was that the Rising Sun was definitely a person, and that they were even on the lookout for him, but I had never seriously considered the idea. I'm a scholar, not a mystic, and I wasn't about to be convinced of something that I thought was so ludicrous."

I chewed on my lip, trying to let this sink in. Brother Mancini had said something like this, hadn't he? That the Sons hadn't been pursuing the Rising Sun mythos until the past few hundred years? "So, you're saying that the Rising

Sun stuff might all just be metaphorical? That maybe there is no Rising Sun?"

"No," said Moretti. "I'm saying that's what I believed before I met Ted." He handed the book he was holding to Jason. "However, Ted showed me this."

Jason opened the book. It was very old. The pages were crumbly around the edges. The interior was in a language I couldn't understand. "Is this in Latin?" asked Jason. He turned to the title page. Then he looked up at Moretti. "A book about King Arthur?" he said. "Are you kidding?"

"Not just any book about King Arthur," said Moretti. "This is a book that traces the genealogy of the historical King Arthur."

"Hold up," I said. "King Arthur is a myth. He wasn't real."

"He was certainly real," said Moretti. "His name might not have been Arthur, however. He is known chiefly to historical records by his title Riothamus, a Latinization of a Brythonic word meaning 'king-most,' or high king."

"Yeah, yeah," said Jason. "I've heard that theory. But there are at least five others, all with evidence claiming that someone else was the historical King Arthur. The fact is we don't know anything."

"No," said Moretti, "most people don't know for sure. We do, because we have that book. It's all there. But knowledge like this is best kept safe here, among the Sons. We wouldn't let just anyone know about it."

That also sounded like Brother Mancini. I narrowed my

eyes and started to say something, but Jason interrupted me.

"Who cares, though," said Jason. "Who cares whether or not King Arthur was real?"

"You've heard of the documents connecting King Arthur to the Rising Sun," said Moretti.

"That stuff about Arthur coming back to England is first mentioned in the 12th century," said Jason. "It's a tenuous connection at best. At worst, it's just stupid. People probably patterned the Arthur myth on Jesus Christ."

"No, no, no," said Moretti. "The earliest mention is this book." He took it back from Jason, holding it up in our faces. "And that's not all. Ted believed that the idea that Arthur would return to England was a mistranslation. He thought it meant that Arthur's descendant would save England in its time of worst trouble." Moretti carefully placed the book on the shelf. "I mentioned the book contained a genealogy. The reason that Ted had it was that it clearly points out that he, Edgar Weem, is a descendant of King Arthur."

I furrowed my brow. "I feel like I'm stuck in *Holy Blood, Holy Grail*," I said. "Next you'll be telling me that book also connects Weem to the bloodline of Jesus Christ."

Moretti snorted. "Jesus Christ didn't exist. He was an invention of the Jewish rabbis, created entirely to quell a revolution."

"What?!" I said, my jaw dropping.

"It's just a theory, Azazel," said Jason.

"Right," I said. "So Jesus isn't real, but King Arthur is. I suppose the Easter Bunny and the Tooth Fairy are historical figures too."

"Actually," said Moretti, "there is some very intriguing mythology surrounding—"

"Let's stay on topic," said Jason. "So Weem convinced you that the Rising Sun was real because he was descended from King Arthur?"

"Well," said Moretti, "the evidence was quite compelling. The Sons have always been tied quite strongly to England, and Ted was English himself. The idea that the Rising Sun might not be the culmination of the King Arthur mythos in addition to everything else that he was, well, I couldn't deny the possibility.

"Ted really felt that the Rising Son would be born soon, and that he would be born to someone of his own family. Due to his own professed celibacy, of course, he didn't then think that he would have anything to do with it."

"Really?" said Jason. "Sure. So what changed his mind?"

"Your mother, of course," said Moretti. "It was her idea."

"Oh sure it was," I said. "I'm sure she was gung-ho to be part of all that sick, ritualistic sex with her teacher. Gross." Why did men always blame the girl for that kind of stuff? Weem had been the adult. It had been his fault.

"Doesn't matter," Jason said. He stood up. "Professor, all of this has been interesting, but I have to admit, I'm underwhelmed. I don't care who I'm descended from or what ridiculous things my father decided to do. The fact is, being followed all over the world by people who are trying to capture me or kill me or kill my girlfriend is really, really grating on my nerves." He held his hand out to me and helped me to my feet. "We'd hoped to find some kind of evidence that we could use to extricate ourselves from this mess, but I think you cleared it up for me back there. It doesn't matter what I believe or what evidence I find. Those men, and you apparently, are functioning on faith. And they're not going to stop believing. Not for any reason." He turned to me. "So I guess we're screwed."

Jason and I started for the doorway.

Moretti moved in our path. "No, Jason, you aren't. You saw how many men there were. And more are arriving daily. They are dedicated to you, body and soul. They will protect you until the death. I wouldn't call that being 'screwed.'"

Hmm. He kind of had a point.

"Besides," said Moretti, "it seems that the campus community has become quite supportive of you."

"Yeah," I said. "We're like suddenly really popular. Do you have anything to do with that?"

"What could I possibly have to do with that?" said Moretti. "It is the two of you. Your power compels. It has done so before. It will only grow."

I swallowed. I didn't think I liked the sound of that. I didn't want to be compelling.

"I assure you," said Moretti. "You are safe here. You are safe on this campus. We are watching. We are protecting you. You are too important to be damaged."

And then, creepily, he knelt down in front of us.

* * *

Jason sighed as he sat down heavily on a pew in the old church. "Normally, I'd say let's just get out of here," he said.

After leaving the library, we'd sent the Weem twins on their way and come inside the assembly hall to talk. It was kind of our spot.

"Leave?" I said.

"I've been thinking about it for awhile," said Jason. "I've been thinking that we aren't having any luck getting into the library, and that the school year's almost over, and that we're gonna have to figure out what we're doing next."

Funny. I hadn't thought about what we were going to do next. I guess I'd been too caught up in my dreams to worry about anything else.

"Those Brothers all bowing down to us," Jason said. "That's really strange."

"Yeah," I agreed. "And everybody suddenly being our best friend on campus is really strange too."

Jason nodded. "Yeah." He motioned me over to him. "Come sit down with me." I did. He put his arm around me and brushed a stray hair out of my face. "I don't like it, and I think it's creepy, but Moretti's not wrong. If we stay here, we have an army protecting us. Maybe it's not such a terrible idea."

"But school is going to be over soon, like you said."

"I don't think those Brothers are going anywhere. We don't have to either. We'll just stay. Until ...I don't know, until this whole thing blows over."

"Blows over?" I didn't think that was going to happen.

Jason kissed me. "It could happen," he whispered.

"With people kneeling down to us? I don't think it's blowing over. I think it's getting worse."

"But we're safe," he said. "I think we're actually safe."

God. That sounded too good to be true. But I wanted to believe it so badly. I lay my head Jason's shoulder and clung to him as tightly as I could. Safe. It was such a nice word.

* * *

The prom was Saturday. I'd barely had a chance to think about what I was going to do with my hair and makeup. I'd told the girls at the party that I was just going to do it myself, and that was what I planned to do. But usually, for events like this, I liked to do a trial run day, where I tried a bunch of different hairstyles, took pictures of them, and decided which one I liked. That Friday night, I bounded up the steps to my dorm after classes, about to ask Palomino if she minded if I used her digital camera and possibly her laptop. When I got in the room, however, it wasn't just Mina in there.

My dorm room was crowded with the fifteen most popular girls in the school. They were sitting in chairs, on both of our beds, and on the floor. Mina was sitting in the middle, chatting with all of them. When they noticed me, all of their eyes lit up.

"Amy!" said Fairie Weem. She and her sister were both sitting on my bed, each hugging one of my pillows.

"Hi," I said. "Um, am I interrupting something, Mina?"

Palomino shook her head, beaming. "Absolutely not. We'll all here for you."

"Me?" I said. Great. More weird people worshipping the ground I walked on. Really, really great.

Faruza patted a square of bed next to her. "Sit down," she said. "Come on, sit down."

I put down my books and went to sit down next to Faruza. "So," I said. "What's up?"

"Well," said Fairie, "you remember how Faruza and I were talking about how you and Jason give all the time and you never get back, and we wanted to know what you wanted?"

"Yeah," I said. "And thanks for helping us get into the library." Not that it really mattered anyway, now, did it?

"Well," said Faruza, "I got to thinking that you might not tell us what you really wanted, so I went to your roommate, because I figured who would know better, right?"

Palomino grinned.

I was not feeling particularly good about all of this for some reason. "Mina," I said, "what did you tell them?" I could think of at least ten really embarrassing things I'd confided in to Palomino. Who knew what she'd said.

"Okay," she said, smiling. "Don't be mad, okay, because I know this is something you were worried about, because you were asking me about it. And I just thought that if we got a whole bunch of people here, we could really, like, talk about it. You know? Just girls."

"What did you tell them?" I repeated.

"Don't be embarrassed, Amy," said Faruza, "because honestly, you are totally normal."

"Oh my God," I groaned.

"We brought diagrams," spoke up one of the other girls, and she whipped out a poster board. Her name was Rita. She was German—very tall, and very blonde. I looked at the diagram, and I felt my face get really hot. I turned to Palomino. "You did not," I said. "You did not tell them about that."

"Look it's fine," said Fairie. "Like half of the girls here haven't ever had one either."

I looked around the room. A bunch of girls raised their hands. "Really," said one of them, "this is like a public service announcement or something. Because nobody ever talks about this stuff."

"Especially not to guys apparently," said another girl.

Faruza nodded. "George can never find anything on my body without my help."

"You guys are back together?" I asked.

"You said you liked him, right?" she asked, looking worried.

"No, he's fine. I like him fine," I said. I took a deep breath and looked out at the girls in the room. "Okay, well, you know this is sweet of you guys and all. But I don't think that we all need to gather in my room and talk about ... this. Not really. I'm fine, really. And thank you so much, but—"

"No," said Mina. "You were asking me how they happened. And I don't know. So I figured, we'd get a bunch of together and pool our knowledge, and by the end of the conversation, we'll all be orgasm experts."

I buried my face in my hands.

"So," said Rita. "The first thing to talk about is the clitoris."

I looked up. She was gesturing at the diagram. "Whoa," I said. "Can we just not say that word? I mean, it sounds like the name of disease or something. Like, 'I can't go out. I caught clitoris.'"

Everyone giggled.

"What do you want to call it then?" asked Mina.

"I don't know," I said. "I think I'm comfortable with just not talking about it, actually. And put that diagram away."

Rita put the diagram down. "Maybe the diagram's a little advanced," she admitted. "We also have copies of *Cosmo*. Who's got the magazines?"

Several people pulled out magazines. Within a few seconds, they were spread open in front of me. I looked at the pages, cocking my head in confusion. I pointed at a picture. "What are they doing?"

"Oh," said Faruza. "That's the kama sutra issue. I think that's a little off-topic for now." She picked up the magazine and closed it.

"Look," said Rita, "according to *Cosmo*, the most important thing to remember is that, unless the guy you're with is a total jackass — in which case you shouldn't have sex with him anyway — he really wants to make you happy."

"Yeah," said another girl. "But all guys are really, really

stupid about this."

"And embarrassed," said Fairie. "Because it makes them look like they're bad in bed or something."

"So," said Rita. "We have to help them."

"Because," said Faruza, "let's face it. We have to help guys with everything."

Everyone laughed again. I couldn't help it. I smiled a little. "Okay," I said. "So we have to help them." Maybe this wasn't a totally terrible idea. Maybe. I could listen for a little while anyway.

"There are two kinds of orgasms," said Rita, holding up an issue of *Cosmo*. To avoid saying the word that Amy doesn't like, we'll call them ... internal and external."

"Oh God," I said. "That's even worse."

Rita just grinned. "For most girls, the internal ones are harder."

"Not for me," said Palomino. "That's the only kind I have."

Fairie glared at her. "Lucky you."

Mina beamed.

"Don't worry about the internal ones," said Rita. "Start with the external ones and go from there."

The talk seemed to go on forever, and I was extremely embarrassed the entire time. Maybe everyone else was too, considering we all kept erupting in giggles every five minutes. More than once, I just wanted it all to stop, but another part of me was too curious, so I kept talking and kept listening. I even looked at Rita's diagram. Which kind of made sense.

Finally, I'd been read about five different magazine articles and listened to several girls tell me that, like me, they hadn't been able to figure out how to have orgasms either, and they sometimes thought it bothered their boyfriends more than it bothered them.

"I just don't get it," a girl named Lissa was saying. "I'm the one who's not getting off, and he gets all pissed off about it. And that really doesn't turn me on."

I knew what she meant.

"But this should help, right?" said Rita, waving the diagram around.

"Put that away!" I said. "I don't want to look at the diagram anymore."

We all laughed, but Rita did put it away.

"It helps," I said. "I mean, yeah. I feel like I kind of understand the whole thing more now, but I still just don't know how to even like bring it up." I looked around at the other girls. "Like, if I tried to talk to my boyfriend about this, I would get really, really embarrassed. And besides that, how am I supposed to explain to him what to do without using really technical words that sound like diseases and making everything like robotic or some-thing."

"Yeah, I get that," said Lissa. "Like if I'm telling him, 'Do this. Do that.' That's not going to be very sexy."

"Don't tell him anything," said Fairie, giggling. "Just take his hand and move it where you want it and show him what to do."

I considered. Maybe that would work. Assuming I even had one of these external buttons or clitorises or whatever we were calling them. Assuming I could even figure out where it was. That diagram was totally strange looking.

"Well," said Rita. "Prom's tomorrow, girls. I hope all of your after prom experiences are, well, memorable."

Everyone laughed again.

"Are you and Jeremy getting a hotel room in town?" Faruza asked me.

"Um ..." I shook my head. "No, you know, we can't really afford stuff like that."

"We're switching dorm rooms," said Palomino. "And I'm letting you guys stay here. I'm going to the guy's room. And I'm making this sacrifice because I love you. Chance promises he's going to clean, but I don't believe he knows how."

More laughter.

"How do you sneak in and out of each other's dorm rooms?" asked one of the girls.

"Magic," I said. "And fire escapes."

* * *

That night I had a dream. It wasn't a nightmare, but it was vivid. I wasn't in the dream. I could see everything that was happening, but it was like I was a ghost or a being with no body. In my incorporeal form, I hovered inside the parlor of Michaela Weem's house. It looked different than I remembered. It wasn't covered in dust. There weren't cobwebs clinging to the corners. The furniture was different.

Several overstuffed couches slouched against the wall. They were patterned in some kind of delicate floral pattern. Michaela Weem was sitting on one of the couches. A man sat next to her, older, maybe in his late thirties or early forties. His hairline was starting to recede, but his face was still quite attractive. He looked like Jason.

He was holding a leather-bound book. He looked disappointed and discouraged. "You wrote it all down?" he asked.

"It was my diary," said Michaela Weem. "I was a teenager. I wrote things down."

"This has to be destroyed," said the man.

Michaela rolled her eyes. "Give it back to me."

"It's evidence of what we did. If the Sons got hold of this, everything I've worked for could be destroyed immediately."

"Well, that would be terrible, wouldn't it?" Michaela's voice dripped with sarcasm. She snatched at the book, but the man pulled it out of her reach.

"You can't keep this," he said.

"Give it back to me!" she said, and she lunged for him, her fingers scrabbling against his, trying to pry his fingers off the book.

The man shoved her. She fell back against the couch and cracked her head against the wall. The man stood up. "It has to be destroyed," he said.

Michaela touched the back of her head gingerly, tears springing to her eyes. Then she vaulted off the couch, grabbing at the book again.

The man captured her wrist with one hand and squeezed. "Stop," he said. "I'm going to destroy it."

"But it's my diary!" said Michaela. "It's my own personal thoughts and feelings, and I want it." She grabbed for it again.

The man slapped her face. She stumbled back, her hand on her cheek, her eyes full of hatred and anger. "Don't," she whispered. "You'll wake Jude."

The man strode across the room and put the leather book inside his briefcase, which was sitting next to the doorway. Turning, he said, "And what's this I hear about you and Arabella's daughter? You've got some group of backwoods crazies worshipping your ridiculous rabbit god?"

Michaela seethed. "I had my hand in bringing the abomination into this world. I will do my part to rid the world of his evil."

The man threw his hands up in the air. "This is why I can't come back here anymore. That abomination you talk about is our son. And frankly, it's just sick that you want to hurt him."

"You know what we did!" Michaela cried. "It's all there in my diary. You know what we did. How could anything that came from *that* be anything but an abomination?"

I floated into the hallway outside the parlor. A small boy with dark hair was creeping across the floor in the darkness. His hand darted into the briefcase and retrieved the leather diary. Then he snuck back up the stairs.

"I won't be back here, Michaela," the man was saying. "I took vows. I break them every time I see you."

"Vows?" she spit out. "What about the vows you made to me? In sickness and in health?"

"Your sickness is too much," said the man.

"Where is he?" said Michaela. "Where is the abomination?"

"You'll never find him," said the man. He walked into the hallway and picked up his briefcase. "Besides, he has a lot he needs to learn if he's to fulfill his destiny. His upbringing has to be perfect."

I awoke with a jolt because Palomino's alarm was going off. I threw a pillow at her. "It's Saturday!" I said to her.

It was Saturday. It was the day of the prom. And I wasn't sure, but I thought I'd just had a dream about Michaela and Edgar Weem. And Jude, as a little boy. And that leather book he'd had. Where was it? I needed to find it. I'd put it in my pocket. Had I thrown those pants in with my dirty laundry?

"Mina!" I said. Her alarm was still going off.

Palomino turned off the alarm. "Sorry," she mumbled sleepily.

I rolled over, enjoying the silence. And slipped back into sleep almost immediately.

* * *

There were about five people pulling my hair in completely different directions. We were standing in front of the mirror in Faruza's and Fairie's gorgeous suite, where they had a bathroom the size of a small country. The mirror was enormous, and everyone was trying to help me get ready. Since I'd told everyone I planned on doing my hair and makeup myself, everyone had jumped on the bandwagon, and we were all getting ready together. It was a mad house.

"I was really going to do this myself," I protested, trying to swat people away from my hair.

"Don't be silly," said Faruza. "We're all here."

Rita tapped a picture in an open magazine, which the girls were trying to copy. It was a complicated updo with tendrils of curls falling out of it in a tousled look. It was very pretty.

"Jason likes my hair down," I said.

"Boys always say that," said Fairie. "They say they want everything simple, but they're just saying that because they don't understand what they want."

Or maybe they really did like things simple — girls with no makeup who wore their hair down. And maybe we just did all this fussy dressing up stuff for other girls, not actually for boys.

Faruza yanked my head sideways and began rolling up a section of my hair with a curling iron. I guessed I was just going to have to sit tight.

Within twenty minutes, my hair was completely and totally curled. I surveyed my face in the mirror, surrounded by corkscrew curls. They were pretty. Rita put her hands on my head and began running her fingers through them.

"What are you doing?" I asked her. I'd really liked my corkscrew curls.

"Achieving tousled perfection," she informed me. "Trust me."

While Rita and the Weem twins were using an entire box of bobby pins on my head, pinning up my tousled curls, the phone in the dorm room rang. Palomino ran to answer it. We could hear her in the bedroom.

"What?" she was saying. "Why?" She was quiet for a few seconds. "Okay," she said finally and hung up.

Palomino came into the bathroom. "You guys aren't going to be happy," she said.

"What?" said Fairie.

"That was the dorm mother," she said. "Campus is on lockdown. Apparently, there's some kind of external threat. They didn't say what, but she said it sometimes happens if one of the kids is in danger of being kidnapped or something."

"Yeah," said Rita, "when that Norwich girl who graduated a few years ago was nearly kidnapped, the campus went on lockdown."

"Anyway, the dance is still on," said Palomino, "but no one can leave campus until we get the all clear."

"Wait," said Fairie. "That means no hotel rooms after the dance?"

Mina nodded. "Yeah. That's what she said."

"That means no parties," said Rita.

"I'm calling my dad," said Faruza.

I excused myself to the hallway and called Jason. This whole thing kind of worried me. He picked up after a few rings.

"What's up?" he said.

"Did you guys hear about the lockdown?" I asked.

"Yeah. Some of the guys down the hall are really pissed off because they booked expensive hotel rooms. Kinda sucks for them, I guess."

"It's an external threat. You don't think it has anything to do with us, do you?"

"Us?" he said. "Why would it?"

"What if it's the Sons? What if they're trying to get to us?"

"Jesus, Azazel. You worry about the Sons way too much. They don't even know where we are."

"Yeah, but they don't seem to have much trouble finding us. And now that we're like the most popular people on campus, we're not exactly low profile. The head said we were special. Moretti knows who we are. George might. Lots of people might."

Jason sighed. I could tell he was moving from wherever he was because the sounds in the background got muffled. "Okay," he said finally. "There is an army of Brothers in the basement of the library. They are all armed and trained to fight. We are safe, or did you forget that conversation we had?"

"I just ...I ..."

"Azazel, it's prom. One day, that's all I want. I want one

completely normal, perfect, high school memory, okay? I am going to come and get you, and I am going to give you a corsage, and you are going to be wearing that dress you were carrying, and then we are going to dance and have fun and nothing bad is going to happen. Okay?"

I sighed. "Okay."

The background noises returned. They sounded kind of electronic. "I love you."

"I love you too," I said. "What are you doing?"

"Chance and I are playing video games," he said. "What are you doing?"

"Getting ready for the dance," I said.

"It's not for hours," he said.

I rolled my eyes. Boys.

* * *

When Jason saw me, his eyes lit up. I had been a little worried, especially since my hair was up, and I was wearing a lot more makeup than usual. But the dress Palomino had helped me pick out was definitely perfect.

And it looked like ...

Jason and Chance were waiting for us in the foyer of our dorm. They stared up at Mina and me as we descended the steps. It did feel perfect. Like something out of a Molly Ringwald movie.

When I reached Jason, he held out my corsage. "You look beautiful," he murmured. "I'm afraid to touch you. I don't want to mess you up."

I laughed. "Don't be silly," I said, and I kissed him.

And then he had lipstick on his face. I tried to wipe it off. "Sorry," I said.

He grinned. "I don't think I really care if people can tell I've been kissing you."

The corsage was simple and pretty—white lilies on a bed of babies breath. "The florist said it would go with everything," he explained, "and I totally forgot to ask what color your dress was."

I twirled. "You like it?"

"I love it," he said, putting his arm around my waist and leading me out of the dorm.

In Bramford, we would have had to drive to the prom, probably in a limo, which was the tradition. Since we were only going across campus to the main hall, however, we walked. Mina and Chance walked ahead of us, hand in hand, occasionally whispering things in each other's ears. I smiled looking at them. I wouldn't have wanted my brother to be a teenager father if you consulted me, but I was glad he was with Mina. They seemed happy and, besides the worry about the baby, they were carefree. No one was chasing them and trying to kill them. More than anything, that was what I wanted for my little brother. I didn't want him to ever have to worry about that kind of violence.

I shuddered, thinking about my dream about Chance. In the dream, I'd had to pick between Chance and Jason. In reality, I hoped I never had to make a choice like that, because I didn't know what I'd do.

The campus was decorated for prom with paper lanterns

strung along the walkways. Candles were lit on each of the steps to the entrance of the main hall. Inside, the room didn't look much different than it did most of the time. It wasn't like proms back in Bramford, where the walls of the gym would be covered in paper, with cardboard cutouts of pillars and fountains that contained balloons. There was also was no ubiquitous disco ball in the middle of the room.

Instead, the room had been set up with two rows of round tables, each covered in a white linen table cloth, with fine china and silverware settings. Each table had a centerpiece of white roses. Someone had taken the time to light the very old chandelier that was in the middle of the room. The chandelier was lit entirely by candles. I looked up at it, wondering if it would drip wax on the dance floor. The dance floor wasn't nearly as large as it might have been at a prom in West Virginia. It was only the wide aisle between the tables.

They had put up different curtains than the ones that usually decorated the main hall. These were white with gold patterns woven through them, and they swept the floor. The windows in the main hall were quite tall, since the ceiling in the room was vaulted, so the curtains were pretty impressive. Overall, the room had a feeling of understated elegance, but no hint of gaudiness or excess. It was beautiful. It was gorgeous. It was definitely a room to have a perfect high school memory in.

The evening was soon underway. There was a sit down dinner, brought to us by waiters in tuxedos. Because we were in Italy, it consisted of about a trillion courses. I was terrified of dropping food on my dress, so I ate carefully and didn't stuff myself. While we were finishing dessert, the music started and the lights came down. The first song came and went without anyone entering the dance floor. But during the second song, couples began to wander out into the aisle and dance. Chance and Mina, who were sitting with us at our table, left. I spotted Faruza and George. Fairie was dragging her date out with her.

Jason and I sat at the table alone. I was poking the remains of my flan with my fork. I'd really been too full to take more than a few bites. He smiled at me.

"I guess this is the part where we dance," I said.

"About the dancing," he said. "I'm not really very good at it."

I took my napkin off my lap and threw it over my flan. "Oh come on," I said. "What do guys really have to do when dancing?" I gestured to Faruza and George. George was standing behind Faruza with his hands on her waist while she ground her butt into his pelvis.

Jason laughed. "Yeah, okay. Like you're pulling that move off in your dress."

"I thought this was supposed to be our perfect high school memory," I said to him. "My perfect high school memory involves dancing."

"Slow dancing, though, right?" he said. "Like where we just stand next to each other and sway?"

"Jason!" I said.

"Give it a second," he said, smiling.

The second song was ending. It was quiet for a few minutes, and then the sound of a screaming guitar solo overtook the room. Jason grinned and stood up, holding out his hand.

"Guns and Roses?" I asked, grinning at him. Jason really liked Guns and Roses. "Did you set this up?"

"'Sweet Child O' Mine,'" he said. "It's as slow of a song as they have."

I was laughing, but I put my hand in his and allowed him to lead me onto the dance floor, which had largely cleared, because the girls weren't totally sure how to grind to this.

Jason put his hands on my waist. I wrapped my arms around his neck. And we started swaying. "Sweet Child O' Mine" might have been one of Guns and Roses' slower songs, but it had a relatively quick tempo, so we had to sway pretty quickly.

Jason smiled down at me, looking deep into my eyes and started mouthing the words to me. I just laughed and buried my face in his tux. He lifted my chin and whispered in my ear, "Looking at you does take me away to a special place."

I playfully poked him. "Yeah," I said. "That's because you are *special*, Jason."

He grabbed the hand that I'd poked him with and wrapped it back around his neck. "I mean it." And he was serious. "I don't know what I'd do without you."

My grin melted into a small, happy smile. "Me either," I said.

"You're like the other part of me," he said. "Without you, I feel like half a person."

I knew what he meant. I just nodded.

And with our eyes locked on each other, silly smiles on our faces, he lowered his lips to mine and kissed me. And there was nothing sweeter on earth than kissing Jason's lips.

Jason insisted on only dancing to slow songs, but I eventually got Palomino to dance with me a couple of times, when I could pry her and Chance away from each other. They were constantly making googly eyes at each other, even if they were across the room from each other. It was nice, seeing the two of them happy again.

Of course, the weird popularity continued. Everyone in the room stopped to compliment my hair or my dress or to tell Jason and me how awesome we looked. And the DJ played essentially anything I asked him to play. The night wore on. Then the head of the school stopped the music and took a microphone to speak. The waiters from before were weaving through the crowd and handing out tall crystal flutes filled with champagne. We were all allowed one glass, since the drinking age for beer and wine in Italy was sixteen. Fairie whispered in my ear not to drink it yet, though. We were going to use it to toast the prom king and queen. Well, they didn't call it the prom king and queen, but that was basically what it was.

Currently, the head was droning on and on about it. "Every year, here at the Sol Solis School, the faculty selects a male and female student who we feel embodies the spirit of the Sol Solis School. These students are high academic achievers, participants in the events the school's activities, good citizens, and are students who their peers look up to. These students are given the honor of being recognized as the Primo and Prima of the Spring Formal.

"During many of our past years, the process of choosing two such students has been an arduous affair, but this year, two students immediately stood out to all of us, and we unanimously chose them with very little discussion. I know that each of you here will also recognize how much these two students are the obvious choices this year, and will join me in congratulating Amy Smith and Jeremy Black as this year's first couple."

At first I looked around for the people who had those names. Then I remembered that that was us. Jason and I exchanged a stunned glance. We were the king and queen of the prom? Really?

I didn't know what to do with my glass of champagne, but Faruza took it from me.

Jason and I walked up to the front of the room amid resounding cheers and applause from the rest of the student body and the teachers. It didn't die down even when we reached the front of the room. In fact, it seemed to go on forever.

It was cool, but it was still, well, weird. I kept waiting for the head to shush everyone, but he didn't. He just let the applause and cheers continue. He was still clapping himself. When it finally did start to die down, he said, "I think we can all agree that it's been a pleasure interacting with these two. They truly are an asset to the school."

More cheers and applause. Jason and I just stood there, frozen, feeling like idiots. We waited again for an agonizingly long time for the cheers to die down. Why did everyone suddenly like us so much? What was going on?

"All right," said the head. "We will now all lift our glasses to the Primo and Prima of the Sol Solis School. Cin cin!" (Which is how they say "cheers" in Italy.)

"Cin cin!" echoed the rest of the people in the room and then they all sipped at their champagne.

I wanted my champagne. I felt like I needed a drink to fully deal with the fact that everyone thought Jason and I were the best thing since canned peaches.

"And now," said the head, "the traditional dance between the Primo and Prima."

Music swelled behind us. Jason took my hand and led me out onto the dance floor. When I looked up at his face, his eyes were shining. He grinned down at me. "This is perfect," he whispered. "It's better than anything I could have imagined. This is all I've ever wanted."

I felt immediately guilty. Here I was contemplating how weird the whole thing was, and Jason was enjoying it. We were at a dance. We'd just been crowned the king and queen. We were living the teen dream. Why did I have to pick everything apart and look for the danger? Why couldn't I accept that something good was happening to me? If I just lay my head on Jason's shoulder and felt the warmth of his arms around me, maybe I could just soak up the incredible excellence of this moment, like Jason was doing. Maybe I could—

Of course not. The reason I couldn't accept that something good was happening to me was that nothing good ever happened to me.

And that simple fact of my life was made perfectly clear when I heard the crash of breaking glass.

Déjà vu.

The glass of the windows shattered to the ground, and I could only think about my Aunt Stephanie's house. November. My parents sitting around a table. Bullets exploding through their heads. Blood arcing out and spilling on the table, on my Aunt Stephanie's white carpet.

And the Sons of the Rising Son bursting in through the windows shooting.

Just like they were doing now. At my prom.

CHAPTER EIGHT

May 10, 1990

So it hasn't happened yet. Jed wants to make sure it's perfect. Plus, heaven forbid we actually did it for fun instead of for procreational purposes. So, he sent me to some doctor who taught me how to chart my cycle and figure out when I'm fertile. And that's when it will happen. The doctor says there's about a four day window when I could get pregnant. We figured out when those four days would be. And we'll be going all over the country and the world to get the blessings of as many powers and traditions as Jed thinks we can squeeze in. In four days.

I'm excited. But I'm scared. I've never done it before. I wonder if it's really going to hurt.

Jason and I hit the floor immediately, as slivers of glass flew through the air. We could hear screams. I tried to look up to see if everyone else was taking cover, particularly Mina and Chance, but Jason was covering my body with his own, and I couldn't see anything. The music was still playing in the background, but over it, I could hear the sounds of feet crunching the broken glass and of bullets ripping from the muzzles of guns.

"Do you have a gun?" I whispered furiously to Jason.

"No," he said, sounding disappointed in himself. "You?"

"It really doesn't go with my outfit," I muttered.

I struggled under him again, trying to get a look at what was going on. I managed to peer out beneath his arm. All I could see were feet in black boots and the streaks of prom dresses as people ran for the exits.

"What is going on?" I hissed at Jason.

Abruptly, he got up and yanked me to my feet. I barely had time to register the fact that the Sons who'd burst in through the windows were being gunned down by Brothers, who were streaming into the main hall from the entrances and through the broken windows.

"Run!" Jason said.

I took two second to jerk the high heels I was wearing off my feet, and then we did run, clutching each other's hands. We were flanked by other students and teachers, also running out of the main hall. I looked around frantically for Chance and Palomino, but I couldn't see them.

"Where's Chance?" I asked Jason.

He stopped. "Dammit," he said. We both scanned the room for a glimpse of either one of them. It was pandemonium. The DJ had fled, and his sound equipment had been knocked over. The tables were lying on their sides, rolling around. Tablecloths were crumpled on the floor, dishes broken. And among all the debris were running people. People tripping over chairs. A girl howling when she stepped on a broken piece of glass. The Sons and Brothers crouching behind pieces of furniture for cover, their bodies already littering the ground. And, I noted, to my horror, there were at least a few other bodies. Bodies in bright colored dresses or tuxedos. Was that a black dress? Was that Palomino?

But no, her hair was dark.

"Chance!" I screamed.

"Azazel!" came a reply.

I whirled, looking for Chance. But instead of Chance, it was Professor Moretti screaming my name. He corralled the two of us and tried to push us towards the exit. "You have to get out of here," he said. "It's important that you survive."

"Where's my brother?" I demanded.

"Your who?" said Moretti, looking confused.

I twisted around Moretti, gazing out into the ruins of the main hall. Were he and Mina already outside?

Suddenly, Moretti grabbed my shoulders and pushed me to my knees. It hurt, and I cried out. But in the next second, Professor Moretti's chest turned red as a bullet struck him. Right where my head had been. His eyes registered shock for a second, then they went dull, and he crumpled to the ground. He was dead.

A tiny gasp escaped my throat.

Yeah. Perfect high school memory all right.

Well screw this. I wasn't sitting around watching people die while they were trying to protect me. I shot a glance around my immediate surroundings, until I saw one of the dead members of the Sons. I crawled over to him.

"Azazel!" Jason whispered furiously.

I just retrieved the man's gun from his hands and waved it at Jason.

He nodded. "Good idea," he said, and within a few seconds, he had his own gun.

We settled in behind an overturned table, peering out to squeeze out shots at the Sons. For a while, it was going pretty well. No one had any idea where our shots were coming from, and we were taking down Sons pretty easily. I hadn't shot a gun in months, but I was doing well with my aim. I even hit one of the Sons squarely in the head, which reminded me of their signature shot. Always in the head. Jason did it too.

Jason, of course, was doing better than I was. He was a crack shot, always hitting his target. Right in the head.

Maybe it was the precision of Jason's shots that tipped them off, but the Sons figured out that it was Jason and I behind the table shooting at them, and they concentrated their effort on us.

Bullets started tearing through the wood of the table, splintering it.

Jason and I both went face down on the floor, flattening ourselves.

I was beginning to wonder if our best idea wouldn't be to get out of the main hall. Where was the exit?

Jason probably already knew where it was. He checked exits the minute he got in a room, and he'd taught me to look for them too, and to keep their location in my head at all times. But I was slipping, and I couldn't remember. I rolled over on my back, my gun leveled at my feet, and craned my neck behind me to look.

Okay. There it was. Maybe twenty feet, but there were overturned chairs and broken glass in our path. Could we crawl there?

And then I heard it. "Azazel!" yelled a voice.

Chance.

I saw him then. He and Palomino were crouching in the corner, not ten feet from us. They were behind a table like us. Chance had his arms around Mina, and she was clutching the lapels of his tuxedo, hiding her face in his shirt.

The fire Jason and I were drawing from the Sons was too close to them. A stray shot could hit them.

I couldn't let that happen.

Another bullet burst through the wooden table Jason and I were behind. It skimmed between us. Too close for comfort.

Jason was still face down, but he was starting to crawl for the exit. "Let's go," he said.

I shook my head. "Chance," I said, gesturing with my head.

More bullets came through the table. I closed my eyes and pressed my cheek against the floor.

If one of those bullets went a little off course, it could kill either Mina or Chance. And Mina was pregnant with my niece or nephew. I didn't have a lot of family left. They were it.

I shot one last glance at Jason, who seemed to be quickly contemplating the distance between the door and Chance.

And, in a flash, I understood my dream. Here it was. I had to choose between protecting Jason and protecting Chance.

Jason could take care of himself.

I stood up.

"No!" Jason screamed.

I opened fire in the general direction of the Sons, not bothering to look or aim as I dashed to Palomino and Chance. A bullet grazed my cheek. It stung and blood started to trickle down my face. I wiped at it furiously.

"Run," I screamed at them. "They don't care about you. They care about me and Jason! Run now, while they're not looking at you."

I took my eyes away from them and surveyed the room. Quickly, I took in the Sons who were firing at me. There were maybe only three. I took careful aim and pulled the trigger. The shot caught one in the stomach. He went down, but I didn't know if he was dead.

I turned back to Chance and Palomino. "Run," I said furiously.

"Zaza—" Chance protested.

"Go!" I growled.

They got up and started for the exit in a crouching, halting run.

And that was when the bullet lodged itself in my arm.

It really hurt.

But I didn't make a sound. I just looked at it. Looked at my shredded skin. At the flow of red blood. And thought, *Well, at least it's not my shooting arm.*

I took another shot at the Sons. And that was when I realized the gun I had was out of bullets.

"Fuck," I muttered. I usually reserved that word for periods of time when circumstances were really, really dire.

I looked around me, searching for another dead guy with a gun that I could get to easily. As I did, I couldn't help but notice that the room was littered with dead men. It was difficult to tell the Sons from the Brothers. They were dressed alike. But there was no one standing anymore except the two Sons who were shooting at me. The Brothers might very well all be dead. But they'd done their job well. There were bodies everywhere.

And none of those bodies were particularly close to me.

I looked back at the two standing Sons. They were going to kill me, I realized. This was it. I was going to die.

At least Chance was safe.

Then I noticed it. It was a sound I didn't think I'd ever heard before—a kind of strangled half-sobbing cry of rage. It had been going on since ...since I'd been shot.

The head of one of the Sons exploded.

I was confused. Or maybe I was getting lightheaded from the loss of blood.

Jason was on the other side of the room. He was behind the Sons.

How had he gotten there?

And he was making the noise. His face was twisted, ugly, kind of a sneer. Almost a smile. He'd just shot one of them. I'd never seen Jason move so fast.

The other one, the guy who'd shot me—Jason tackled him, knocking his gun on the floor.

The man hit the floor with a thud. Jason was on his feet. I'd never seen him move so fast. He grabbed the guy by the collar and wrenched his body off the ground. Then he flipped his gun over in his hand so that he was holding it by the barrel and began to bash the man in the face. Blood spattered onto the floor. Onto Jason's face.

Jason threw the man onto the floor, and Jason ground his foot into the man's face. I heard a crunching noise and the man twitched. Then he was still.

Jason didn't stop though. He kicked the man's face again and again.

And the face didn't look much like a face anymore. It was mangled and meaty, features askew.

Jason was still leering or smiling or whatever he was doing.

I started forward. "Jason," I said.

He didn't look up.

"Jason," I said again, walking shakily across the main hall to him.

When I was so close that I could touch his shoulder, I did.

And he looked up, startled.

"I think he's dead," I whispered.

Jason's face was white with fury. He backed away from the man, his breath coming in gasps. "He shot you," he gulped out.

"I'm okay," I said. But that lightheadedness ...

Jason stripped off his tuxedo jacket and wrapped it around my arm. He started to lead me away, out of the main hall. We gingerly stepped over the bodies.

This was our style all right. Wherever we'd been, we left a mess. We weren't exactly great guests.

"So," I said to Jason, "you were saying that we were safe here?"

He glared at me. "You're bleeding," he said. "Let's joke later. Okay?"

* * *

I was in a hospital bed when Jason and a Brother came into the room. Jason was carrying a bundle of clothes for me. I'd asked him to get them from Mina.

Apparently, those hotel rooms that the rich kids had booked turned out to be useful after all. The campus had pretty much been immediately evacuated. Students were all being sent home. Chance and Palomino were already at the airport, booked on flights back to the States.

I was going to be released soon. The gunshot wound wasn't too bad. It had entered the fleshy part of my arm and missed most of the muscle, just going through fat. I'd never really liked the fact that my arms were a little pudgy at the top, but I was pretty grateful now. I'd been stitched up and bandaged up. The staff had instructed me to change the bandage often, apply antibiotic ointment and watch for infection. My stitches would supposedly dissolve on their own, so I wouldn't need to come back to the hospital.

"How are you?" Jason asked, looking concerned.

I grinned. "These pain meds are awesome!" I said, giving him a thumbs up.

He smiled, but came over to sit next to me and hold my hand. "It kills me that you got hurt," he said. "I should have been watching."

"Not your fault," I said. "Maybe trying to provide a diversion so that Chance and Mina could get away was not the brightest of plans."

He kissed my forehead. "You're brave, Azazel. I've always said so."

The Brother who had come in with Jason was looking uncomfortable. Let him. As long as he didn't start kneeling to us, I didn't really care. "So," I said to him, "how many of the Brothers survived?"

He shook his head. "Two of us, including me," he said. "The other is in intensive care."

That was bad. "I'm sorry," I said.

"Many are lost in pursuit of the Purpose," said the Brother. "It is a deep honor for us to die in your service."

Oh gross. "Okay, well, don't do us any more honors," I said. "I don't like people dying for me at all."

"Me either," said Jason. "This is Haversham," he introduced me to the Brother. "He wants to take us somewhere remote."

"Remote?" I said.

"I have access to a private plane," said Haversham, "and I know of a very small island off the southern coast of Africa. I don't think you would be discovered there."

An island? That could be kind of cool, maybe. It would be warm. There would be an ocean. Then I remembered

Florida. That hadn't really turned out really well. I shook my head. "They always find us," I said. I looked at Jason for reinforcement.

"I don't know if they would," said Jason.

I bit my lip. "Hand me my clothes," I said.

Jason gave me the bundle he was holding. "If we just disappeared, maybe this whole thing would blow over."

I shook my head, looking at the outfit Jason had brought me. "You said something like that before," I said. But I didn't really think it would happen. "But they're obsessed with finding us, Jason."

"Of course they'd look for us," he said. "But if they couldn't find us, after a while, they'd give up."

"And if they didn't? Would we just spend the rest of our life on an island?"

"If we were together, would that really be so bad?"

I considered, unfolding my pants. "Hey, I wore these pants a week ago," I said. "I haven't even washed them yet."

"They don't look dirty to me," said Jason. He changed the subject back to the matter at hand. "Think about it. It would be somewhere that no one has ever heard of us. We could just ...be. No one would be chasing us. We could relax."

These were the pants I'd worn the night I'd found Jude and Jason, weren't they? And there was something in the pocket ... The leather journal I'd taken from Jude! I pulled it out. I'd had a dream about this thing. I couldn't believe I'd forgotten all about it.

"What's that?" Jason asked.

"Jude had it," I said. I opened it up and began to read from one of the pages. "'Ted says we need to gather as much power as we can to imbue to our son—the Rising Sun. We're leaving the Sol Solis School for Rome.'" The dream! I looked up at Jason. "This is Michaela Weem's diary. It explains everything that she and Edgar Weem did to create you."

Jason looked confused. "How do you know that from reading one sentence?"

"I had a dream ... I just know, okay. And I think this is important." I didn't think I would have dreamed about it if I weren't supposed to do something with it. I paused, examining the ramifications of that statement. I'd thought the word "supposed." Meaning that I thought there was some kind of destiny wrapped up in the journal. That I thought something was meant to be. That went against everything I'd ever thought. "Jason, I don't want to go hide on island and pretend this is going to go away. I don't think it's going to go away."

Jason reached out his hand for the diary. He flipped through it. "What else are we going to do, Azazel?"

I took a deep breath. I couldn't believe I was actually going to say this. "What if it's true?"

"What if *what's* true?"

"What if you really are the Rising Sun?"

"Oh, and then you're the Vessel of Azazel?" he asked. "Then I think you're supposed to kill me, right?"

"I assure you," said Haversham, "there is no doubt in my mind that you are the Rising Sun. And you," he gestured at me, "are his consort. You complete and feed each other. Your duality is echoed in countless mythological traditions."

"Yeah," said Jason, "we know that you think that. But we—" He broke off and looked at me. "I thought we were going to make our own destiny."

"By running away and hiding on an island?"

He didn't say anything.

"Things happen to us, Jason. Weird, weird things. Most recently, I think we made an entire campus of people like us."

"Okay," he said. "That *was* weird. But it's just like everything else that happens. It happens *to* us. We don't control it. It just happens. And, yeah, you're right. It's weird."

"I don't know," I said. "I mean, before the Sons went nuts in Shiloh, I sincerely wanted us to get out of there alive. And when you came back to life, I really wanted you back. And tonight, at the prom, you said that it was perfect. I mean, before the Sons came in. We got crowned prom king and queen. Some part of you wanted that. Some part of me wanted it. We might not know how we're doing it, but I think, maybe, we are controlling it."

Jason kept flipping through the diary. He was quiet for a long time. Then he looked up at me. "Maybe," he said.

"So," I said, "maybe we could find out more. I mean, maybe we use this diary. Retrace Michaela and Edgar Weem's steps. Maybe if we knew more, we could figure out how we're doing what we're doing. And then, if we really were as powerful as they seem to think we are ..."

"We could make them stop bothering us," he finished.

I nodded. "Yeah."

Jason stood up. He walked back and forth in front of my hospital bed several times. Finally, he stopped. He turned to Haversham, suddenly all business. I was reminded of the time, back in Bramford, when he'd given orders to my father like a commander in the army. There was something inside Jason that was good at this — at leadership. "Okay, if Azazel and I are going to do this, we'll need a little bit of cover. That means, Haversham, you are to take the plane to the island, and act as if we are with you, should anyone ask. Don't tell anyone, no matter who they are, or what their allegiances are, that we're anywhere else. Can you handle that?"

Haversham raised his eyebrows. "I feel that I must voice my own concern for your safety. After all you are too important to — "

"Can you handle that?" Jason cut him off sharply.

Haversham bowed his head. "Indeed," he said.

"Good," said Jason. "Secondly, we're going to need money, and we're going to need transportation. I have a contact in the states that I usually go through for credit cards and stuff, but I don't think she'll be able to help us here. Can you help us with that, Haversham?"

Haversham considered. "A car is no problem, sir. However, since the Brothers have been cut off from the Sons, we haven't had much access to funds. I might be able to put together some cash — maybe a few thousand euro — but it would take me several hours, at least."

Jason's eyes widened. "A few hours, a few thousand euro? That should be more than sufficient. Thank you."

"Of course," said Haversham. He bowed his head again.

"And one more thing," said Jason.

"Sir?"

"Stop with the bowing stuff."

"Yeah," I agreed. "It's totally creepy."

PART TWO

Battle not with monsters lest you become a monster, and if you gaze into the abyss, the abyss gazes into you.

-Friedrich Nietzsche, *Beyond Good and Evil*

CHAPTER NINE

To: Ian Hoyt <ihoyt@risingsun.org>

From: Arabella Hoyt <arabella.hoyt@gmail.com>

Subject: This is ridiculous

Ian,

First it's taken your boys months to find them, when they were right under our noses the entire time. Then I get news that you've botched it yet again.

A bloodbath at the Spring Formal and my grandson headed back to me on a plane? And my granddaughter, I understand, is still out there, somewhere, with that wretched thing. You were supposed to destroy him. He's an eighteen-year-old boy. How hard could it be?

Arabella

I closed the door to the hotel room after me, tossed the shopping bag on the bed, and collapsed on it. Jason came out of the bathroom, a towel around his waist. Beads of water glittered on his chest.

And his hair ...

I got up and went to him, putting my hands on his head.

Which he'd shaved.

"Oh Jason," I murmured. Jason's hair hadn't been cut in awhile. It had been getting to this shaggy, unkempt sort of stage, which I'd really, really liked. He looked completely different, like a baby bird or something, plucked clean. I rubbed my hands over the short, soft stubble.

"You hate it," he said.

I did. "No," I said. "It's just different."

He nodded. "Yeah, that's the idea."

Jason had decided that since we were on the run again, and no one was going to have much of any idea where we were, it was probably a good idea to change our appearances. With any luck, it would take them time to trace Haversham's plane, which they would believe we were on. By that time, hopefully, we'd have figured out what to do with our power. That is, if we actually had any, and we could actually use it. Still, we weren't sure exactly how long it was going to take us to follow Michaela's journal. And we weren't sure if that would even help us. If it did, we didn't know if it would take months of practice to hone our skills. We needed every advantage we could get.

Jason crossed to the bed, opening the shopping bag I'd brought with me. "What'd you get?" he asked.

One of the things I really despised about this whole being on the run thing was that I always had to leave my clothes behind. I'd had a fabulous wardrobe in Bradenton, which we hadn't been able to go back for. And now, when I'd just started to get a nice collection of clothes again, we had to leave those too.

Jason pulled a few pairs of jeans out of the bag. He surveyed them. "These are for me?"

"Yeah," I said. "And don't start complaining about the style of Italian guys' clothes. We're trying to blend."

Jason rolled his eyes, but tossed them on the bed. He

pulled more clothes out of the bag, including some underwear I'd purchased. He held up a pair of bikini briefs with little pink polka dots on them. "These are for you, right?" he asked, grinning.

I snatched them away from him. "If I'd known you were going to comment on everything I bought, I would have bought you tighty-whiteys."

He smiled. "I'm sorry," he said, laughing. "It's very sweet, you buying underwear for me."

I threw the panties I was holding at his head.

He pulled them off his face. "What?" he said, looking innocent. "It's very domestic. I like it."

"Shut up," I said. "I am *not* domestic."

"Okay, fine," he said. He pulled out a box of hair dye and eyed it. "Red, huh?"

"What?" I said. "You said it had to be a different color than what my natural color is."

"Yeah," he said. "But red?"

"What's wrong with red? I mean, what choices did I have? Black's not that much different than brown, and I guess I could have gone blonde, but stripping color out of your hair is really hard on it and—" I broke off. "You wanted me to be blonde, didn't you? God! Boys."

"No," said Jason. "I didn't want you to do anything. I like your hair the way it is. And red is ... very different." He turned the box over in his hands. "It's also the color of Lilith's hair."

I grabbed the box away from him silently and went into

the bathroom. I wasn't even going to respond to that comment, because it was stupid, anyway. I hadn't picked up this color of hair dye because I wanted to look like Lilith. Sure, I'd envied Lilith's looks during our entire friendship. And yes, there had been a time when I was really worried that Jason wanted Lilith and not me. But that wasn't why I'd picked red. It really wasn't.

I opened the box and began taking stuff out of it. Gloves. Several bottles. The instructions.

Which were in Italian. Well, there were pictures. It appeared that I needed to mix the contents of the first two bottles, then squeeze it all over my hair, and then leave it on for 25 minutes. The other bottle was apparently conditioner or something.

Jason appeared in the doorway. "You know I was never going to do anything with Lilith."

"I never said you were," I said, twisting the top off one of the bottles. God. That didn't smell very good.

"Wait," said Jason, "we should cut your hair first." Oh right. I'd forgotten we were cutting my hair too. I recapped the bottle. Jason reappeared with scissors. He gestured for me to take off my shirt. "We'll put a towel around your shoulders. We don't want your clothes dyed or anything."

I fingered the edge of my shirt. I bit my lip.

Jason moved close. "You're the only girl I've ever wanted. You have to believe that."

"It's not about that, Jason," I said. "I don't like hearing her name." I pulled my shirt over my head forcefully. I reached for a towel and draped it around my shoulders. "I killed her."

I faced the mirror. Jason stood behind me. He picked up a comb and dragged it through my hair. Then I heard the first sound of scissors slicing through my hair. A lock fell down to the floor. I stared at it.

"You know," said Jason. "She was trying to kill you at the time. It was self-defense. I know it's not easy. But you can't keep beating yourself up about it."

"I think I could have talked her out of it," I muttered.

The scissors cut through my hair again.

"She was saying all this stuff," I continued. "About how she was never going to be loved and how ... I don't know. I was getting to her. I think I could have made her let me go. I think I could have helped her. I think, in the end, she was just really hurt and confused. And I just ... I just shot her. And her head. It was all —"

"Stop," said Jason, cutting off another lock of my hair. "She had a knife to your throat. She was working for the Satanists. I'm not saying she deserved to die, Azazel. But I'm saying you had to do what you did. If she'd killed you, I would have killed her."

Yeah. He probably would have. But after Jude had shot Jason in the head, and Jason was lying on the ground, and I thought he was dead, I hadn't gone after Jude, had I? If Jason had been dead, would I have ... "I just don't like talking about her," I said.

Jason snipped again. He was quiet for a minute, just

cutting and looking at his handiwork. "I've been thinking," he said, "about your nightmares and stuff. I think that this has all been harder on you than it is on me. I mean, Azazel, you were betrayed by everyone you ever cared about. And the people you had to shoot ... they were people who were close to you. I've never been close to anyone like that. Except, well, except you." He turned my face to look at him and cut the pieces of my hair, right at my chin. He checked to see if they were even. Then he gazed into my eyes. "It makes sense why it hurts you so much. That's all I'm saying. But I've never blamed you for anything. And I don't think you should blame yourself."

I looked at myself in the mirror. My hair was cut in a bob, barely reaching past my chin. I touched it. Jason had done a good job. "What about Anton?" I asked the mirror.

Jason didn't say anything.

"Didn't he betray you?" I said.

Jason just breathed.

"Do you blame yourself for that?"

Jason handed me the bottle I'd recapped. "You should dye your hair now," he said.

He left the bathroom. I heard the television in the hotel room flip on. It was in Italian. What was he going to do? Just sit around staring at people speaking a language he didn't understand?

I probably shouldn't have said that to him, I thought as I began to mix the hair dye. Jason had been trying to reassure me and to help me. Not only hadn't I accepted it, but I'd thrown Anton in his face. It wasn't a spoken rule, but I knew better than to mention him, especially not to mention the fact that Jason had killed him. Anton had been the closest thing to a father Jason had ever had.

Once I had dye all over my hair, I did the best I could to clean up the hair that was on the floor from my hair cut, and I put the box of hair dye in the trash. The twenty-five minutes I was supposed to wait passed pretty quickly because I couldn't stop thinking. Was Jason right? Was I blaming myself for something that wasn't actually my fault? After all, I didn't blame Jason for killing Anton. He'd been defending himself. He'd been betrayed and confused. Was I being harder on myself than I was being on Jason?

But if I could forgive myself for what I'd done to Lilith and my brothers, what would that mean that I would become? While I didn't necessarily blame Jason for what he'd done, there was some part of him that had gotten hardened by all of it. I remembered the look on his face while he was beating the member of the Sons to a pulp at the prom. He'd been lost in his vengeance then. And I remembered the way he'd been about to kill Jude without even telling me about it. Sometimes I felt like Jason was slipping away from me.

I got in the shower to rinse off the hair dye. When I got out, I noticed that the television wasn't on anymore. I rubbed my hair with a towel, staring at myself in the mirror. Wow. My hair was really red, wasn't it? I didn't look much like myself either. Was that what was happening to Jason and me? Were we becoming something else?

I went into the bedroom, still wrapped in my towel. Jason was sprawled on the bed, reading Michaela Weem's diary.

He looked up at me. "Wow," he said. "That's red."

"Yeah," I agreed. "Listen, I'm sorry I said anything. You were just trying to help."

Jason snapped the diary shut. "I don't blame myself," he said. "I don't, and I haven't in a while. And I don't want to read this diary anymore." He threw it at me.

I caught it. I looked from the diary to Jason. I'd made him angry. I shouldn't have said anything.

"You know why I don't want to read it?" he asked me.

I shook my head.

"Because I don't want to think of her like that," he muttered. "I don't want to think of her like a teenage girl, having normal regular emotions. I don't want her to be a *person*, Azazel. Because I killed her. And I killed Anton. And I've killed ..." He stood up from the bed and went across the room to the window. He pulled the curtains open and looked out into the night.

I set the diary on the bed and padded over to him. I put a tentative hand on his back. He turned to me. "What's happening to me?" he whispered. "What's happening to us?"

I grabbed his hands and kissed his fingers. His knuckles. His palms. He pulled me close, his lips against my ear. "Sometimes, I think if I can just be close enough to you ..."

"That it will all just go away?" I finished.

"That it does. Go away. That the only thing important then is you and me and our bodies."

I kissed him. "Let's make it go away," I whispered, untucking my towel so that it fell away onto the floor.

Jason's hands skimmed my bare skin, spanning my waist and crushing me against him. And it was so desperate, so immediate, so hungry, that I didn't have time to think to tell him where to put his fingers or how to try to please me.

It was only afterwards, when the hotel room was dark, and Jason was gently snoring next to me in bed, that I lay awake, watching shadows on the ceiling and feeling unfinished. I bit my lip, wondering why everything had to be so complicated. When guys had sex, it seemed to be entirely made for their bodies. There were no extraneous zones, places that needed to be stimulated by anything other than the act of intercourse itself. Was it some kind of cruel joke that our most sensitive place, our place of deepest pleasure was just a few inches too far away? Why?

Instead of thinking about it too much longer, I just got up and started reading the diary. If Jason didn't want to read it, I would.

* * *

Brother Mancini wasn't happy to see us. We knocked on the door of the monastery and asked for him. When he arrived at the door, he ushered us into his office, trying to take care that no one saw us. Once inside, he slammed the door to the office. "I thought I made it clear why the two of you shouldn't be here," he said.

205

Jason lounged against the door to the office. I sat down in a chair across from Brother Mancini's desk. "Well, we were having lots of fun at school," Jason said, "until a bunch of guys with guns came in and shot up our prom."

We were in Rome. We'd taken a train that morning. Brother Mancini was our first stop.

"I'd heard about the incident at the Sol Solis School, of course," said Brother Mancini. "And I'm sorry. But there is absolutely no way you can stay here. We'd offer you shelter, but we are at capacity with all the defectors from the Sons. I'm very sorry."

"That's not why we're here, Brother Mancini," I said. I held up the diary. "We're here about this."

Brother Mancini looked flustered. He sat down at his desk. "I don't know what that is."

"It's Michaela Weem's diary," I said. "She mentions you."

"Michaela Weem?" Brother Mancini was blank.

"Michaela Weem," said Jason. "She says she and Edgar, her soon-to-be husband, came through the monastery about eighteen years ago. Ringing any bells now?"

"I'm sorry, no," said Brother Mancini. He was starting to look less flustered and more annoyed.

"My parents," said Jason.

Recognition flitted across Brother Mancini's face. He stood up from his desk, going for the door. "Listen, I'd love to chat with you two, but I don't know anything about that, and since it really wouldn't be prudent for our guests to see you—"

Jason was still lounging against the door. He put his hand on the knob just as Brother Mancini reached for it, blocking him.

I spoke up. "Michaela says you directed the two of them to a guy named ..." I had this page marked. I opened up the diary to look. "...Cornelius Agricola." I closed the diary. "This of course was after she and Edgar went to Coliseum and made love in the moonlight while chanting Latin spells."

Brother Mancini's face had gone ashen. He moved away from the door. "What are the two of you up to? I thought I explained to you that it was highly unlikely that there was anything to the idea of the Rising Sun."

"Funny thing," said Jason. "Just recently, Azazel and I were able to make everyone in the entire school think we were really, really awesome. And we have no idea how we did it. I'm not saying I'm the Rising Sun. But, you know, I did come back from the dead."

"We found this diary," I said. "We thought if we could figure out what Edgar Weem did to create Jason, maybe we could understand what we were doing."

"Well," said Brother Mancini, "Cornelius Agricola is dead."

Jason and I exchanged a look. Even I could tell he was lying.

"I don't think he is," said Jason. "Why don't you just tell us where he is, and we'll be out of your hair."

Brother Mancini shook his head quickly, moving back to

his desk. "No," he said. "You don't want to see Cornelius."
He began straightening piles of papers on his desk.

"Why?" I said.

"He's not exactly a very stable person," said Brother
Mancini, stacking the piles on top of each other.

Jason raised his eyebrows. "We can handle unstable," he
said. "We can handle a lot of things."

Brother Mancini just kept shaking his head. "No, I don't
think so," he said. "I won't tell you where that man is. In
fact, I don't even think I remember. And maybe he is dead.
God help us, maybe he is." He looked up at us with a
strained smile. "Well, if that's all, then the two of you should
really be on your way, shouldn't you, then?"

"We're not leaving until you tell us where to find
Cornelius Agricola," I said. "What's so unstable about him
anyway?"

Brother Mancini crossed himself. "The Reddimus Order
may not be the most traditional in its beliefs," he said.
"Certainly, we are students of pagan religions and
mythology. Perhaps not all of us see things as black and
white. But, I must tell you, if there is evil in the universe,
Cornelius Agricola serves it. And it has been my misfortune
to have to deal with him." He stood up again. "But that is all
I will say about him. You won't get anymore out of me, and
I refuse to tell you where he is."

Brother Mancini went back to the door. Jason didn't
move.

"Evil, huh?" asked Jason. "Well, Azazel and I know a

little bit about that, considering she's imbued with the spirit of a Jewish demon, and I'm the devil incarnate, so that's really not going to scare us off. If this guy's so bad, why do you even know who he is?"

"No!" said Brother Mancini, putting his hand on the doorknob. Jason settled firmly against the door. "I won't talk about it. You won't make me. You two need to go."

Jason caught my eye above Brother Mancini's head. "Don't be difficult, Brother Mancini," he said. "We'd really like this to be a pleasant visit."

"Yeah," I said. "Just tell us where he is." I reached into my jacket for my gun. I just put my hand on it. I didn't take it out.

"I've told you I won't," said Brother Mancini. "You can't trap me here in my own office."

I slid the gun out. "Brother Mancini," I said. "Please just tell us what we want to know."

At the sight of the gun, Brother Mancini began muttering to himself in rapid Italian. He retreated into a corner of the room, his hands in front of his face, cowering away from us. Jason pushed away from the door, drawing his own gun. I stood up. We advanced on Brother Mancini. Both of us leveled our guns.

Brother Mancini's eyes were wide. "Listen," he said. "Cornelius Agricola is not someone you can just have a chat with. If you knew what he'd done and why he forces the Order and the Church to allow him to stay in the city, you wouldn't want to go there."

"So tell us," said Jason.

"No," said Brother Mancini, crossing himself again.

"We don't want to shoot you, do we, Azazel?" Jason asked me.

"No, we don't," I said. "Thing about shooting people is that it's always messy."

"Fine!" said Brother Mancini. "Fine, I'll get you his address. But put away the guns!"

* * *

"We weren't really going to shoot him, were we?" I asked Jason as we strode out of the monastery.

Jason handed me the slip of paper Brother Mancini had given us with Cornelius Agricola's address on it. "Only like in the leg," said Jason, "if he really wouldn't have given us the address."

I nodded. That sounded reasonable. "It was kind of cool, wasn't it?" I said. "I mean, standing over him with our guns like that. It felt, I don't know, kind of powerful." I looked at Jason. "Do you think that's bad?"

He shrugged. "We didn't hurt him. Don't worry about it."

Okay. I wouldn't.

CHAPTER TEN

June 1, 1990

It does hurt. We only did it twice so far. Once was at the Coliseum. We did it at midnight, while intoning a chant in Latin that Jed taught me. It hurt. Afterwards, I told Jed that I loved him. He told me I shouldn't say things like that. That we were doing this for a specific purpose, not for personal pleasure. I should have said, "Good," because there wasn't much pleasure for me anyway.

Brother Mancini of the Order of Reddimus directed us to Cornelius Agricola yesterday. Last night, we went to see him. Jed was very excited, because Cornelius apparently has access to some kind of power that he could imbue into the child. I didn't get to find out much about what it was, because they talked without me.

It was strange and weird. I had to drink from several really disgusting tasting drinks. Then they smeared my body with something that smelled horrible. Jed and I did it again, in dark, with just these candles. And Cornelius Agricola watched. I don't like him.

Today, I feel tired. We only have two more days in my window of fertility. Jed hasn't told me where we're going next.

Brother Mancini had made Cornelius Agricola sound pretty dangerous. The entry in Michaela's diary hadn't. She'd said she didn't like him, but nothing more than that. I hadn't had the chance to read beyond her entry on Cornelius

211

Agricola, though. Maybe she talked about him more later. I wished the diary was like Google, and it had a search function. It didn't though.

Jason and I decided the best course of action was to be cautious. I had to admit that I didn't like the fact that Brother Mancini had seemed so frightened of Agricola. I was curious about why, but if it were really, really bad, maybe it was better that we didn't know. We approached Agricola's house with our guns drawn. It was a tall house and connected to the other houses on the street. Most of Rome was like that. All of the houses looked like a wall. The street and sidewalk met the edge of the foundation. There weren't any trees or yards. The city was completely covered in stone. It was as if the original builders of the city had wanted to eradicate nature or something.

The entrance to Agricola's house was a tall, metal gate, made of twisting wrought iron. It wasn't locked. Jason swung it open, and I followed. That was when we both took out our guns. Inside the gate was a courtyard. There was a fountain in the center. When we looked up, we saw a balcony. Dozens of hanging plants dangled in our faces. Jungle-like and dark, the courtyard gave me a touch of the creeps.

Jason went first. We tiptoed across the courtyard to a door across from the gate. It had an old, iron knocker on it. Jason raised it and dropped it. The sound was a resounding boom. We both jumped a little.

Nothing happened. We waited.

"You think he's not home?" I whispered, tightening my grip on my gun.

Jason took a look around and then raised the knocker again. It hit the door and made another loud booming sound.

Still nothing.

"Should we come back?" I wondered.

Then there was the sound of shuffling feet from behind the door. It opened. A short, wizened woman stood on the other side of the door. She had stringy white hair, olive colored skin, and she was quite rotund. "*Buongiorno?*" she said.

"Uh," said Jason, keeping me behind him. "We're looking for Cornelius Agricola."

The woman looked confused. She let out a string of Italian words.

Jesus. This was stupid. Why were Jason and I trying to get around in a city where we didn't speak the language?

"Um," I said, "*Inglese?*" (Which was essentially the extent of my Italian. It meant English.)

"Ah," said the woman, looking saddened. "*No Italiano?*"

"No," I said.

"Cornelius Agricola," said Jason. "Does he live here?" He pointed at the ground, as if that was supposed to somehow mime "live."

"Agricola," repeated the woman, still looking confused.

There was a thud behind us.

Jason and I whirled, raising our guns. I didn't have a

chance to see what had fallen behind us, however.

Before I could think, someone or something kicked both my gun out of my hands and my feet out from under me. I fell back, my head cracking on the stone of the courtyard. And everything went dark.

* * *

I woke up in a darkened room, my back to Jason. We were sitting on the floor and we were chained up. The chains looked like chains from some medieval dungeon. They were heavy, and they attached to large metal shackles that encircled our ankles and wrists. The room itself was dark and stone, with no furnishings except some whips and chains hanging on a far wall. The only light came from a grate high in the ceiling, where a shaft of light fell down directly on Jason and me. I gulped. What had we gotten ourselves into, exactly?

I nudged Jason. "You awake?" I whispered.

"He's awake," said a voice. Not Jason's. The voice was deeper and older than his, with a heavy Italian accent.

I didn't say anything else. My gun was gone. I'd had it in my hand when I'd been knocked out. I noticed now that both our guns were hanging underneath the whips. Whoever had us was taunting us, putting our weapons in sight but out of reach. This sucked. It didn't seem likely that this guy, if he actually was Cornelius Agricola (the lady at the gate hadn't seemed to recognize the name), was going to be real helpful. He probably wasn't going to tell us anything.

"I've been waiting for him," continued the voice. The

man who was speaking strode around the circle and into my vision. Apparently, he'd been standing in front of Jason. He was a tall man with broad shoulders. His head was shaved, and he had a goatee. The way he glared at me from under his eyebrows projected something sinister. I didn't like it. "You, though," he continued. "I didn't think there would be a girl." He smiled. "But that will make things even more interesting."

Interesting? What was this guy planning to do to us?

"Sit tight, lovelies," he said and left the room, shutting and locking a heavy door behind him.

We were quiet for several minutes after he left. I was expecting something to drop in through the ceiling or crawl out through some grates in the floor that I couldn't see. Something like poisonous snakes or some deadly gas. But nothing happened.

"He said he'd been waiting for you," I said. "Do you think he knows who you are? Do you think he's Cornelius Agricola?"

Jason was rattling his chains, examining them. Trust Jason to be practical, only concerned with trying to get us out of the situation and not with the motives of our captor. "These are old shackles," he said. "I don't think they were made for women. You might be able to slide out of them."

I tested one of them, trying to pull my hand out of it. It seemed pretty tight to me. Plus it was hard to move my limbs since they were connected to such heavy chains. "I don't think so," I said.

"Try," said Jason.

I dragged the chains closer so that my hands were close enough to touch. I held onto one of the shackles and tried to slide my hand out of it. It slid up over my hand, but caught on the knuckle of my thumb. I tried to push it farther. It wouldn't go. I folded my thumb against my hand, making that part of me as small as possible. It slid a little further up. Then it caught and wouldn't slide any further. "No," I said. "I can't."

Jason twisted, flinching as he did so. He was straining against his chains. He checked my progress. "You've almost got it," he said. "Keep trying."

"It hurts," I said.

"Keep trying," he insisted. He moved his hand forward to help me, but his chain didn't reach far enough.

I grasped the shackle again and tried to force it over my hand. It scraped my knuckles, drawing blood. "Ouch," I said. But it had moved forward more, so I kept struggling with it.

More scraping. More bleeding. And then—success! My hand was free! Awesome.

"It worked," I told Jason. "I have a free hand!"

"Good," said Jason. "Keep going."

The second hand was easier to free, but I scraped it up even worse, probably because I knew it could be done and wasn't as careful of myself. With both hands free, I started on my feet. I shrugged out of my shoes and socks and started to try to get the ankle shackles off. At first it seemed hopeless. I pushed the shackle down as far as I could get it. It slid down over my heel, but bit into the skin of the top of my foot, drawing more blood.

Then I had a vague memory from when I was a very little girl. I couldn't have been more than three. My mother was in her bedroom, putting on a pair of very tight jeans. She couldn't get the end of the jeans over her heel. I remembered the way she'd pointed her toes, like a ballet dancer. Then she'd yanked the jeans up. They were tight on her ankle, like a second skin.

This shackle was bigger than those jeans. Of course, it was also not made of fabric. Still, I tried it, elongating my foot and pointing my toes. The shackle slid right off. "Got a foot!" I told Jason. The second one came off just as easily. I was free!

I stood up, going around to face Jason.

"Good," he said. "Good job." He smiled at me.

"How do we get you out?" I asked.

"We don't," he said. "My hands and feet are too big. I've tried." He held up his hands, which were just as scraped as mine, but still encased in their shackles. "Instead, you've got to get the guns and wait behind the door. When he comes back, you shoot him. Then hopefully he's got keys on him, and you can get me out."

It wasn't an awful plan. "But," I said, "if he's Cornelius Agricola, we still want him to tell us about what he did with Michaela and Edgar Weem."

"Well, don't kill him," said Jason. "Just disable him."

"So, where do I shoot him?" This guy looked pretty big. I wasn't sure if he'd go down with a shot in the leg. If it came to fighting hand to hand, I'd never be able to match him.

"Go get the gun," said Jason. "Let me think about it."

It turned out to be a moot point. I couldn't reach the guns. They were too high on the wall, out of my reach. I tried jumping. I couldn't even get my fingertips to brush them. Jason was taller than me. If we could get him free, he could probably reach them.

But Jason assured me that he couldn't get out of his shackles. I told him to keep trying. I surveyed the door. It opened into the room, so it was possible that I could hide behind it when it opened, like Jason had said. "Maybe I could trip him," I said. "When he comes in?"

"And then what?" said Jason.

"Well," I said, "if he falls down flat on his face— How far can your chains reach?"

Jason crawled forward. "Maybe," he said. "Maybe I could reach him. I could get a chain around his neck or something. But you'd have to help. If you ran up and kicked his head from behind, that would hurt him. Keep him down. It might work."

We didn't have a better plan, so it was what we went with. I positioned myself behind the door and waiting for the man to come back. He didn't come back. I got sick of standing and sat down behind the door.

It felt like hours passed. But we didn't have any way to measure the time. The light from the grate over us seemed to be dimming. Moving. Was it early evening? Late afternoon? We didn't know.

"You know what's been bothering me?" I finally said. "Two people at the school said that they started thinking about us on Friday."

"What?" said Jason.

"Faruza or maybe it was Fairie. And the head. When I asked them when they started to think we were special or whatever, they both said they did on Friday. And that was the day that I found you with Jude."

"So?"

"Well, every other time something weird has happened to us, it's been right after we kissed," I said. "And we did kiss on Friday. Do you remember?"

"We kiss every day, Azazel. Weird things don't happen every time we kiss."

"Yeah, but do you remember that kiss? It was a pretty intense kiss."

Jason didn't answer for a second. "Yeah," he said. "I do remember. And right before we were kissing, I was wishing like hell that I could just be normal and enjoy high school."

"Were you? Because I was wishing that we had someone who supported us," I said.

"Huh," said Jason.

"We got our wishes, didn't we?"

"Do you think that's how it works?" he asked me. "Because before the Sons went nuts in Shiloh, I was totally wishing that we could get out of that situation."

"And when I thought you were dead, I could hardly accept the fact that you were. I wanted you back."

"Huh," said Jason again. "Maybe we should ditch this whole tripping him plan and just wish really hard that he'd come let us go. And then make out heavily."

I laughed. "You think so?"

"It wouldn't hurt anything would it?" Jason asked. "Plus, the whole thing doesn't sound unpleasant."

I laughed again.

"Come over here," Jason said.

I went to him. I sat down next to him. I touched his face and his chest.

"Now wish," he whispered.

I shut my eyes. I wished as hard as I could. With my eyes still closed, I felt Jason's lips press against mine. They were sweet and soft and familiar, and they still made me feel like the entire world was splitting apart and falling away. I clung to him, our kiss deepening, our mouths opening, our tongues entwining. When we broke away, I sighed.

We waited. The guy didn't come back. The wound on my arm itched. I scratched at it. Jason scolded me about messing up my bandage. We waited some more.

"I guess that didn't work," I said finally.

"Maybe," said Jason, "we didn't do it right. Maybe we should try again."

"You just want to kiss me again."

"I'm that transparent, huh?" he grinned. "Wish again," he said and kissed me. We kissed for a long time. Jason couldn't really touch me because of the fact his hands were in shackles, but he kept whispering to me to get closer. Eventually, I ended up straddling him, our bodies pressed tight against each other. I was running my hands over the stubble on his head, which actually felt really cool. I was getting more and more used to it.

Of course, that was when the door opened.

And I wasn't nearly close enough to trip him. The sound startled me, and I remembered that was what I was supposed to do. So I leapt to my feet and lunged for the guy. Not only didn't he trip, he caught me and drove me up against the wall, kicking the door closed behind him. He pinned me, his hand around my neck.

"Yes," he said. "You're definitely making things interesting."

The man was strong. He lifted me off the ground, pushing me up the wall. My hands went to my throat instinctively, prying at his fingers, trying to keep him from choking me. The man just laughed.

I couldn't breathe! I couldn't count the amount of times people had tried to strangle me in the past year. Really. Couldn't this guy come up with something original? And considering he was trying to strangle me, I was pretty sure that meant our little kissing-wishing maneuver hadn't worked.

I tried kicking at the man. That only made him laugh more. I looked around the room frantically. Jason was making frantic gestures to look to my left. It was hard to move my head, considering I was being strangled, but I managed to twist it a little.

The guns!

The man had lifted me up higher. I should be able to reach the guns, which were hanging below the whips and chains to my right. I reached out, my hand scrabbling against the wall. I knocked one of the guns off the wall, and it clattered against the floor.

Damn it!

The world was going white around the edges, and the man was grabbing at me, trying to move my arm down. I groped for a hold on something—anything—over there.

My fingers closed around a chain of some kind. I yanked at it with all my strength, and it came free. It was heavy, and I had very little control over it as I swung it back toward the man.

As it swung around, I was able to see what it was I'd grabbed. It was a ball and chain, the ball as the end heavy and made of iron. The ball swung wide and clobbered the man in the back. He buckled from the force of it, letting out a growl, and dropped me.

I hit the ground hard, and the ball had bounced against the man and was swinging back around. I dropped it, rolling out of the way, and crawled to the dropped gun. The metal ball clattered against the floor. Gun in hands, I rolled over onto my back, aiming in the general direction of the man and flipping off the safety.

My arms weren't steady as I pointed the gun at him. He

was lumbering forward, the expression on his face one of pure rage. I was still trying to get oxygen back into my lungs, but I managed to say, "Keys," to him.

He was coming for me.

"Stop," I gasped.

He grabbed at the gun, like he was going to wrench it out of my hand. So I pulled the trigger. He was already putting pressure on the barrel of the gun, so the shot went wide, but it caught him in the opposite shoulder. He let go of the gun and cried out.

I got to my feet, still breathing hard. "Give me the keys, so I can get Jason out," I said.

I was waving the gun in his face, and he was clutching his bleeding shoulder, but he still hesitated. Finally, he dug a set of old keys on an iron ring out of his pocket and flung them on the floor. I bent down to pick them up, keeping my eyes and the gun trained on him.

Holding the keys, I stood up. "Stay where you are," I said to him, backing away. When I reached Jason, I handed him the keys. I didn't watch him, just listened to the sounds of metal scraping metal. Instead, I watched the man, who *was* staying put, still clutching his bleeding shoulder and looking royally pissed.

"Azazel," said Jason. "I can't get the right one off my hand."

I only looked down for a minute. Jason had freed his legs and his left hand, but his right hand was still shackled. I was about to hand Jason the gun, so that he could cover the man while I unlocked his shackle, but in that short period of time, the man had made his move.

He tackled me, knocking the gun out of my hand. It skittered across the floor, far out of my reach. I was underneath him, the full weight of his body pressing down on me. He pinned my hands down above my head with one arm—the one with a bleeding shoulder, if you could believe it. He pulled back his other fist. He was going to hit me! I cringed.

And Jason dove into the man, knocking him off me.

I pulled myself out of the way. Jason and the man were wrestling on the ground. Jason was on top of the man, his hands around the man's neck, squeezing.

The man entwined his legs with Jason's and forced them over so that he was pinning Jason. He punched Jason several times in the face.

Wait. This looked familiar. I'd seen Jason make that move before. Back in Bramford. At the Nelson farm party.

Jason reached up and pushed several fingers into the wound on the man's shoulder. The man cried out, thrusting Jason's hand out of the wound. Jason took the opportunity to punch the man squarely on the chin. The man's head whipped to the side. Recovering, the man drove his fist into Jason's nose. Jason started bleeding.

Shit.

Maybe I should stop sitting here watching this like a damsel in distress and find the damned gun.

I caught sight of it and ran to pick it up. The man was

sitting up, punching Jason again and again. There wasn't any chance I'd hit Jason instead of the man. So I took careful aim and pulled the trigger.

Click.

No! Out of bullets? I stared at the gun. We'd stolen it from the Sons when they were shooting up the prom. Jason had told me the name of these kinds of guns once, but I couldn't remember. Still, it seemed to me that these were the kinds that held about thirty bullets. But who knew how many times the gun had been fired before I picked it up on the floor of the prom? Jason and I needed more ammunition.

I looked from the gun to Jason and the man. The other gun was on the other side of the room, still hanging on the wall. I couldn't get to it, could I? Maybe I should try. Maybe I could grab the ball and chain and throw it up there. Maybe it could knock off the gun.

Jason's head thudded against the floor. His face was broken and bleeding. He groaned.

I ran for the gun. Halfway across the floor, I heard the man howl. I stopped and turned to look. He was lying on his back. Jason was standing over him, kicking him repeatedly in the groin.

"Get the chains," Jason called to me.

At first I thought he meant the ball and chain over by the door. But then I realized he meant the chains in the middle of the room. He wanted to chain up the man. I sprinted to Jason and the man, stopping to grab one of the shackles. I dragged it to the man, clamping one around his wrist. It locked when I snapped it closed.

"Wait," yelled the man.

Was he crazy? I ran to get another shackle.

"I don't think you're who I thought you were," said the man.

I yanked the shackle across the floor, reaching for his hand.

"You're Jason, aren't you?" the man said to Jason.

Jason held up his hand for me to stop. I paused, but I wasn't really sure why. So the guy had mistaken Jason's identity. Big freaking deal. Like that made any difference. He'd chained us up, nearly strangled me, and beaten Jason's face mangled and bloody. We should definitely restrain him, no matter what he was saying.

Jason folded his arms over his chest. "Who'd you think I was?" he asked.

"Michael Jude," said the man. "He's your brother, right? I had a picture. You two look an awful lot alike."

Okay. Intriguing and all. I gestured with the shackle at Jason. "Who cares?" I said.

The man twisted to look at me. "I don't mean you any harm," he said. "I was expecting the other one. Not you." The man's face was pretty messed up too. Jason had held his own. He held out his hand to Jason, the one that wasn't shackled. "Cornelius Agricola," he said.

Jason just stood there for a second. Then he moved forward and shook the man's hand.

"You're amazing," said Agricola. "It's been over twenty

years since a man's bested me in a fight." He grinned, and it looked horrible because there was blood in his mouth. "I am getting a little older," he said. "But you were well trained. And I consecrated you to both Mars and Mithras myself. I'm in awe."

Jason shrugged. "Well, I wouldn't have beaten you if I hadn't gone for the groin. Fought dirty."

"No such thing," said Agricola, grinning even wider. "How about letting me out of this shackle?"

"No freaking way," I said.

"Azazel," said Jason.

"You two were just beating the living crap out of each other, and now you're shaking hands and complimenting each other?" I demanded. "This guy is dangerous. We leave him chained up."

"Your young woman is smart," said Agricola. "Listen, I offer you my word. I swear to you on my faith in the great power of the bull and its purifying blood. I will not harm you."

"Screw your word," I said.

"Azazel, I believe him," said Jason. "Besides, we did come here to talk to him, didn't we?"

I couldn't believe this. Maybe it was some kind of ridiculous male code or something. Guys could just punch each other and be friends right after. Who knew why? It was weird and disturbing and stupid. But we did want to talk to Cornelius Agricola. And I supposed what he said kind of made sense. Maybe.

"Why'd you think Jude was coming?" I asked.

"Jason's father told me he probably would. Edgar said Jude was in possession of a journal that mentioned me and that the boy would be following the journal through Europe. Edgar wanted the boy contained and the journal returned to him."

"So you're in touch with Edgar Weem," said Jason. "And doing him favors?"

"Ted and I are old friends," said Agricola. "I used to train his Brothers in hand to hand combat. Years I did that."

"Well," said Jason. "Last I checked, Edgar Weem wanted me dead, so I don't think I'm actually going to let you go."

Thank you, Jason. At least he was being slightly reasonable.

"Dead?" Agricola laughed as if that were ridiculous. "Jason, you're his pride and joy. He doesn't want you dead."

I stood by Jason. We both folded our arms over our chests.

"All right," said Agricola. "Perhaps he wanted you to think that. Ted always had a tendency to make things more complicated than they needed to be. I told him if he really wanted to destroy the Sons to just set a bomb, but no, no, no. He was convinced about all of this Rising Sun business and wanted to make you to do it for him."

Jason and I exchanged a look. "Destroy the Sons?" said Jason. "I thought I was supposed to unite the world under a global government."

"Let me out of my shackle, and I'll tell you all about it,"

said Agricola. "And we can all get cleaned up. Maybe have some food?"

Jason looked at me questioningly.

"I promise I won't call Ted," said Agricola. "I swear."

I *was* hungry.

* * *

About an hour later, we were sitting at the table in Agricola's dining room. The old woman from the door was bustling about in the kitchen. She was Agricola's mother apparently. She'd already set out several plates of food. First course stuff. *Antipasti.* There were slices of gorgonzola and mozzarella, a plate of prosciutto and salami, a bowl of olives, some roasted red peppers, and a basket of bread. I could probably make a meal out of this, but Agricola assured us there was more coming. Much more.

They really did know how to feed you in Italy. Agricola's mother came into the dining room, carrying a wine decanter. She sat it down on the table and sat down with us. "*Mangi. Mangi,*" she said.

"Eat," translated Agricola. He reached for a plate and dipped himself some roasted red peppers.

While we filled our plates with appetizers, Agricola and his mother chatted easily in Italian. Jason and I ate quietly. Thus far, everything seemed okay. Agricola was being very hospitable. He'd allowed Jason and I to shower and had his mother prepare this massive feast for us. I wasn't sure if I trusted him or not, but the food was really, really good. Still, I was curious. What did Agricola know about Weem? Why had he said that Weem wanted to destroy the Sons? It didn't make sense. Up until a few months ago, Weem had been very high up in the Council, practically the head of the Sons. If he wanted to destroy them, why had he worked for them for so long? I wanted to ask Agricola about it, but I wasn't sure how. Besides, he and his mother were still talking.

Eventually, his mother went out of the room to bring out the first course. Agricola told us that he'd been explaining to her who we were and that she would be dining in the kitchen so that we could talk.

"She doesn't have to do that," I said. This woman was preparing our food. It didn't seem right that she also had to eat in the kitchen.

"It's not a problem for her," said Agricola.

She brought in a several bowls and a large dish of pasta. Linguine with onions and tomato sauce. We served ourselves portions of pasta and Agricola's mother left the room.

"So," said Agricola, "I must admit, I'm curious. How did you happen to get this instead of your brother?" He held up the diary.

"Can we have that back?" I said.

Agricola hesitated, then slid it across the table to me. "I was to give it to Ted," he said, "but I'll give it back to you as a gesture of good faith."

"Jude's dead," Jason said shortly, digging into his pasta.

Agricola raised his eyebrows. "Ted will be saddened," he said. "He said that the younger boy was unruly, however."

"I don't think Edgar Weem is going to care," I said.

"You don't know him," said Agricola. "I'm sure he's appeared cold and aloof to you, but he's not a bad man. He has his weaknesses, but so do we all. I know that he is quite proud of you, Jason."

"Yeah," said Jason. "Well, see that's what I don't get. Because he had one of the Brothers watching me this winter, waiting to see if I got too violent. According to that guy, Edgar Weem said that when he made me he 'created a monster.' And that if I screwed up too much, he'd have me killed."

Agricola shrugged. "Ted always wanted you to be violent," he said. "Not in an undisciplined manner, of course, but he created you to be a deadly warrior. And it seems he succeeded." Agricola smiled. "I can't say enough how impressed I am by your abilities. Perhaps he only wanted you watched because he wanted to keep tabs on your progress. I'm certain he never intended to have you killed. He's your father, after all."

"I don't have a father," Jason muttered.

"I'm sure he'd approve of that sentiment, as well," said Agricola. "But I'm afraid I still don't understand. You took this journal from your brother. Killed him —"

"We didn't kill him," I interrupted. "Someone else did."

"I see," said Agricola. "But I don't know what this journal is. Ted wouldn't explain. He said that if I found it, I'd probably read it, and that he couldn't stop me. But he wouldn't go any further."

"It's Michaela Weem's diary," said Jason.

It was occurring to me that Agricola was asking the questions and not the other way around. Was he pumping us for information? When he had what he wanted, would he just lock us back up again? Maybe that was why he'd had no problem giving back the diary.

"Who?" said Agricola.

Jason looked surprised. "She was here with Edgar Weem. Eighteen years ago."

Agricola still looked blank.

"My mother," Jason said finally, but he didn't sound like he liked saying the words.

"Ah! Yes. She was a pretty girl. You do take after her quite a bit. I don't know if I ever knew her name."

Really? "In the diary, she says that you watched her and Edgar have sex. And you didn't bother to find out her name?" I asked.

Agricola turned to me. "You are quite a girl, aren't you?" he said. "You handle a gun well. And Jason, you do rely on her quite a bit, don't you?"

"She's reliable," said Jason.

"She's your weakness," said Agricola. "Women always make men weak."

Sexist bastard. I clamped my mouth shut. No wonder he didn't know Michaela's name.

"No," said Jason. "You're wrong about that. Before Azazel came along, I didn't have anything to fight for. Fighting without purpose makes a man weak. Having a purpose strengthens your resolve."

I shot Jason a grateful smile.

Agricola raised an eyebrow.

"Besides," said Jason. "She held her own." He nodded to Agricola's shoulder.

"Touché," said Agricola. "So your mother's diary, then."

"It explains how she and Edgar Weem went about trying to conceive me," said Jason. "Azazel and I thought that if we knew more about where I came from, we could figure out … Do you believe in the Rising Sun?"

"Of course not," said Agricola. "But I do have my beliefs. They are older than those of the Sons. And they are far less democratic. I don't believe all gods are the same god. I don't believe that all religious traditions are equally valid. No. I worship Mithras, and I worship Mars. I am a warrior and a soldier, and those are my patrons. I believe that the power I summoned to bestow on you, Jason, was very real indeed."

"I guess that's why we're here," said Jason. "We want to know what exactly that power was. The diary is pretty vague on what actually happened."

Agricola raised his eyebrows. "I'm not sure the details of the ritual are really a good dinner conversation."

"Because they're gross?" I asked.

"Not gross," said Agricola, giving me a withering look. "They are sacred, powerful actions. But they might not be appetizing."

"Did you make her drink the bull semen?" I asked.

"I thought you didn't know about the ritual," said

Agricola.

"It's vague," said Jason.

"So you did?" I said.

Agricola sighed. "Maybe I should start at the beginning," he said.

"Okay," said Jason.

Agricola took a deep breath. "I've known Ted for quite some time, as I said. For years, I was on the Sons' payroll, because I trained the Brothers in hand-to-hand combat. Ted and I spoke often during this period. He and I talked about ancient religions, which was his deepest interest. He sometimes shared with me concerns about the organization he worked for. He was worried that the Sons were losing their faith. He didn't feel that they were following the true path anymore, but had been seduced by the call of power and money. In those early days, he used to talk to me about the Sons' messiah. The Rising Sun. He said that the way things stood, if the Rising Sun were to arrive, he'd clean house in the Sons, in much the way that Jesus did with the moneymakers in the temple.

"A few years later, he contacted me again. He was a teacher now, at a school the Sons ran for rich kids. But now he had a crazy idea in his head. He said that the Sons needed to be stopped. Destroyed. They were too corrupt. And he was going to do this by bringing forth the Rising Sun. When I asked him how, he started spewing all this ridiculous nonsense about King Arthur and genealogical lines."

"Yeah," said Jason. "We've heard that too."

"The long and short of it was that he wanted my help to perform a fertility ritual on him and some girl he was bringing with him. He wanted the blessings of Mars and Mithras on the child, because he felt that the Rising Sun would need to be a great warrior in order to destroy the Sons.

"I told him that I worshipped the gods of soldiers, and I didn't know much about fertility. He suggested an initiation of sorts into the Mithraic mysteries for both him and the girl. I told him this was blasphemous. Women weren't allowed in the Mithraic mysteries. We worked out a compromise. I initiated Ted, but not the girl. She was however, bathed in the blood of the sacrificial bull and, as a measure of fertility, drank the bull's semen."

"Sacrificial bull?" I said. "You killed a bull?"

"The mysteries are mysteries for a reason," said Agricola. "I can't tell you what transpires in the ceremony. It is a sacred secret."

I guessed I knew enough about that ritual anyway. Bathed in bull's blood? Eeww.

"Further," continued Agricola. "I consecrated you to Mars and blessed you with a warrior's spirit. Or rather, I consecrated their union, should it produce offspring. Which it apparently did."

Jason was quiet for several seconds. Then he said, "Did you do anything that might make me, like, come back from the dead?"

Agricola raised his eyebrows. He did that a lot. "You

died?"

"I got shot in the head," said Jason. "I wasn't breathing. I didn't have a pulse. And then Azazel kissed me, and I woke up."

Agricola laughed. "Well, it sounds like something Ted would want his Rising Sun to do. No. I don't have access to power like that. I have no idea."

"I thought Mithras was a dying god," said Jason.

Agricola shook his head. "No Mithras sacrifices a bull, which he is tied to symbolically. But he himself does not die. And the bull doesn't come back to life. It's not a seasonal religion, you see. It isn't intended to explain why the crops die. Instead it is about fighting always against the evil that surrounds us."

I couldn't help laughing a little.

"Why are you laughing?" asked Agricola. "I don't think that was funny."

"It's just that Brother Mancini told us you were evil."

"That is because Brother Mancini serves the Catholic Church, which is the most evil institution in the world. I fight against it. Brother Mancini doesn't appreciate that."

Oh. Well, with everyone thinking everyone else was evil, it sure made things confusing, didn't it? I guessed this was why my parents hadn't believed in evil, just constructive and destructive consequences. Maybe fighting against evil was really the only evil that existed, because it allowed people to do things they wouldn't otherwise do. If their enemies were evil, then all bets were off. They had to do whatever they could to get rid of those enemies. It all seemed so primitive.

"But this warrior power stuff," said Jason. "That could easily be explained by the fact I was trained by the Sons. And the fact I was able to beat you is probably because you used to train the Sons, so I know your techniques. Overall, how is there any proof that what you did to Michaela and Edgar had any affect on me?"

"Proof? Is that what you're looking for?"

"I don't want to be this Rising Sun thing," said Jason. "I don't care if I'm supposed to be establishing a global government or destroying the Sons. I just want to be left alone. I told myself that the Sons were just nuts. That there was no Rising Sun. But this weird stuff keeps happening. And I just want to know why."

"You think I can answer that question?" asked Agricola.

A rock sailed through the window in Agricola's dining room. It shattered the glass and landed in the middle of the pasta dish.

CHAPTER ELEVEN

To: Arabella Hoyt <arabella.hoyt@gmail.com>

From: Ian Hoyt <ihoyt@risingsun.org>

Subject: Working on it

Arabella,

I assure you that we are as concerned about the situation as you are. The two of them loose on the world represents a serious threat to the organization. We had a lead that they were on an island of the coast of Africa, but that seems to be a dead end.

I'm checking out a report that they're in Rome. I'll be sure to give you updates on the situation.

Ian

Through the hole in the window, we could hear shouts. "Let him go!"

Agricola stood up and went to the window. He looked out. "It's the Sons," he said.

Jason and I were also on our feet. "The Sons?" I said. "Since when do they throw rocks? They always come in shooting."

"Not the Brothers," said Agricola. "Those ridiculous ex-Council members that are taking refuge with the Reddimus monks." He turned to us. "How exactly did you find me?"

"We asked Brother Mancini for your address," I said.

"Yeah, but he didn't want anyone to know we were there," said Jason.

"Apparently, they found out," said Agricola.

I stepped over to the window. Below us, in the courtyard, were a throng of about twenty aging men. They were wearing suits. "Release the Rising Sun!" one of them yelled.

"I believe your public awaits," said Agricola.

Jason and I just looked at him.

"Well, go on," he said. "I'm not hiding you here while they cause further damage to my property. You'll have to leave."

"Is there a back door?" Jason asked.

Agricola snorted. "Out," he said. "Sorry we weren't able to finish dinner. And that I wasn't more help."

He ushered us through the dining room and down the stairs, depositing us in the courtyard. When the men saw us, they all fell to their knees.

Jason and I rolled our eyes. This kneeling thing was getting so old.

"We're fine," said Jason. "And stop kneeling to us."

"Yep," I said. "On your feet. All of you."

Jason took my hand, and we started for the gate. It was dark outside now. I hoped we'd go to a hotel. I needed to read more of the diary to figure out what our next move was. Of course, maybe my idea wasn't panning out so well. Agricola hadn't been much help. We didn't know anything else that was useful, and Jason had gotten his face beaten in.

The Sons swarmed after us. Lovely. Outside the gate, I paused to look at them. "Okay," I said. "Thanks for coming after us and all, but as you can see, Agricola didn't hurt us.

He isn't even evil. So, why don't you guys go ahead home, and we'll catch up another time."

"We can't let you wander off," said one of the Sons. "It's too dangerous."

"Yes," piped up another one, "Hoyt is looking for you. He wants you dead."

"Somebody always wants one of us dead," said Jason. "We're used to it." To me, "Don't talk to them. Let's just go."

The Sons formed a circle around us. "You must come to sanctuary," they said. "Not even Hoyt would dare to harm you in the Reddimus monastery."

We were surrounded. Jason sighed. "We should just shoot our way out," he said.

"We don't have guns anymore," I said.

"Dammit," said Jason. He looked out at the Sons. "Can you guys get us guns?"

* * *

They brought us guns. They also brought us wine and food and gave us a private room together. They managed to find us laptops with internet access. They brought in beautiful, expensive sheets and intricately woven rugs. When I mentioned that I was sad to have lost all my clothes, someone took our measurements and arrived later with shopping bags full of clothes for both of us.

Brother Mancini was not happy with this turn of events. "This is a monastery!" he raged as they piled the luxurious items into our room. He stood in the doorway, his hands on his head.

"This is the Rising Sun and his consort," said one of the Sons.

"We offer you sanctuary and you repay us in this way? I should just turn you all out in the street!" Mancini raged.

"Try it, and we'll throw you out," said another of the Sons.

"Sorry Brother Mancini," I tried.

"You don't speak," he said to me. "The both of you are the spawns of Satan, with your guns and your threatening and striding out of here earlier without worrying about who might see you or what they might do. You've brought this upon us, and may God forgive you for your sins!"

Then he stalked off.

The Sons who'd been bringing us stuff bowed low. "What else can we do for you?"

"Stop bowing?" I said.

"But we must show our respect."

I sighed. They weren't going to stop bowing.

"We're fine," said Jason. "Leave us for the night. We'll speak more in the morning."

The Sons nodded their assent and trooped out of the room, closing the door behind them. Jason flopped down on our bed, which was swathed in pillows and silk comforters. He grinned. "Well," he said. "This isn't all bad."

I lay down next to him. It wasn't bad. It was nice. "So we're going to stay here tonight?" I said.

"Definitely," he said, putting his arm around me.

I opened the diary. "Let's see where we're headed next," I

said.

"What, you don't want to stay here and be bowed to and waited on hand and foot?" he teased me.

"I want to find someone who knows more than Agricola did," I said.

Jason sighed. "Maybe we're just barking up the wrong tree here. Maybe it doesn't matter how I was created. Maybe it's not me. Maybe it's you."

"What?" I put the diary down. "Me?"

"You know, you've been there too, when all the weird things have happened. And God knows some weird Satanist mumbo-jumbo rituals have been done over you too. I mean, we're considering the possibility here that being consecrated to Mars or making love in the moonlight of the Coliseum while chanting Latin is what's causing us to be able to do what we do. Why not being the Vessel of Azazel?"

"Because ... Because Michaela Weem made me happen. It wasn't Satanism they believed in, it was just her, and her obsession with Rabbit and whatever else she thought."

"Edgar Weem made me happen," said Jason.

"True," I said. "I don't know." I was quiet, flipping through the pages of the diary. "So, are you saying we should just give up? Stop following the diary? Stop trying to find this stuff out?"

"No," said Jason. "I don't know." He sighed. "Where did they go next?"

I looked at the diary, flipping past the entry on Agricola. I read quietly. "Tuscany," I reported. "A woman. Her name was Agnes. There's no last name." I kept reading. "She had a cauldron, apparently."

"Does it say anything else about where this woman was?"

"No," I said. "It's a short entry."

"Maybe we can skip her," said Jason. "Who's next?"

"I don't think we should skip anyone," I said.

"How are we are going to find this lady? You propose we just go to Tuscany and start knocking on doors? You know how big Tuscany is?"

I sighed. I flipped the page. I gasped. "No way," I said.

"What?" said Jason.

"After Tuscany, they went to New Jersey." I handed him the diary.

"Oh my God," said Jason. "Your grandmother?" He kept reading. "Your grandmother's a gypsy?"

"We can't go there," I said. "She doesn't like you. And she has ties to the Sons. To my great-uncle who's like the head of the Sons. Dammit!"

Jason gave me back the diary. He got off the bed and began pacing in front of it. "Who's next?"

"That's it," I said. "She was only fertile for four days. That was their four days. The rest of the entries are about going to Shiloh. It says that she and Edgar waited two weeks to see if it took, and she was pregnant. After that, she starts talking about morning sickness and hating Edgar. Which is weird, because she liked him before."

"Great," said Jason.

I tossed the diary on the floor and rolled over, burying my face in a pillow. Well, so much for that idea. I lifted my head. "Next time I have an idea, Jason, remind me that they're always bad."

He came back to the bed and sat down next to me. "Your ideas are not always bad."

I sat up, and began ticking them off on my fingers. "Ms. Campbell. Aunt Stephanie. Florida—"

"Florida was great."

"No, it wasn't."

"Well, bad stuff happened there, but it wasn't because of Florida."

"Going to see Sutherland," I said. "After he carried me off from the target range. That was a great idea."

"Look, I've had bad ideas too," said Jason.

"Like?"

"Like the prom," he said. "And I thought you were paranoid in Florida."

"I *was* paranoid."

"But you were also right. People were out to get you."

I flopped back on the bed. "What are we going to do now?" I asked the ceiling.

"Do a Google search for Agnes in Tuscany?" he suggested.

I glared at him.

"Maybe," he said, "we should wish really hard for all the answers to come to us while kissing heavily."

I laughed. "That was another of my ideas that didn't

work!"

"It might have worked," said Jason. "He did come back. And after we beat him senseless, he was actually kind of nice."

I wacked him with the pillow. He yanked the pillow away from me. "What?" he said. "Don't you want to kiss me, Azazel?" He began tickling me and kissing whatever part of me he could get his lips on—my elbow, my shoulder, my nose. I struggled away from his hands, laughing and gasping for breath. "Stop! Stop!" I told him, trying to push him off me.

Jason pinned me down with his legs, forcing himself on top of me to keep tickling me. I punched at his chest, grabbed at his hands, still laughing. "Stop!" I said again.

"No, no," he drawled, imitating a redneck accent. "I'm going to learn you, woman. If you don't kiss me, you get tickled." He caught my hands, which weren't having any effect on him anyway and pinned them above my head. Then he kissed my lips, long and sweet. And he stopped tickling me.

My giggles faded into sighs. Within a few seconds, his hold on my hands loosened, and I was free to let my hands roam over his back and to play with the stubble on his head.

"I like the way your head feels," I said.

He broke the kiss, propping himself up to look at me, one eyebrow raised.

I playfully punched him again. "You know what I meant," I said. Then I couldn't suppress a slightly wicked grin. "But I guess you could take it the other way too."

He rolled over next to me, pulling me into his arms. I snuggled against his shoulder.

"Last night," he murmured, "I was kind of ... I mean, I know you didn't ... finish. I'm sorry. I didn't even try."

I ran my fingers lightly over the stubble on his head, trying to think of how to respond.

Jason started talking again. "I want you to — "

Impulsively, I grabbed Jason's hand and moved it onto my body.

"Azazel?" he said.

"Shh," I said to him.

I put my hand over his, guiding him over my skin, showing him where to put his fingers. For a couple of seconds, I was frightened, because it felt like before, when Jason had tried to do this. It felt like nothing. I closed my eyes, trying to listen to my body, ask it where it wanted to be touched. And then, together, we found it. The place.

I moaned.

"Like that?" Jason asked. He sounded surprised and turned on all at the same time.

"Yeah," I breathed, removing my hand and letting Jason's stay there.

"That's good?"

"Yeah," I said, half choking on it. That was *very* good.

It took forever. It felt really good, but it took forever. Several times, I was just kind of lost in the sensation of it, floating in this warm, sweet feeling, and I suddenly remembered how long it had been going on. I snapped my head a few times up to ask Jason if he was getting bored or if his fingers were getting tired. The third time I did it, Jason growled in my ear, "Shut up, Azazel. I'm not bored. And I love those little noises you're making."

But then, several centuries later, it happened. It was a bursting feeling. It was like flowers opening up or a sweet crescendo of thunder across the sky. It was lovely. I opened my eyes and saw Jason looking at me, and I started crying. He brushed the tears away from my cheeks. "Was that okay?" he asked.

Like he had to ask.

* * *

I was dreaming. In my dream, I was reading Michaela Weem's diary, but I was sitting inside an old house. There was a cauldron boiling over an open fireplace, and whatever was inside it smelled delicious. The room was lit entirely by firelight and candles. It was cozy. I snuggled under a quilt, sitting on an overstuffed easy chair.

A woman sat opposite me in a rocking chair. She had long white hair that reached down to her waist. Her face looked so young, however—unlined. Her eyes were wide and eager, like a child's. She was knitting.

"How am I going to find you?" I asked her.

"I have come to you," she said. "You don't have much time."

"Why not?" I wanted to have time. I liked being in this house. I could stay here forever. It was so warm and nice.

"They're coming for you," she said. "They're always coming for you, aren't they?"

"Mmm," I said. They always were.

"I had hoped you could come to me," she said. "I had thought you might. But things have changed." She smiled at me. "For two people on the run, you sure do have a tendency to come in guns blazing, don't you?"

The guns. I shook my head. "I don't like shooting people."

"Of course you don't." She smiled again. "But wake up, Azazel. I'm outside."

"Can't I just stay here?" I asked.

"Wake up," she said. "Come outside."

I opened my eyes, and I was inside the monastery. Jason was asleep beside me. It was quiet. I sat up. Come outside? Weird dream.

Come outside, repeated the woman's voice in my head.

I looked down at Jason. He looked so peaceful and beautiful sleeping like that. And I eased out of the bed and put on a pair of jeans. I was going outside. Sure it was a stupid idea. Sure, it had just been a dream. But that dream about Chance and Jason had led me to the basement of the old church. And that dream about the diary had ...

I moved quietly through the darkened halls of the monastery. When I opened the door, I opened it onto a silent, dark street in Rome. It was after midnight. The air was cold. Goosebumps broke out on my arms. I hugged myself. There was no one out here. It had only been a dream.

I reached for the door knob.

"Azazel," said a soft female voice.

I whirled. There she was. The woman from my dream.

"Agnes," I said, and I knew that it was her.

She nodded. "Walk with me," she said, reaching for my hand.

Her hand was warm and strong. I could feel her calluses against my palm. And once I was close to her, it didn't seem nearly as cold anymore. We walked through the silent streets, away from the monastery. Everything seemed beautiful, bathed in a deep blue moonlight. There was no one on the streets. No one at all. She led me through the streets of Rome as if she had done it many, many times.

I was surprised when we arrived at the Roman Forum. I didn't know if we could get in at night. During the day, you had to pay to tour it. But Agnes led me over steps and around walls and before I knew it, we were there. I stared up at the splendor of it. These buildings were thousands of years old. They had majestic columns and long staircases leading to their entrances. They were in ruins—but they were still standing. When Jason and I had visited earlier this spring, it had been awesome. But now, in the dark, standing here, looking up at what was left of ancient Rome, I felt as if the buildings were whispering to me, telling me their secrets.

Agnes squeezed my hand. "We will sit here," she said. "In front of the Atrium Vestae." The House of the Vestal Virgins. How long ago had it been that I'd designed a Vestal

Virgin Halloween costume?

We sat down.

"You must have questions," she said to me.

Of course I did. What were they?

"Are you the Agnes from the diary?" I asked her.

"Yes," she said. "I blessed Michaela and Ted's union. I prayed to the goddess Hecate that Jason would be a powerful being, a blessing to the earth."

"So powerful he could come back from the dead?" I asked.

She laughed. "That would be up to him, now wouldn't it?"

What? I didn't understand. I realized that I should probably be finding this entire experience extremely weird, but I didn't. There was something about Agnes that made me feel very, very relaxed. I trusted her. Maybe that was stupid, but I did.

She smiled. "You want to know what happened. What I did for my part to help create Jason."

I nodded. That was why we'd been looking for her.

"I can tell you that," she said. She took my hand. "Eighteen years ago, a man and a woman checked into my little inn in Tuscany. That is what I do, you see. I am an innkeeper. I have run my little inn my whole adult life. My mother ran it before me. It is a charming place. I didn't think anything of the visitors who arrived, not really. I noticed that the girl seemed much younger than the man, and that she looked tired and sad."

As Agnes spoke, I felt like I could see what she was talking about. I envisioned the small inn, an old, old house of two stories. It was built of stone. Inside, it was rustic and comfortable. There were quilts hanging on the walls, rugs hugging the wooden floors. Each of the rooms had a fireplace. But when Michaela and Edgar arrived, it was summer. No fires were burning. Instead, air conditioners chugged in the windows. They arrived in the evening. The sun was hanging heavy in the sky. Edgar was carrying the luggage. Michaela hung behind him as he checked in and paid for the room.

Agnes' words swirled into what I was seeing. I both heard her and didn't. Instead, it was as if I were there. Like my dream about the diary, I floated in the corner of the room, looking down on what was happening.

Agnes was standing at her check-in desk. She had a feather quill pen, which she was using to mark down the number of nights Edgar and Michaela would be staying. They couldn't see me, but Agnes did. She waved at me and said, "I gave them their keys, and I wouldn't have given them a second thought."

Edgar and Michaela trooped up the stairs to their room. Agnes opened the novel she was reading and settled back in her chair. She wore reading glasses, perched on her nose. Edgar Weem came back down the stairs.

Agnes stood up, marking her place in her book. "Is there a problem, sir?"

"No," said Edgar. "I wanted to ask you something,

actually."

"Certainly," said Agnes, smiling her best for-the-customer smile.

"We heard some things about you in the village," said Edgar. "You grow herbs. I saw your garden when we arrived."

Agnes seemed unsure of herself. "You're talking about the fact that some of the villagers think I'm a witch."

"Yes," said Edgar. "I am. Is it true?"

Agnes hesitated.

"Because," said Edgar, "we are trying to have a baby, and I had hoped that if you would be willing, you could lay a blessing on the two of us."

Agnes nodded in recognition. "I see," she said. "I do suppose there might be something I could do. You believe in the blessing of an old woman you have never met?"

"Yes," said Edgar, smiling. "I do." He was actually a good-looking man. For an old guy.

Agnes turned to me. "So," she said. "I agreed to meet them that night, after the evening meal. I was planning to bless their union, a similar blessing to the one traditionally made at weddings. I gathered my herbs and prepared them in my cauldron."

The scenery around Agnes changed suddenly. She was in the room where I'd seen her in my dream, bustling about and dropping herbs into the boiling water. The fire was hot. Every so often, she would wipe her brow with her apron. She was humming to herself. Behind her, Michaela entered.

Michaela looked so young. Her hair was long and black. She had braided it, but wisps of hair were coming free of the braid and framing her face. She was wearing a sundress. She clasped her hands behind her back and cleared her throat.

Agnes turned to her. "Yes?" she said.

"Ted said that you were a witch," Michaela blurted.

"I prefer a different word," said Agnes. "I am only a simple woman. But I do seek the power of the goddesses and study the wisdom of the Tarot and of the stars. Are you concerned about the blessing your husband asked me to perform?"

"No," said Michaela. "I am not concerned about this one." She looked away from Agnes and there was a haggard look in her eyes. To the floor, she said, "He's not my husband."

"You do seem quite young," said Agnes. Agnes crossed to Michaela, touching her shoulder. "And somehow sad."

Michaela looked at Agnes, tears in her eyes. "I said I would do this because I love him. But he doesn't love me. I wondered if there was something ... a charm, maybe, or a spell. To make him care about me? I could pay you."

"Oh my dear," said Agnes. "That is not what magic does. Magic cannot force anyone to do things against his will. We ask magic to change ourselves, not to change our environments."

Michaela shook her head. "Ted doesn't think that," she said.

"Well, I must admit I am curious. Why, if he doesn't love

you, does he want you to bear his child?"

"Not his child," said Michaela. "Not really. This will be *the* child."

Agnes looked confused. "I don't think I understand."

"Ted believes this child is going to save the world. There are prophecies. He thinks we are fulfilling them. He thinks we're conceiving some kind of messiah."

"And you?"

"I used to think so too. But last night ..." Michaela shook her head.

The sound went away, even though their lips still moved. Agnes' voice came up, like a voice-over on a movie. "She began to tell me things," said Agnes. "She poured out the whole story to me. It was tragic and heartbreaking. She was young. I could see that she was losing her innocence. That she was becoming embittered. And the man she was with was responsible for it. I began to wonder if it would be the right thing to do to bless the two of them. I began to wonder if I shouldn't instead try to find some way to get the girl away from the man she traveled with.

"After she left me, I turned to my cards." I saw Agnes sitting at a table, turning over Tarot cards. "I had quite a strange reading. Every card I turned over was from the major arcana. When this happens in a reading, it means that the subject of a reading is in play, and that there is little you can do to change it. It means that powerful forces are at work." Agnes glanced over her shoulder, where I was hovering next to her. "Let me show you the reading," she said.

I settled close to her and stared at the cards. They were arranged in rows. The center looked like a cross. Agnes turned over the first card, the one in the very center. "The World," she said. "This card tells what the reading will concern. The present situation. The present situation in my reading was the world. Generally, this card means that one cycle of life is ending and another is beginning."

Agnes turned over another card and placed this one over the first card. "This card," she said, "represents the immediate challenge to the present situation. I drew The Tower. That card refers to a situation in which a structure must be demolished to make way for something new." She pointed to the illustration. "You see how the tower is falling apart in the picture? How the people are falling out of it?"

I nodded.

"I wasn't sure what this meant. The immediate challenge was that the entire world needed to be destroyed to make room for something new? I turned over the next card." Agnes turned over the card. I looked at it. It said, "The Emperor." But the card was upside down. "This card represents the mind," she said. "It represents the structured world. The world of rules. It is upside down. In this position, the position of the distant past, it indicates that the perversion of the structured world has influenced the need of the world to change radically."

Agnes turned over the next card. "This is the position of the recent past," she said. The card was the Magician. "This card represents the ability of the individual to transform things through his will. I surmised that this card represented Ted. According to Michaela, he had decided to create the Rising Sun. To bring about change."

The next card was the card that revealed the best outcome of the situation. "The Sun. Clearly, here it represents the Rising Sun, I thought. Also, it is a card of extreme optimism and positivity. So it seemed that in regards to the immediate situation, the best outcome was that the Rising Sun did indeed emerge."

The last card in the cross revealed the immediate future. "The Wheel of Fortune," said Agnes. "Meaning that destiny and fate were in play. And that in the immediate future, I would play my part."

She moved to the final four cards, which were in a row to the right of the cross. "This seventh card reveals factors affecting the situation," she said. She turned it over. "The Devil, upside down. The Devil is the representation of the dark side with humanity, or within yourself. It represents desires, or lusts, destructive forces that lurk within each of us."

I interrupted her. "What does that mean, it affects the situation?" It was pretty obvious this Tarot card reading had as much to do with Michaela and Edgar as it did with Jason and me.

"Simply that," said Agnes. "It will come into play. It does not mean that it will overcome the situation and destroy the final outcome. But it could. It is part of the whole."

She turned over the next card. "External influences. Things out of control," Agnes explained. The card was the Hanged Man. "This card refers to the idea that one must make sacrifices — like the Hanged Man's sacrifice of freedom — to gain knowledge and wisdom."

Agnes turned over the next card. "Hopes and fears," she said. "Death. The card that represents a shift or transition to a new level of life.

"Finally," said Agnes, "is the outcome of the situation. Overall." She turned over the last card. "The lovers," she said. Agnes looked over the cards, her brow furrowed. "At the time," said the voice-over of Agnes, "I wasn't entirely sure what to make of the reading. I knew it strongly directed me to take part in something which was directed by Fate. I knew that implied that great good could come from the situation. But there were aspects of the reading that did not make sense to me. Why did the reading say that the final outcome of the situation was the Lovers? Where Michaela and Ted to become the lovers?

"I supposed it was possible, but it seemed unlikely. The kind of love represented on the card was a kind of perfect love, the combination of a duality to create a beautiful harmony. In some ways, it seemed to me that Ted had abused Michaela. I didn't see how a perfect love could come from a union like that.

"I was also confused by the appearance of the Devil and of the Hanged Man. Where these cards meant for me? Where they meant for Michaela? Or where they meant for someone else? Someone who hadn't come into the picture yet?"

Agnes turned to me, away from the cards. She grasped my hands. "I think they were meant for you," she said.

"Me?" I said.

"I think the Lovers card refers to you and Jason. That this whole situation was to culminate in the two of you. You and Jason have been entwined since before your conception, in ways that I don't think either of us understands. The seeds were planted here, when Michaela began to express her dissatisfaction with Ted. And the Devil card, that has special significance to you, doesn't it?"

The Satanists. "Yes," I said.

"Study this layout. Remember these cards," said Agnes. "I show them to you to guide you. To help you make your choices. If the cards are correct, the fate of the world is at stake here. The world will be changing." She smiled at me again. "But more on that later."

The scene changed. Ted and Michaela were standing in the room now. They were holding hands. Agnes placed a wreath of flowers on Michaela's head. Her voice-over continued. "I only knew that I had a role to perform in a greater scheme, and that I must do it. I didn't bless the union of Ted and Michaela, however, but I blessed the child they would conceive. I believed that the cards had told me that he or she would bring about some kind of phenomenal change in the world. I believed that it was important that I bless the child with the power and grace of the goddesses."

Agnes gave Michaela and Ted each a goblet, and they drank. She sang to them in another language. The three all kneeled, their hands raised to the ceiling.

And then the vision swirled again. When it stopped moving, I was back in the Roman Forum, holding hands with Agnes. It was still dark outside. I shook myself. That had been strange. "So you blessed Jason," I said. "You imbued him with power?"

Agnes laughed, and it sounded like wind chimes. "I can't imbue power," she said. "Power comes from within. Power comes from the goddesses. Power comes from the earth. I don't control these things."

I sighed. This had all been very, very interesting, but we really weren't any better off than we had been. "Jason and I can do things," I said. "We don't know why. We don't know how."

"And you wanted me to tell you," said Agnes.

"I hoped ..."

Agnes stood up. She helped me to my feet. She gestured at the Forum. "This was once the hub of the civilized world," she said. "Once, this place and the people here controlled everything."

I looked around. Sure, I knew this. This was a majestic place, full of the echoes of ancient power. But I didn't understand exactly why that was important.

"How did they do it?" she asked me.

"Well, they went and killed a bunch of people," I said. "They took them over and then they taxed the heck out of them."

Another laugh from Agnes. "Certainly," she said. "But how did they become the most powerful? How did they create a society that was so advanced? Democracy. Aqueducts. Religious tolerance. How did all of this come to the Romans?"

"I don't know," I said. "I guess they just thought of that stuff."

"It was their time," said Agnes. "They had an explosion of knowledge and power and creativity. There have been other such times in the world. It hasn't always been the Romans, but there have been other times. And then it was no longer their time. Things began to fall apart."

I gave her a sharp look. "You read Yeats?"

"Hmm?" she looked confused.

"Nothing."

"Changes happened. Have you ever heard of the crisis of the Roman empire?"

"No," I said.

"It was a period of time," she said. "In the third century, when the empire nearly collapsed. But right around the end of it, something happened. The planet Pluto entered Capricorn."

"I thought Pluto wasn't a planet anymore," I said.

"For astrological purposes," she said, "it is a very important entity. Very powerful. Pluto symbolizes the hidden undercurrents within us and society. It represents what is hidden coming to the surface. When it enters

Capricorn, the sign of hard work and goal-oriented views, it means that things can get done. For that period of time, when Pluto was in Capricorn, the Empire was able to hold off the darkness, to keep things from falling apart. It took another hundred years afterwards for the Empire to really break apart."

This was interesting. I guessed. "Why are you telling me this?" I asked.

"Pluto has been in Capricorn during some interesting historical periods," she said. "It may have been there when King Arthur was fighting off the Saxons." God. King Arthur again. "We can't be sure when King Arthur lived, but the dates seem to line up. It was in Capricorn when Martin Luther nailed his Ninety-five Theses to the door of his church. It was in Capricorn when the American Revolution happened." She looked at me. "And Pluto entered Capricorn last November."

"Really?" I said.

"It is a sign," she said. "We are on the cusp of the Age of Aquarius. Things are changing. And I'm sure you've thought about the fact that 2012 and the end of the Mayan calendar are only three years away. This is a time of great change and a time of great power. You and Jason are part of it. The Tarot reading showed that to me. Your influence will be felt. It will happen. You may not know how. But you are part of something very big."

I took a second to let all of that sink in. People had been telling me all about destiny and fate for the past year. People had been telling Jason and me that we had important roles to play. This woman was saying the same thing. But somehow it was different. Maybe it was just because it wasn't primarily concerned with either of us exactly. It was about bigger things, things that were happening in the world. It was about everything, on a global level. But still, it was the same song and dance. The world was destined to change. Jason and I were supposed to be part of it.

"Do you think this change that's going to happen in the world is a New World Order?" I asked. "Is it a global government?"

"I don't know what it's going to be," said Agnes. "No one knows. No one understands the future."

"But you're saying that you do. You're saying that these signs predict what will happen." This was the problem. I didn't want to be a plaything of fate and destiny. I'd promised myself over and over that I'd make my own destiny. I didn't want to be forced into doing anything. "You're saying that Jason and I don't have a choice."

"Choices are all we have," said Agnes.

"That doesn't make sense," I said. "If the future is all set like that, if I have a destiny, then I don't have a choice."

Agnes laughed. "This isn't *Oedipus Rex*, darling. That isn't the way destiny works. Listen, all that anyone can ever predict, by looking at the stars, or by reading cards, or by searching ancient prophecies, is that you and Jason will be forced into situations over and over again where you will have a massive influence on the fate of important things. But it will be up to you to decide what to do in those situations. You've made decisions before. You'll make them again."

I blinked. "You mean there can be destiny and free will at the same time?"

"I mean that there are influences beyond ourselves that we can't control," said Agnes. "That will always be, no matter what you believe. What you can control, Azazel, is the way you react to those influences."

I bit my lip. Okay, I guess that made sense. So the way Jason and I had been reacting thus far was to run away. To try to protect ourselves. And I'd been worried that the things people had told me about our being evil were coming true. I thought of the Tarot card spread that Agnes had showed me. It was a factor at play. Our violence. "You don't think that we're evil, then?" I said. "Or destructive? Or violent?"

"Why do you ask me that?"

"Because there were visions," I said. "There were visions that Jason was going to kill tons and tons of people. And that he was going to eat me alive. And then some people said that Jason would have been fine, but that I was his dark force. That I was the destructive half, and that I would drive him to become evil. And then Jason is always hitting people and shooting people, and I've been shooting people too. And sometimes it seems like all there is between us is blood and terror and running and hate and fear."

"The Devil card," said Agnes. "It's an influence."

"That's all. Just an influence?"

"There is no way to know what will happen in the

future," said Agnes. "Earlier this week, I did a reading that indicated you and Jason would come to see me. This morning, I did a reading again, and it became clear that you two would not be coming."

"So you came to me."

"Best as I could," said Agnes. "There is something deeply powerful within you. And within Jason as well. I've never felt anything like it. You speak of visions, Azazel. You have had visions, too, though."

"Me? No, I haven't."

"Your dreams."

"They're just nightmares," I said.

"They are not 'just' anything. They are the way that I can communicate with you. Truthfully, perhaps, you brought me to you more than I came to you. You must trust yourself. Jason has been trained to act without thinking. You examine things. You worry over things. But until you come to believe that you can make the right decisions and that you will do the right thing, you will never be truly able to wield your power. Jason needs your concern for balance. But you also need his daring resolve. You must act. You must not doubt."

The sounds of birds chirping carried through the forum. I could see that the sky was starting to lighten.

"You must go back," said Agnes. "It is late."

I wanted Agnes to walk with me back to the monastery, but she said she had to go in an opposite direction, so I made my way through the silent streets alone, trying to think about what she had said. None of it made much sense to me.

She said that I had to be confident to wield my power. She said that I did have choices, but that I was also bound to a destiny. Overall, she'd said absolutely nothing definite. It was much different from the way the Sons behaved or from the way the Satanists had behaved. They were certain. They were sure of themselves.

Maybe that was it. She'd said I needed to be confident in myself. Trust myself. But hadn't my parents been certain that Jason was evil? And hadn't that exact certainty caused them to do absolutely horrible things? Weren't the Sons sure that Jason was really the Rising Sun? Hadn't Edgar Weem been certain that he should do what he'd done to bring Jason into the world? I didn't know if I wanted to be certain. I was afraid that if I was certain, I would excuse all kinds of atrocities that I committed in the name of that certainty.

Of course, it wasn't as if I hadn't already committed atrocities. I flashed again on Lilith's demolished, bloody face. I felt sick.

When I got back to the monastery, I slid in bed with Jason, who didn't wake up. I closed my eyes and was asleep almost immediately.

I awoke to the sound of gunshots.

CHAPTER TWELVE

September 5, 1990

Arabella Hoyt has opened my eyes. In the time we spent with her, I have realized that I have been completely wrong about everything I thought about Jed. He has used me. He destroyed me. And the thing that may be growing inside me is not a force of good. It is a force of pure evil. I have been deceived. I must do what I can to end this horridness.

Jason sat up straight in bed. "Did you hear that?"

I was up too. It was midmorning. The sun was up. Streams of light came in through the narrow windows, drawing bright rectangles on the floor.

Jason was on his feet, shrugging into a shirt and checking to make sure his gun was loaded. I followed suit. I wished my hair was longer. I would have liked to pull it back into a ponytail. Instead, I just shoved it behind my ears. Our guns drawn, we crept to our door. Jason kept me behind him as he opened the door. The hallway outside our room was silent. We listened again.

"I heard shooting," Jason said to me.

"So did I," I said, peering around him.

We listened. There wasn't any noise now, but it wasn't dead silent. We could hear the sounds of the streets coming from behind us. Cars beeping. People chattering in Italian as they passed by. But within the monastery, we heard nothing. Jason pulled the door shut.

"What do we do?" I asked.

"Maybe nothing's wrong," said Jason. "Maybe it was a firework or a car backfiring or something."

"Maybe," I said.

Another gunshot. A scream.

"No," I said. "That was a gun."

"Yeah," said Jason. He took a deep breath. "Okay, then. Say goodbye to your clothes."

I glared at him. "Are we going to try to go out the front door?"

"Don't see why not," he said.

I grabbed a bag and shoved some clothes and one of the laptops into it. "Let's just try to take some stuff with us, okay?"

"Whatever," said Jason. "Let's go."

He opened the door again and we eased out of the room. Our backs against the wall (well, my stuffed-full bag against the wall, anyway), we crept down the hall, holding our guns. We didn't see anyone.

Our room was relatively close to the entrance. We only had to go down one hall, make a left, and then we'd be right at the door. We moved quickly but cautiously, glancing around for danger. At the end of the hallway, Jason stopped me. He peered around, gun out.

We heard another gunshot, much closer now.

Jason snapped back around the corner. "The Sons," he reported.

"You can see them?" I asked.

"They're at the entrance," he said. "They shot a bunch of monks."

"Oh my God," I breathed. "I thought we were safe here. I thought this whole city was sanctuary."

"They attacked us in a church before," said Jason. "I don't think sanctuary much matters where we're concerned."

"How many?" I asked.

"I don't know," said Jason. "But a lot. Maybe twenty. And who knows if they don't have reinforcements waiting somewhere."

"Should we kiss and try to drive them crazy?" I asked, trying to make a joke.

Jason grabbed me by the neck and kissed me fiercely. "No," he said, pulling back. "I think we should look for a back door."

He grabbed my hand, and we fled back down the hall. It had been a while since Jason and I had lived in this monastery. Still, we knew our way around pretty well. I didn't remember there being a back door, though. "What back door are you talking about?" I asked Jason.

He shot a look over his shoulder as we ran. "The kitchen," he said. "There's a door in the kitchen."

"Well, we're going the wrong way!" I said.

Jason yanked me to the right, hard, and we emerged in the cloister. The cloister was a covered walkway that surrounded a square courtyard. I pointed across the courtyard to the other side of the monastery. "The kitchen is over there," I said.

"Yeah," said Jason. "We're going across the courtyard." And he pulled me along with him.

More gunshots echoed from inside the monastery. Jason and I scurried across the courtyard and back inside the monastery. We emerged in a small hallway. The door to the kitchen was right in front of us. We could hear the sound of screams from the main entrance. Jason threw the door open, and we rushed inside.

We were greeted by the sight of several ex-members of the Council cowering in front of the sink. At the sight of us, they immediately bowed their heads. Geez. They were in fear for their lives, and they were still doing the bowing thing?

Jason pulled me forward. "Ignore them," he said. We headed for the door.

"Don't!" said one of the ex-Council members.

"They've sealed off all the exits," said another.

Jason stopped short as we saw that there was body in front of our exit. Immediately, he pulled me away from it. We clattered into the stove. He addressed the ex-Council members. "They're outside the door?" he asked.

They nodded. "Briggs tried to get out. They shot him."

"This is *sanctuary*," said Jason. "What is Hoyt thinking?"

"We think they're going to go through every room and just shoot everyone," said another ex-Council member. "It's Hoyt's way of showing us what he'll do if we stand up to him."

"They're looking for us, though, right?" I said.

They nodded.

"Jason, we've just got to go engage," I said.

"What?" he said.

"They're killing all these people because of us. We can't just let them die."

"No, it is an honor to give our lives in your service," said one of the ex-Council members.

"Maybe for you," I conceded. These guys were messed up in the head. "But not for the monks here. They don't want to die for us."

"It's screwed up," said Jason. "We should have gone to freaking Africa!"

"Jason, we can't let them shoot monks!"

"There are twenty of them at the main entrance. Who knows how many of them are surrounding the monastery," said Jason. "We go out there shooting, we could maybe take down half of them. But not all of them. They'll kill us."

I sighed. He was right. But it was sickening the amount of people who had been killed in the crossfire of this hunt for Jason and me. At the Sol Solis School, it was one thing. At least those men had been Brothers, trained to fight and prepared for dangerous situations. These monks, however, were peaceful. They'd offered us a place to stay. They'd hidden us. I leaned against the stove, scratching at the bandage on my arm. It was still itchy.

That reminded me that the bandage hadn't been changed recently. I planned to do it this morning. I hoped it wasn't getting infected. I tried to examine my wound through the bandage.

"Don't play with that," Jason said.

I dropped my arm, studying the gun in my hand. I'd already been shot once by the Sons. I didn't think I wanted to be gunned down, even if it meant that they stopped shooting monks. I was lucky they hadn't killed me at the prom—

Lucky. "Jason," I said. "How likely is it that one of the Sons would miss a shot? You know how the Brothers are trained. If you meant to shoot someone in the head, would you miss and shoot them in the arm?"

Jason looked at me like I was crazy. "If I shoot someone in the arm, it's because I meant to shoot them in the arm," he said.

I held up my arm. "Why didn't they kill me? I was standing in the open. I was an easy target."

Jason's eyes narrowed. "That is weird," he admitted. "I was so glad you were alive, I never thought to question it."

"Maybe they're not trying to kill us," I said. "It's only hearsay that they are."

"So then, what are they doing?" Jason said. "Why are they here with guns, shooting everything in sight?"

I didn't know. I had no idea.

"Even if they don't want us dead," said Jason, "they aren't trying to do anything nice to us."

No. I guessed they weren't. I sighed. "So, I guess we try to get out of here."

"There was another plan?"

No. It was just that I had wanted to minimize the violence, somehow. Keep people alive. I turned to the ex-Council members. "How many of them do you think are at the door?"

They shrugged. They didn't know.

Were there more at the entrance than at this door?

They thought so. Probably.

"So," said Jason, seeing where I was going with this. "You think we should just try to shoot ourselves out of this door?"

I shrugged. "Unless you have a better idea."

We surveyed the door. It opened into the kitchen, which wasn't great. If it had opened out onto the street, we might have been able to use it as a shield. Maybe. It was a wooden door, after all. It wasn't exactly impervious to bullets. We decided to stay low. We figured the Sons outside would assume that whoever was opening the door was standing. So we would lie flat, our guns out. Jason would reach up and open the door a few inches, just enough so that we could see what we were dealing with. From there, we'd just have to see what happened.

First we had to drag Briggs' body away from the door. His wound left a smear of blood on the floor. We were going to have to lie on the blood smear. Gross.

Jason and I got in position. He reached up for the knob and eased the door open. Almost immediately, there was a volley of gunfire, but it went over our heads. So far, so good.

I was watching through the opening of the door as Jason

pulled it open. Quickly, I assessed the situation. There were seven members of the Sons in the street. I shot as soon as I had a clear view. Carefully aiming, and remembering to breathe, I squeezed off three shots. They hit home perfectly. Three head shots. The men I'd hit crumpled to the ground. Jason was with me. He shot the other four.

Well. That had been easy.

We scrambled to our feet and out the door. Jason pulled it shut behind us.

"It's them! It's them!" yelled a voice.

And Jason and I were immediately swarmed by at least ten more members of the Sons. We opened fire.

They were everywhere, coming from all sides of the building. Some had been hiding behind cars. Others had been on the roof of the monastery. I got off several good shots. Jason got off even more than me. We took down at least five more of them. But there were so many.

Then someone kicked the gun out of my hand and someone else tackled me from behind. I went down on the ground, my chin skidding against stone. I bit my tongue and tasted blood in my mouth. I cried out.

They were on my back, handcuffing my arms and feet.

I twisted, looking for Jason. He was fighting with a group of men who were on him, slinging punches everywhere. "Azazel!" he yelled to me.

"Jason!" I screamed.

The Sons who had me hoisted me into the air. Two men had my feet and another three held my head and upper torso. They were taking me away. "Jason!" I screamed again.

The last image I saw of him was the Sons finally overpowering him and forcing him to the ground. He was struggling and yelling my name. I strained at the handcuffs. I tried to wrench my head so that I could bite at the hands of the men who held me. But I was trapped. We rounded a corner. I couldn't see him anymore.

CHAPTER THIRTEEN

To: Ian Hoyt <ihoyt@risingsun.org>

From: Arabella Hoyt <arabella.hoyt@gmail.com>

Subject: Where are you?

What is going on? You aren't answering any of the numbers I have for you. You said you had confirmation that they were in Rome and you were moving in. So help me, if you screw this up again, Ian, I don't know what I'll do.

I'd better hear from you soon.

Arabella

The Sons shoved me in the back of a car. One of them sat with me. I thrashed ineffectively, yelling at him. I don't know what I said. I was beside myself, angry, frightened, and concerned for Jason. I didn't know what they were going to do with him. Tears were rolling down my cheeks. I probably threatened him. I probably begged for Jason's life. I probably swore and swore at him.

"Can you make her shut up?" asked one of the Sons as he started the car.

The man in the back seat with me pulled out a syringe. He plunged the needle into my arm.

The world started to fade away into blackness.

The last thing I remembered hearing was someone saying something about an airport ... .

* * *

Everything hurt. My wrists were sore and chafed. My

chin and teeth ached. The gunshot on my arm throbbed. I moaned and rolled over in bed.

Bed?

Where was I?

My eyes snapped open. I was in a bedroom. There were expensive sheets on the bed I lay in. The walls were painted pink, but they had been plastered with posters. Familiar posters. Bands I liked. Movies I'd watched. They were *my* posters. From my old bedroom, back in Bramford. There was a bookshelf in the room too. It seemed to be filled with *my* books. But this wasn't Bramford, and this wasn't my old room. It was just all my stuff.

"What the hell?" I muttered.

"Zaza?" said a voice. Someone rushed over to me.

"Chance?" I said.

Chance threw himself at me and hugged me in bed. "Oh my God, you're okay!" he said.

"Ow," I said. "Chance, you're killing me here."

He sat up, perching on the bed next to me. I pushed myself into a sitting position, groaning when it hurt as bad as it did.

"Sorry," said Chance.

"Where am I?" I demanded.

"It's good to see you too," he said sarcastically. "I wasn't worried about you or anything when you and Jason just disappeared from the school after the whole prom got shot up."

"Where am I?" I repeated.

"Grandma's," he said.

Grandma Hoyt's house? "In New Jersey?" I said.

Chance nodded. "Yup. That's where she lives."

"I went to sleep in Rome," I said. I'd been out for the entirety of a fourteen-hour plane flight. Whatever that guy had given me in the car must have been really, really good. "How did I get here?"

"Grandma said that you were in an accident and that some of her business associates in Italy found out about it. They were able to get you sent back here. But when you got here, you were totally out. I thought you were like in a coma or something."

I threw the covers of the bed aside and got up. Jesus! That hurt even worse. That tackling thing they'd done to me must have really damaged me. "I wasn't in a coma," I said. "I was drugged. A bunch of men jumped Jason and me. They tied me up and knocked me out. And I ended up here."

"Where is Jason?"

"You don't know?" I asked.

"I asked Grandma about it, and she said no one knew where he was."

"Really?" I said, hopeful. Maybe Jason had gotten away. Maybe ... I started for the door to the room. "I've got to find him," I said. I had my hand on the door before I realized I was wearing a frilly, full-length nightgown. I looked down at it. "Ugh," I said. "Where did Grandma Hoyt get this?"

Chance shrugged. "It's kind of cute on you, though."

"I'll have to change," I said. I crossed the room to the

closet. It was empty. There was a chest of drawers. It was empty too. "Okay," I said. "I have no clothes."

"Yeah," said Chance. "Well, maybe we could go to the mall. I have a credit card. We could get you something."

"I don't have time to go to the mall," I said. "I don't know where Jason is. And the last time I saw him, he was being wrestled to the ground by like ten guys with guns. I have to find him."

"Yeah?" said Chance. "Well, I don't know where my girlfriend is either."

That made me pause. "Mina?" I said. I had assumed Chance and Palomino were okay. After they'd been sent home, away from us, I figured everything would be fine.

Chance sighed. "It's my fault," he said. "She was freaked out about the baby and everything. I told Grandma about it. I thought she could help. But she called Mina's parents, and they shipped her off somewhere to one of those places where they send girls so they can have a baby and then they take it away so no one will ever know."

"Oh my God," I said. "You're kidding."

"I can't even call her or talk to her. They won't tell me where she is. And Grandma says I'm forbidden to ever see her again."

"Chance, I'm so sorry," I said, hugging him. I meant it to be comforting, but it was kind of silly, since Chance was way taller than I was. He was growing like a weed. He hugged me back, though.

"I was freaked out," he said. "I mean, we're kids. I'm not

ready to be a dad. But this is just wrong. Nobody asked us. They just took her away. And they're gonna give our baby — my baby — to some strange couple somewhere. I'll never even see him!"

"No," I said. "Chance, that is not going to happen. Once I find Jason, he and I will find Mina, and we will get her out of there. I promise you that."

"Yeah," said Chance. "I saw the way you guys were shooting at the prom. Zaza, where did you learn to shoot guns like that?"

I sighed. "That's a long story. For now, I just have to get out of here." Where was I going to go? How was I supposed to find Jason? I decided to concentrate on the more pressing issues. "I'm going to need to borrow some of your clothes," I said to Chance.

He sized me up. "They're not going to fit you," he said.

"I'll need a belt," I said. It was so annoying. I'd carried that bag with clothes and the laptop all the way out to the street outside the monastery. I must have lost in the scuffle with the Sons. I seemed to be cursed never to keep a closet full of clothes.

Chance shrugged. "You can try, I guess," he said.

We went to his room. He gave me a pair of his shorts. They were really long, so they fit me like pants. I cinched the waist up as best I could with a belt and threw one of his t-shirts on over the whole thing. I didn't have a bra, which really sucked, because I felt like I was wearing pajamas, flopping all over the place. But it was better than the stupid nightgown.

As we headed down the steps, I considered my options. I didn't know where Jason was, so I was going to have to find someone who could help me find him. Who did I know who could do that? Maybe if I could get in touch with Hallam? I had no idea how to do that, though. If Jason had been captured by the Sons, though, he could very easily be —

No. I wasn't going to think that. I'd held Jason in my arms when I thought he was dead before. I'd gotten him back. He couldn't be dead now. No.

The important thing was to get out of this house. "I'm going to need a car," I told Chance. "Do you know where Grandma Hoyt keeps her keys?"

"*We're* going to need a car," said Chance. "I'm coming with you."

I stopped on the stairs, looking up at Chance, who was behind me. "No way," I said. "You can't come, Chance. It is way too dangerous. I can't take care of you. And I won't let anything happen to you. I have lost way too much of my family. You are all I have left. You stay here where it's safe."

"I hate it here," said Chance. "And if you and Jason are going to get Mina, then I have to come with you. I have to help her. I can't just sit here."

"I don't care if you do hate it here," I said. "You're not coming, and that's all there is to it." I turned and continued down the steps. Chance hurried after me.

"You can't just leave me here," he said. "I'm going!"

"Going where?" said a voice.

Grandma Hoyt floated in front of the steps. She was a tall woman with gray hair, which she pulled into a severe bun at the back of her head. She always dressed impeccably. Today, she was wearing a cream-colored suit. Her arms were folded over her chest.

"Hey Grandma," I said. "Listen, thanks for getting me out of whatever you got me out of back there. But I can't stay. I have to go. I don't know where Jason is."

"Jason is at the Sons' headquarters in England," said Grandma Hoyt. "And you're not going anywhere. He's been arrested by their internal police. There will be a trial, and I have no doubt he'll be executed for his crimes against the organization. You'd do well to stop thinking about that boy. He's the past."

Trial? Executed? Crimes? "Grandma," I said. "I don't think you understand."

"No, Azazel, I don't think you understand," said Grandma Hoyt. "Your great-uncle and I have been searching for you all over Europe for the past several months. I've been beside myself with worry ever since you got mixed up with that boy. Now when Weem was heading the organization, there wasn't much I could do. But now that Ian is in charge, I've been able to get you home and safe and sound. And I've been able to do what I could to eliminate the threat of Jason."

I was stunned. I'd known that weird things were going on with my grandmother for some time. She had ties to the Sons. And she'd been helping my brothers Gordon and

Noah earlier this spring. But I hadn't thought that she thought Jason was a threat. "That's why you were helping Noah and Gordon?" I asked. "Because they were trying to kill Jason? You want him dead?

"Child, I never wanted him conceived," said Grandma Hoyt. "Now you march back up those steps and put any ideas of getting out of here out of your head. You are my only blood descendant, and I'll be hanged before I allow you to bring shame to the Hoyt family."

I didn't move. This was so bad. What was I going to do? "You can't talk to me like that," I said. "I stopped being someone's child a long time ago. I'm leaving. You can't stop me."

"Maybe I can't personally, but I'm sure the armed guards on every door and at the gate can," she retorted. "Up the steps!"

* * *

Grandma Hoyt refused to actually give me any clothes. If I didn't have clothes, I couldn't run, or so she said. She forced me to attend dinner in my nightgown. We ate in the formal dining room—Chance, Grandma, and I all gathered at the end of the long, narrow table. I was going to refuse to eat. I sat sullenly at the table, staring at the elegant drapes and the garish modern art on the walls. When they put the food in front of me, however, I realized I was famished. And refusing to eat was kind of childish, anyway, wasn't it?

I dug in. Grandma Hoyt kept up a steady banter of lighthearted conversation. Well. Not really conversation, because neither Chance nor I said anything. Instead, it was a monologue. She talked about the parties of the season, who was getting married, and what designers they were using for their dresses. She said that later on, perhaps when I calmed down, we needed to work on planning my coming out party. I was a bit old to be a debutante, she said, but I needed to be presented to society. I was her granddaughter, after all. She may not have had much say in my upbringing thus far, but she was going to make up for that.

I glowered at her over my boiled potatoes and peas. I hated this woman. I wasn't going to do anything she suggested. I'd checked out the doors after she'd said they were all guarded. She was right. There were burly men at every exit. Through the window, I was able to see the gate to her estate. It was also heavily guarded.

I didn't know how yet, but I was going to escape from this fortress, if it was the last thing I did.

Dinner lasted an interminably long time. Afterwards, I went to my room. Chance asked if I wanted to talk. He was really confused about what was going on. "Who are the Sons?" he wanted to know. I wasn't in the mood to explain. I apologized but said he was just going to have to be patient. Eventually, I would explain everything.

I just wanted to be alone. In my room, I examined the windows. I was on the second floor. I didn't know if a drop out of the window would harm me terribly. I could unlock the window and probably get the screen out. While I was checking this out, I noticed that there were a bunch of large

Doberman pincers wandering around on the grounds. They looked mean. So that meant if I jumped out the window, I was going to have to get past the dogs. I could possibly scale the fence that surrounded the property, and maybe if I was lucky, there wouldn't be any guards on the opposite side. But in doing so, I'd probably set off some kind of alarm. And, of course, I didn't have a gun.

If I tried to escape and failed, Grandma Hoyt would probably triple the security. Who knew, maybe she'd handcuff me to my bed or something. No. I needed to do this right. I was going to have to plan. And I needed something waiting for me once I got out. I wondered if Father Gerald could get me in touch with Hallam. There was no phone in my room, but I did have a computer.

I looked up Christ is King Catholic church in Shiloh, Georgia on the internet. I found a phone number, which I scribbled on a piece of paper and stuck in the pocket of my nightgown. (It had pockets. Go figure.)

I was considering whether or not I could make friends with the kitchen staff and get some food to bribe the dogs with, like a big steak or something, when there was a soft knock on my door.

"Who is it?" I yelled.

"It's your grandmother."

Go away, I thought. But I wasn't going to give her the satisfaction of speaking to her, not even to tell her to get lost.

She opened the door and came in. I plopped down on my bed, my back to her. Gently, she sat down next to me.

"Azazel," she said, "I wanted to talk to you."

I didn't look at her.

"I know," she said. "You hate me. You don't want anything to do with me. You think I'm ruining your life." She reached over and tucked a strand of my hair behind my ear. It was a tender gesture. A motherly gesture. I pulled back from her, as if she'd stung me. "I know you can't see it now," she continued, "but I'm doing this for your own good. One day, you'll look back on this, and you'll see I was right."

Was she insane? I untucked my hair from behind my ear.

"We really need to get you an appointment with a decent stylist," she mused. "That color is absolutely terrible for your skin type."

Oh my God. The love of my life was going to be executed across the ocean. It was her fault. And she had the gall to talk about hair stylists?

"Listen," she said. "I wanted to come in to talk to you. I know you're angry. And I'll give you time to calm down. But I wanted to explain to you a few things. I don't know if you understand exactly what's happening here."

"I understand perfectly," I said. "You're keeping me prisoner while you have my boyfriend killed. It's sick and horrible. You're an evil person."

She sighed. "I thought you might think something like that. Let me try to start at the beginning. You never met your grandfather—Grandpa Hoyt. He died before you were born."

What did my grandfather have to do with this?

"I would have never met you if my parents hadn't been killed by the Sons," I said. "They killed your daughter. Both of your daughters. Why don't you hate them?"

"The Sons didn't do that," she said. "Edgar Weem did that. He gave those orders." When she said Edgar Weem's name, it was like she was saying a particularly disgusting word. She reminded me of Michaela Weem. Then she clenched the comparison. "Vile man. Vile."

Michaela had said those exact same words. I suddenly turned to my grandmother with interest.

She continued. "Your grandfather was a complicated man, Azazel. A good man, but not without his weak-nesses. When I met him, I was barely older than you are. I did not come from a wealthy background—"

"Yeah," I muttered. "You're a gypsy or something, right?"

Anger flashed in her eyes. "I've done a lot of work to cover up that fact. I don't know how you discovered it. But, yes, my family was Roma. We traveled in a caravan throughout the United States. I had always been both blessed and cursed with dreams—visions more accurately. And I saw him coming. Your grandfather." She smiled then. "He was so beautiful then. Very charming. I was besotted with him from the moment I dreamed of him. When he arrived, coming to our carnival, I was not surprised to see him. But I was surprised when he seemed to take an interest in me.

"We had a whirlwind romance, the way only young

people can. His family was against it. They wanted him to settle down with someone proper. Someone who befit his social standing. They were horrified when he married me. It was a love match. We were blissful. At first.

"We didn't know it then, Azazel, but our elders were right. Love does not last. All the problems they predicted would happen did indeed happen. Your grandfather tired of me. I was hopeless when it came to fitting in socially, and I had to learn the hard way, pulling myself up to a station of respect within society. And all the while, I had to do this while your grandfather was blatantly unfaithful to me. There were whispers everywhere I went. I was the gypsy girl who'd married into money because my husband had been crazy about me, only to be disinterested in me in just a few years.

"It wasn't easy. As a woman, and an originally poor one at that, I was kept completely in the dark about your grandfather's money and about his ties to the Sons. I knew nothing of who they were. But we did socialize with members of the Sons on a fairly regular basis. It was then I met Edgar Weem. He was young. Quite a lot younger than I was. But so excited, eager, and full of energy.

"The Weems and the Hoyts have never gotten along. There has been a long-standing feud between the two families. Edgar and I both knew this, but we had an affair anyway. It was short. He was far too much my junior, and in the end, he took his vows to the organization too seriously to continue it. He had made vows of celibacy, you see.

"But I was able to learn much about the Sons from Edgar, who was quite open about the organization and about the prophecies with which he was so obsessed. It was clear that your grandfather had absolutely no interest in the organization. Instead, he left that to his brother, Ian. I was able to use my knowledge to make myself invaluable to Ian. After all, I had a certain amount of control over the Hoyt fortune. I used that control to cement my position in the family.

"After your grandfather died, I remained in control of the fortune, instead of having my coffers skimmed by the Sons. We had no male heirs, but it was okay, because I was able to perform the duties your grandfather had performed.

"And that was when Edgar Weem blackmailed me. He had the information that we'd had an affair, and he knew that would ruin me. It would have ruined him if it had come out as well, but he knew I'd never let that happen. He wanted two things from me. He wanted me to bless his union with some ridiculous girl, so that she could bear what he thought was going to be the Rising Sun. And he wanted my financial and influential backing to help him rise in the ranks of the Sons. He wanted to sit on the Council. He wanted to be in control.

"I was livid. First of all, it was insult that he had left me entirely because he wanted to honor his vows of celibacy. Here he was with some slip of a thing, who he was trying to sire a child upon. I hated him for that. And I hated him for trying to use what had been between us for his own gain.

Furthermore, he would be working against the Hoyts, my own family, because he was a Weem. I was siding against my legacy with this horrible man. And I had no choice.

"This Rising Sun he intended to erect would be his child. He would be able to mold the child as he saw fit. And he would wrench the power completely away from the Hoyts. I knew exactly what he was doing. He said it was about noble things, about bringing the Rising Sun into the world. He claimed to believe in the prophecies. But I saw through him. It was a power play, pure and simple. He was a despicable, wretched, scheming man. I wondered if he hadn't orchestrated the entire affair with me entirely for that purpose.

"When he arrived here with that girl, that Michaela, I could see immediately that she had an impressionable mind. So I did the only thing I knew to do. The only thing I could think to stop him. He wanted me to use my gypsy powers to help him and his child. So I used my gypsy upbringing all right. But not in the way he thought. I planted ideas in Michaela's mind. False visions. I thought if I could turn her against Edgar Weem and the child, that she would just get rid of it."

"What do you mean, you planted ideas in Michaela's mind?" I asked. Just how freaking powerful was my grandmother?

"It's a bit like hypnotism," said Grandma Hoyt. "It's something I learned in my carnival days. It's been useful other times as well. When Edgar Weem alerted me that a

Brother named Anton Welsh knew our secrets, I was able to place certain ideas in his head as well. Not the ideas Edgar would have wanted, of course, but then he was too stupid to realize that I was always working against him. Always."

My head was spinning. Grandma Hoyt was responsible for what both Michaela *and* Anton thought? "What kind of ideas did you plant?" I asked, even though I was pretty sure I knew the answer.

"I told them that the child, that Edgar's child, was an abomination," said Grandma Hoyt. "That he shouldn't live. That he would bring nothing but evil to the earth. And I didn't bless him, instead I cursed him, so that my predictions would come true."

"Cursed him?"

"A gypsy curse. I cursed him to descend deeper into darkness as the power inside him — power already bestowed by others — grew. Soon, he won't even be human." She took my hands. "So, you see, that's why I want you away from him, darling. I know you think you love him, and I've felt that way before too, but what you don't understand is that those passionate feelings are adolescent. They fade over time. They don't last. I'm not saying it doesn't hurt now, but it will get better."

I snatched my hands away from her. I was reeling from what she'd just told me. She'd planted the visions in Michaela's head? And the idea that Jason was an abomination? "Wait," I said. "Did you plant the vision of the vessel in Michaela's head?"

"Of course not!" said my grandmother. "I don't know where she came up with that ridiculous idea. I wasn't pleased at all when she didn't just terminate the pregnancy. Instead, she wove this elaborate conspiracy to get rid of Jason, and she involved my own daughter in it. I was less than amused by that."

"Your own daughter you weren't speaking to," I pointed out.

"Because she wouldn't listen to me when I told her that the whole thing was ridiculous and made up," said Grandma Hoyt.

"So the only reason Michaela hated Jason was because you hypnotized her," I said to myself more than her. That was so strange. It made everything different. Suddenly, there weren't any visions stating that Jason and I were evil or that we'd do terrible things together. It was all just ravings of a hypnotized woman. Except ... "Michaela's visions were sometimes right, though," I said. "It couldn't have just been because you hypnotized her."

"She wasn't right," said Grandma Hoyt, dismissing that entirely.

"But she was," I said, and I explained about her prophecy and the men in the church in Shiloh.

Grandma Hoyt shook her head. "She didn't have a vision, Azazel. She put the suggestion in your head. Then you put that suggestion in those men's heads. You planted their insanity."

"I didn't hypnotize them," I said, confused.

"Yes," said Grandma Hoyt. "You did. And this is why I wanted you here with me, Azazel. Neither of my daughters had my gifts. But you are special. They are strong within you. You have dreams as well. Dreams that suggest the future. Dreams that show you things. And you can also exert your power over the minds of others. You are stronger even than I am."

What she said made a certain amount of sense. But I wasn't sure that I actually believed it.

"I can teach you how to control and hone your gifts," she said.

I glared at her. "So that I can be like you? No, thanks."

"What does that mean?"

"Okay," I said, "I get that you're mad at Edgar Weem. He sounds like a big jerk. I'd be mad at him too. So if you have these powers or whatever, why not use them on him? Why didn't you just make him go take a big jump off a building or something? Why this elaborate scheme? And why involve Jason, who was an innocent, unborn child and had never done anything to hurt you?"

"The power doesn't work like that," said Grandma Hoyt. "You can't just go around messing with the minds of everyone you meet. Only impressionable minds can be used. Edgar wasn't suitable."

"Jason was just a baby," I said. "You disgust me. You're a vile woman." I threw her words about Edgar Weem back in her face.

"Azazel, you must wipe thoughts of Jason from your

mind. He is gone. He was a violent, terrible boy. He wasn't a good influence on you. And he would only have hurt you in the end. My curse would have seen to that. The boy is little more than a walking time bomb."

Oh. Screw her curses. Maybe they only worked on impressionable minds too. I stood up from the bed, fuming. I couldn't believe this. My entire life, everything that had gone wrong, was all my grandmother's fault. It was her fault that Michaela had tried to use the Satanists to kill Jason. Sure Satanism was weird and a little gross, but beyond the ritual killing of Jason, it didn't really hurt anybody. If it hadn't been for that, maybe I could have simply dealt with my crazy Satanist family. They might still be alive, too. Essentially, my grandmother's actions had caused pretty much every bad thing that had ever happened to me.

I spun on my heels, staring at her. She sat so prim and proper on the bed, her back as straight as if an ice pick had been rammed up her spine. And as I stared at her, I hated her.

"Do you have any idea what you've done?" I said. "You set things in motion. It's your fault that so many people are dead. And you just use people like they're your pawns. You just move them around. Like Palomino. Taking her away from Chance."

Grandma Hoyt got to her feet. "Palomino is in a facility in the Sons' Headquarters. I assure you, she's quite safe. And it's for her own good."

"Her own good?" How could she be so self-righteous?

Didn't she see what a horrible hag of a woman she was?

"I'm sure I've given you a lot to think about," said Grandma Hoyt. "I'll let you think." She swept out of my bedroom.

I stood, rooted to the spot, seething. All I could think about was what an absolutely terrible person she was and how much I hated her. I tore out of my room after her.

She was standing at the top of the staircase.

"Grandma!" I screamed.

She started and lost her balance. She went tumbling down the steps, crying out.

Chance came out of his room. "What's wrong?" he said.

Grandma Hoyt's body came to a stop at the bottom of the steps. Her neck was twisted in an unnatural way. She was crumpled into sickening position, her legs and arms like a pretzel over each other. And her eyes were wide open, staring up at me. But she wasn't moving.

I took a step back, my hand going to my open mouth. "Oh," I whispered.

Chance clambered down the steps to Grandma Hoyt. He knelt by her, shaking her shoulder. "Grandma?" he said.

I'd just accidentally killed my grandmother.

CHAPTER FOURTEEN

To: Cornelius Agricola <cagricola@it.yahoo.com>

From: Edgar Weem <arthurisreal@hotmail.com>

Subject: Re: Jason

Cornelius, don't worry about anything! You did the right thing, letting them go. The boy needs to follow the path I've set for him to truly achieve his full potential. He is remarkable. You're right.

For this reason, I don't worry about him. There's not a situation on earth he can't get himself out of. He's proved this over and over.

Edgar

The guards weren't at the doors. They were inside, staring at Grandma Hoyt.

"It was an accident," Chance was saying. "She fell down the steps."

I was still at the top of the steps, my hand at my mouth. I was shaking.

But the guards weren't at the doors. It was my only chance.

I vaulted down the steps, carefully avoiding the body, and I shot through the front door. Chance called after me, but I didn't stop. I just kept going.

When I was about five blocks away, approaching a bus station, I realized that I should have stopped and gotten some money or a car or something. I walked to the bus station, wondering what I should do. Should I go back to the house? But no, I didn't think so. There would probably be police and ambulances. They would ask questions. And I couldn't answer them. Besides, I could think of a place that I could go to get money. And a passport, which I was going to need.

There were two people at the bus station. One was a man in a business suit, carrying a briefcase. The other was an elderly lady with a scarf over her head. She saw me immediately, taking me in. I was still wearing the nightgown my grandmother had forced me to wear. I wasn't sure how I looked.

"Are you crying, sweetheart?" asked the woman.

Was I? I touched my face. Oh God. I was. I looked at the woman and blurted, "My grandmother," I said. "She's dead. I just ran out of the house, and I don't have money for bus fare, and I need to go into the city."

"Oh my," said the lady. "You poor dear." She opened her purse and gave me a ten dollar bill. "That should get you into the city. I'm so sorry about your grandmother."

"Thank you," I said, breaking out into fresh sobs.

As I settled into a seat on the bus, I mused that it wasn't true what people said. There were kind people on earth still. Of course, if that woman had known it was my fault that my grandmother had fallen down the steps to her death, she might not have been as nice.

The bus deposited me at the train station, where I boarded a train bound for New York City. I spent what seemed like hours studying the map of New York City in the train, trying to figure out where I was supposed to get off. I finally decided that I would get off at the 33rd Street and 6th Avenue stop because it looked close to Penn Station, and that was where Jason and I had gotten off the bus the last time we'd been in New York, last fall.

Once off the train, I was overwhelmed by the city again. I hadn't been back since our short visit back in November, and it seemed the same as ever. Tall buildings, tons of people, movement everywhere. It had been a long time ago, and I hadn't paid a lot of attention to where Jason was taking me, but I knew that we had walked from here. I found my way to Penn Station and to the place where the bus had dropped us off. This looked familiar.

What had we done after this?

Jason had gone to a payphone. I looked up at down the street until I located it. I went to the phone. Now. Where had we gone from here? Had we walked further up this street or had we turned and gone the other way? I tried as best as I could to hone in on my memory of the situation. To remember Jason's movements. We'd walked up this street. I was almost certain of it.

I walked up the street, to the edge of the block. Had we crossed the street?

I remembered that we'd walked for a long time, and that Jason had been walking really fast. I remembered that I'd gotten out of breath. But I had no idea what turns we'd taken. I'd paid no attention to the names of the streets. I hadn't thought I'd ever need to retrace our steps. I sighed. I didn't think we'd crossed the street here.

But I resolved to remember each of my paths, so that I could come back to Penn Station and try each route, taking different turns, until I found the right one. How many possible combinations could there be? I remembered there was a formula for figuring that out. But I didn't remember the formula, and maybe it was a blessing, because I didn't want to know how hopeless this was.

It was getting dark, and I wandered through the streets of New York City in my white lace nightgown. (The only good thing was that no one gave me a second glance. There were tons of weirdly dressed people on the streets of New York City.) Nothing looked familiar. I tried walking straight for as far as I could. After about a half an hour, I decided that I must have gone the wrong way, and I walked back to Penn Station. I started off again, this time crossing the street.

I repeated this process about four times, taking different streets. I didn't see anything familiar. My feet hurt from walking. I was only wearing a pair of slippers which my grandmother had given me. I was exhausted. It had to be after midnight, and I was freaked out about being in New York City this late at night. Was I going to be robbed at gunpoint? I snorted. I only had a few bucks. No, I didn't think that anyone would try to rob a chick in a nightgown. I didn't look like I had any money.

This had been a really stupid idea. How was I supposed to find an apartment when I remembered next to nothing about how I'd gotten there in the first place? I really should have planned this whole excursion out a little better. But I hadn't had much time to think about what I was doing or where I was going. It only made it worse knowing that Jason was stuck in the Sons headquarters and was probably going to be executed. I didn't know how much time I had, but here I was wasting it wandering around in New York City. I needed money. I needed a passport. I needed a plane ticket.

And then once I was in England, I didn't even know where I was going to go.

Wait. I'd written down a number for Father Gerald and put it in my pocket. I dug in my pocket. Yes. It was still there.

Maybe if I could get in touch with Hallam, as I'd been thinking, I could get some kind of help. Maybe Hallam could ...

I was back at Penn Station after my last failed attempt to find the apartment. I trudged over the payphone that Jason had used all those months ago. Sliding some coins into it, I dialed Father Gerald's number. It rang and rang. I realized it was late, and he was probably asleep. I waited for the answering machine to pick up.

But then there was a sleepy, "Hello?"

"Father Gerald?" I said.

"Yes. Who is this?"

"It's Azazel Jones. You might remember me from—"

"I remember you. What is it now?"

He sounded a little annoyed. I guess he knew if I was

calling, it meant trouble. "Do you have a number for Hallam?" I asked.

"Of course," Father Gerald sighed. He gave me the number. Of course, I didn't have a pen or pencil, so I had to memorize it.

I hung up, put more money in the phone and dialed the number Father Gerald had given me. It too, rang and rang and rang. Then went to voicemail. Dammit! The voicemail identified the number as Hallam's cell phone. It beeped. I took a deep breath. "Hallam, it's Azazel. I-I'm in trouble. Jason's in trouble. The Sons have him. I think they're going to kill him. I need ... Oh, it doesn't matter. I don't have a phone. You can't call me back. But if there's anything you can do to help him ... " Jason had told Hallam that if he saw Hallam again, he would kill him. I hung up the phone. I didn't even remember the number anymore.

I slumped against the phone. What was I going to do? There wasn't anyone else I could think of who might know any of these locations. Wait. I dialed Father Gerald again.

"Didn't the number work?" Father Gerald wanted to know.

"It went to voicemail," I said. "I wonder if you have another number. Sutherland?"

"You want the phone number for Liam Sutherland?" Father Gerald said, like he didn't believe me.

"I'm desperate," I said.

"Where are you?"

"New York City."

Father Gerald sighed. He gave me another number. I memorized it again. And I used the last of my change to dial the number for Sutherland. Just the thought of him gave me shivers. He wasn't a very nice person. He was a rapist and murderer, but he had also helped Jason and I get to Rome.

The phone only rang once. "Sutherland," said the voice on the other end, brisk, British, and alert.

"It's Azazel Jones," I said.

"Azazel!" Sutherland sounded delighted to hear from me. "What can I do for you?"

"I want to know the location of the Sons headquarters in England," I said.

"Can't help you. I don't know. I've never been able to figure that out," he said.

Fuck. Why was this so, so hard? I wanted to cry. I considered hanging up the phone.

"You used to follow Jason around, didn't you?" I said. "When you were trying to find out information on him?"

"Occasionally."

"So, do you happen to know where his ID contact Marlena lives?"

"Actually, there I *can* help you," said Sutherland. "But I'll want to trade."

"I don't know anything!" I said.

"Perhaps we can trade for something else, then," he said, sounding eager. Oh. Gross. Sutherland was so disgusting. "Where are you? In New York?"

"Wait," I said. "Maybe I do have some information." And

I began blurting out everything I'd learned over the past few weeks, from the fact that Edgar Weem was descended from King Arthur to Cornelius Agricola training Brothers, to my grandmother's story. In the middle, a recording interrupted me to tell me I needed to put in more coins. I didn't have anymore.

"Call me back collect," said Sutherland, giving me his number again.

I did. I picked up where I left off, telling Sutherland everything. He might be able to do all kinds of terrible things with this information. After all, he sold it to the highest bidder. But I didn't care. I just cared about Jason.

When I'd finished, Sutherland was extremely happy. "This is wonderful, Azazel," he said. "There's so much I can do with this, especially to the Hoyts." Then regretfully, he added, "I'm afraid you've given me more information than the location of Marlena Cross is worth. I could tell you something else, though, in addition. I do know where Edgar Weem is holing up. He's in Kildare, Ireland. I'm sure if you went to him, he could tell you the location of the Sons' headquarters."

"Deal," I said wearily.

* * *

Marlena still had a mat in front of her door. I still thought it was silly. There wasn't any reason to wipe my feet on it. I knocked, exhausted and sagging against her door frame. After an eternity passed, I knocked again. Maybe she wasn't home. After the third knock with no answer, I slid down the wall, curled up, and fell asleep.

I woke up to someone kicking me. "Wake up, you filthy bum," a British accent was saying.

My eyes fluttered open. "Marlena," I said, struggling to my feet.

"You can't sleep in here," she was saying. "There's a shelter just a few streets down."

"No," I said. "Marlena, it's me. Azazel."

"How do you know my name?" she demanded. She still looked really pretty, with her flawless dark skin. But she didn't have her hair in braids anymore. Instead, it was cut short. It clung to her head in tiny black ringlets.

"I'm Jason's girlfriend," I said.

Her eyes widened in recognition. "You look awful!" she exclaimed, fitting her key to the lock of her apartment and ushering me inside.

"Thanks," I said.

Marlena hung her keys up on the wall near the door. "Well, I didn't mean it like that," she said. She was wearing a jacket, which she shed and threw over one of her couches. Her apartment looked the same, incense and tapestries. I breathed it in. I remembered how the first time I'd been here, I'd found the place frightening and disturbing. Now it just seemed comforting. "Why don't you sit down?" She gestured at her couches.

Gratefully, I settled on a couch. It was soft. I felt as if it hugged my body. I relaxed into it, sighing. I hadn't realized how sore my body was from walking all over New York

City.

"Would you like some coffee?" she asked me.

I sat up. "That would be awesome," I said. I did need to wake up. Who knows how much time I'd lost? I had to get to Jason as soon as possible.

Marlena disappeared into the kitchen. I heard the noise of water coming from a faucet. The click of a coffee maker switching on. "So what are you doing here?" she asked. "Where's Jason?"

"Jason's in England," I said. "They're going to kill him."

Marlena rushed back into the living room. "What did you say?"

"I've got to get there," I said. "I've got to stop them."

She sat down on the couch beside me. "You back up," she said. "And you tell me everything. Who's got Jason? What are they going to do to him?"

I explained as best as I could. While I was talking, the coffee finished brewing and Marlena brought us both a cup. We filled them with packets of sugar and single serving creamers. Marlena stole them from fast food restaurants. The coffee was strong, but I made it sweet with about four packets of sugar. As the hot liquid coursed through my body, I could feel myself becoming more alert. I sped through the rest of my explanation.

Marlena was upset. She paced in the living room, holding her cup of coffee. "So you think this Weem person has Jason's exact location?"

"I'm pretty sure."

She took a long drink of coffee. "We're going to need passports," she said. "And a credit card with a pretty high limit. But I think I have one."

"We?" I said.

"I'm coming with you," she said. "You think I'm going to let Jason be offed by those prigs that have been chasing him all this time? Jason is like the little brother I never had. I won't let anything happen to him."

Well. I'd seen Marlena load a rifle once. She seemed like she could handle herself in a fight. I didn't think she'd slow me down. "Okay," I said. "You can come with me."

"You don't have to give me permission," she said. "I wasn't asking for it."

I considered. "What about guns? Can you get us guns?"

Marlena hesitated. "Well, I know someone who can." She set her coffee down on the coffee table and went back down the hall. She came back with a credit card, which she handed to me. "I'm going out," she said. "I'll be back with passports and guns. You book the tickets. Book them for this afternoon. And use the name on the credit card for the tickets. And for yours, give yourself the same last name and, I don't know, what do you want to be called?"

"Wait," I said. "If we have the same last name, that would mean we're related."

"Your point?"

"Well, I don't know if people are going to believe that you and I are—"

"Oh for Heaven's sake. Maybe your parents adopted a

305

little black girl from England. You ever think about that?"

I shrugged. "Okay."

"Your name is Jane," she said. "Is that all right?"

"Sure," I said.

* * *

Edgar Weem was living in an old stone cottage opposite St. Brigid's Cathedral in County Kildare, Ireland. The little house itself looked sweet and charming, like something out of a storybook. It had window boxes with brightly colored flowers growing in them. The door was white with a quaint iron handle on it. Next to the house was a fenced in garden. I'd expected Edgar Weem to be like an evil warlord, presiding over an ancient castle with a mote or something. The little house didn't seem to fit his personality.

Marlena and I, who were still adjusting to the time change after flying across the Atlantic, had landed in Dublin. Then we'd arranged transportation to Weem's house. Our flight had taken about six hours. It had taken about an hour to get to Kildare. For us, it felt like sometime after midnight. In Ireland time, it was early in the morning — around 6:30 AM. We didn't know if Edgar Weem would be awake yet, but we didn't care.

I rapped on the door. To my surprise, the door opened immediately. Edgar Weem stood there. He was wearing his robe, holding a cup of coffee. He had a receding hairline and his hair was going gray around his temples. But — and here was the weird thing — he was definitely the same man I'd dreamed about and envisioned when I'd been talking to

Agnes. I'd almost convinced myself that the whole experience with Agnes had been a dream. I thought maybe it was nothing more than a product of my subconscious. But this was definitely the same guy. Just eighteen years older.

Edgar Weem made an apologetic face. "Sorry," he said. "I don't want any." He started to close the door.

Marlena wedged her gun in the doorway, blocking the door. "We're not selling anything," she growled.

Edgar Weem opened the door wider again. He looked alarmed.

"We're coming in now," said Marlena. She pushed past Edgar. I followed her. Marlena was really super cool. We'd had a little bit of time to chat on the plane, and she'd told me stories about Jason when he was a little boy, how he'd helped her and her dad with faking car registrations. I was glad that Jason had someone like this. He'd never had a family. Having someone like Marlena was good though. I liked her.

Edgar closed the door behind us, holding one arm in the air and clutching his coffee cup with the other. "I'm afraid I don't know what's going on," he said.

"We're here about Jason," said Marlena. "You're going to help us."

"Jason?" said Edgar. He lowered his hands. "You must be Marlena. And you're Azazel, then?"

So he knew about us? Both of us? I expected him to know about me. But Marlena?

"How do you know who we are?" I wanted to know.

"Well, I've kept close tabs on Jason throughout his life. If two women with guns burst into my apartment talking about him, you two are really the only two choices I would have." He smiled at us. "It's good to meet you both at last." He offered us his hand, the one that wasn't holding his coffee.

Marlena and I looked at his proffered hand and then looked at each other. We both tucked our guns into the waist of our pants (Marlena had gotten me some clothes, so I wasn't wearing the horrid nightgown anymore) and folded our arms over our chests.

"Let's get something straight," said Marlena. "We don't like you."

"You're pretty much a shoo-in for the Worst Father in the Universe Award," I added.

"We're here for information. That's all," said Marlena.

Edgar withdrew his hand. "All right, then," he said cheerily. "Can I get the two of you some coffee?"

"No," I said. "For all we know, you'll drug it."

"I'd like some coffee," said Marlena. "I'll make it myself. You watch Weem."

"Sure," I said. "Have a seat, Edgar."

The inside of Edgar Weem's cottage was just as charming as the outside. There was a small sitting room filled with overstuffed couches and bookshelves. In the corner, there was a working fireplace, although it wasn't burning. Edgar made his way there and sat down. He threw one of his arms over the back of the couch, thoroughly at ease. "Why don't you come and sit with me, Azazel?" he said. "I'd love to get a look at you. You're a very pretty girl. I can see why Jason's so taken with you."

My eyes narrowed. I was beginning to see why both Michaela Weem and my grandmother had found Edgar Weem so charming. I didn't move. Instead, I just put my hand on the butt of my gun warningly.

"Oh, Azazel," he said with a jovial laugh. "You can relax, really. I'm on your side."

CHAPTER FIFTEEN

To: Edgar Weem <arthurisreal@hotmail.com>
From: Renegade Son <settingsun007@yahoo.com>
Subject: Jason and Azazel

Edgar,

I've gotten a message on my phone from Azazel. She says she and Jason are in trouble and she wants my help. Do you have any idea where they are or how to reach them? I'm beside myself with worry.

Hallam

"Listen Edgar," I said. "You are definitely not on my side."

"Call me Ted, please," he said.

Marlena poked her head out of the kitchen. "Get him to tell you where the headquarters are," she said.

Right. I went into the sitting room and sat on a chair opposite Edgar Weem. "We're only here for one reason," I said. "We need you to give us a location."

"You don't believe me, do you?" he asked. "You really think I'm out to get you?"

"I don't care," I said. "I already know more about you than I'd like. I've read Michaela's diary and talked to my grandmother and, well, eww."

He laughed again, a deep chuckle. When he smiled he had little smile lines around his eyes. He looked like a harmless uncle. I didn't like it. "Can I explain to you?" he asked. "Can I tell you why I've done what I've done?"

"Marlena," I called, "how long is that coffee going to take?"

"Not long," she said. "If I can figure out this crazy European contraption, it'll be ready in a jiff."

Okay, then. That sounded like it might be a while. I glared at Edgar Weem. "I guess I can't stop you," I said. "But I don't see how you could really explain anything. You've manipulated everyone around you just to get power. Now that you don't have any, I guess you want to be friends."

"You've got it all wrong," said Edgar. "I never wanted power." He sighed then, and looked sad, suddenly. "No, I often wish I'd never gotten the power that I did. It changes a man, not always for the better. But I've made sacrifices. For the greater good, though, Azazel. I think you'll realize that."

He settled comfortably on the couch. "Let's see," he said. "How shall I start?" He mused for a second, scratching his chin. (Really). "I suppose you know about the longstand-ing feud between the Weems and the Hoyts, don't you?"

"My grandmother told me about it," I said.

"Do you know why it started?"

I shook my head. Like I cared. "Well," said Edgar, "I suppose you know that the Sons are an offshoot of the Order of Reddimus, since you stayed with them in Rome."

"Yes," I said. "I heard about that."

"Well," said Edgar, "the Sons left because they were angry with the Church for creating the Jesuits. This was in the 1500s. I assume you're familiar with the Jesuits?"

"Uh ... something to do with the Spanish Inquisition, right?"

He laughed. "Indeed. The Reddimus monks had been created to combat paganism, but it was no longer an issue with the Church. Instead, the issue in the 1500s was Protestantism. The Church created the Jesuits to combat that issue. They no longer needed the Order of Reddimus. The original members of the Sons were so outraged at having been supplanted that they stole a large amount of money from the Church, and they used it to create a business. They became money lenders. Eventually, they started a bank. They became very wealthy indeed."

Great. Wonderful. Who cared? "Look, really, all we want to know is—"

"Wait, let me continue," said Edgar. "Where was I? Oh, yes, so the Sons of the Rising Sun were always wealthy men. And they had an enormous amount of power. This wealth and power only grew. With the establishment of centralized banks in European countries in the early part of the twentieth century, the Sons were able to create powerful holds on the governments of major world leaders. They controlled countries, not just money. This was big business and also big power. Lots of money and lots of power are always a bad combination.

"The Hoyts have always been a premier family in the Sons, and they began talking amongst the other members about what they could do with this influence. The Sons had always concerned themselves with the era of the Rising Sun, a period of time they felt would overtake the world and change it for the better. The Hoyts saw this period as a time when a global government could be implemented—a New World Order."

"Did they own the Federal Reserve Bank in the U.S.?" I asked.

Weem raised an eyebrow. "Well, yes. Members of the Sons did."

"I've heard this before. This is Conspiracy Theory 101," I said. In my *Da Vinci Code* phase, I'd gotten really into stuff like the Freemasons and the Illuminati. Against my better judgment, I found myself getting interested in what Weem was saying.

"All right, then," said Weem. "But I bet you haven't heard this part. My family, the Weems, didn't think this was a very good idea. We were staunchly on the side of democracy and not manipulating people with our money. Of course, we'd always thought the Rising Sun prophecy to be about a *person*, not a metaphor or time period. We were vocal in our opposition to both the Hoyts and the idea that the Rising Sun would be a period of time when the Sons ruled the world.

"Our dissension held off action for decades, but the discussion of a global government continued. I became increasingly frightened when the discussion began to become more and more serious in the late 1980s. I looked into the prophecies about the Rising Sun deeply. I discovered what I thought was proof that the Rising Sun would be born in the twentieth century. But even this discovery didn't stop the rumbling and scheming of this New World Order. And I became nearly frantic when I learned that the Sons were planning something for 2012. You know the date, yes?"

I nodded. "Yeah. The world's gonna end. Or there's going to be a polar shift or something."

"The Sons have access to a weapon that uses scalar electromagnetics. This is a very powerful technology that can disrupt gravity. They plan to use it in 2012 to create a global disaster that will very much resemble a polar shift. In the aftermath, they will swoop down to care for a wounded planet, and erect themselves rulers of everything."

I shook my head slowly, trying to absorb what he'd just said. "The Sons are going to destroy the world?"

"Not the whole world," he said. "But many people will die. It will be a crisis unlike anything we've ever seen. And the significance of its occurrence in 2012, with the end of the Mayan calendar and the pseudo-scientific rumblings about this polar shift will mean that what's left of the world won't think to question what's going to happen.

"I knew I needed to stop this. I now believed that the Rising Sun was to end the terrible reign of the Sons, not help cement their power in the world. I began to search desperately for the Rising Sun, pouring over prophecies. I was half insane in my desire to stop the Sons. I had discovered a link in my own genealogy and the blood line of

King Arthur—"

"Yeah, Moretti told us about that. And I read Michaela's diary. So I know it was 'her idea' for the two of you to conceive Jason. But I don't care. She was in love with you and you treated her—"

"You don't think I was in love with her?" asked Edgar. "I married the woman didn't I? I fathered two children with her. It's not that I didn't care about her. But you must realize that the safety of the world trumped my own feelings for her or even for our own son. I knew what Jason had to become. He had to grow to be a fierce warrior who could destroy an organization like the Sons. I had to devote myself to making sure he was ready. It wasn't easy. He was my son. Of course I didn't want to expose him to the dangers I exposed him to. But I had to prepare him for his work. His very vital work."

So I was just supposed to forgive Weem for everything now? Because he was trying to save the world?

Marlena came in from the kitchen with two cups of coffee. She handed one to me. "Thanks," I said. "Are you hearing this?"

"Sure," she said. She shrugged. "I always knew Jason was special. If I had to pick someone to save the world, I'd pick him."

I bit my lip. No. It wasn't right. "You're all so stupid," I said.

Marlena jerked her head to face me.

"Not you, Marlena," I said. I stood up, taking a long swig of my coffee. It was black and bitter, but I didn't care. "I mean you guys. Edgar. Michaela. My grandmother. You're all stupid. And you're cowards. My grandmother was mad at you because you broke off your affair with her and then moved on to Michaela. And so she screwed up Michaela's head, ruined my life, and has been trying to get Jason killed for his whole life."

"Wait," said Edgar. "Arabella is trying to kill Jason?"

"You blackmailed her," I said. "You think she wasn't pissed?"

He looked troubled.

I wasn't finished. "Michaela Weem wanted Jason dead. So, she convinced my parents and a town full of people that I was a Vessel of Azazel and that I was supposed to kill Jason. And you, Edgar — *Ted* — you wanted to save the world. So you went around Europe having ritualistic sex and then put your own son through abusive situation after abusive situation, trying to turn him into a killing machine.

"You know what's wrong with all of you?" I demanded. "You won't take responsibility for your actions, and you won't get your hands dirty. Ted, I'm gonna have to repeat what Cornelius Agricola said to me. Why didn't you just set a fucking bomb?!"

Edgar was quiet for a second. Then he cleared his throat. "You can't understand, Azazel, how very powerful the Sons are. There was simply no way that I—"

"No," I said. "Don't make excuses. There is no reason to screw up so many other people's lives just because you don't think you can handle the problem. You're clearly a smart guy, Edgar. I can't help but think that there was some way you could have figured out how to take the Sons down yourself. But you left it to Jason. And so, when you go to sleep at night, I hope that you see the faces of all the people that Jason and I have had to kill. And the faces of all the people who have died trying to protect us. Because you know what? They're all on your hands. You started this. And you didn't have the guts to even finish it."

I sat down on the couch. "Now," I said, "you're going to tell us the location of the Sons' headquarters, so that I can go there and save my boyfriend."

* * *

Marlena and I surveyed the Sons' headquarters from behind some bushes. The headquarters were, indeed, an old castle. It didn't have a mote, though. The castle was hulking, crouching in a clearing in the woods. It sat in a valley, one large round tower surrounded by fortified walls and several smaller turrets. Marlena and I were above the castle on a hill, looking down. Five or six armed men guarded the entrance. Squadrons of others marched in circles around the perimeter.

"Well," said Marlena, "how do you suppose we're going to get in?"

I sighed. "I don't know."

"You think maybe a distraction of some kind?" she asked.

"Like what?"

"Well, maybe one of us could flash them."

I laughed, thinking about suggesting this very thing to

Jason when we were trying to get into the library. "I don't know," I said. "They're celibate men. Maybe they wouldn't care."

"Celibate," she said. "Maybe they wouldn't even know what breasts were."

I laughed again. "Seriously," I said.

"I am serious," she said. "Distraction. Get most of them away from the door and then one of us sneaks in."

"So what would happen to the other one?"

She considered. "Good point."

When Jason and I had been trying to get into the library, all we'd had to do was go up to the door and ask. Of course, everyone at the school had been under some kind of mojo, making them want to make us happy. Still, maybe ... "Let's try this," I said, and I explained what I was thinking to Marlena.

After some discussion, we both leapt out of the bushes and ran to the door, waving our arms in the air. "We surrender!" we yelled over and over again.

The men were startled. Rather than rushing to us, they kept their distance, staring at us like we were nuts. Marlena and I trotted up to the main door.

"We surrender," I said to the men at the door.

"So we hear," said one. "What for, exactly?"

"You don't know who we are?" I asked, pretending to be wounded.

"We're very dangerous enemies of the Sons," said Marlena. "You'll want to take us to your superiors right away."

The men looked even more confused.

"Of course," I said, "if you don't accept our surrender, I suppose we'll just leave then."

"Absolutely," said Marlena.

"Hold on," said one of the guards, grabbing me by the arm. He and another guard opened the door and took us inside. The inside of the castle, oddly enough, was all fluorescent lights and linoleum floors. Inside the door was a man at desk, typing things into a computer. Marlena and I took a quick look around and then both drove our elbows into the midsections of the men who were escorting us. While they huffed and doubled over in surprise, we scampered out of the room and down a long corridor.

Men were walking down the hallway, wearing suits. Marlena opened a random door, snatched hold of my shirt, and yanked us both inside.

The room was an office. There was a man behind its desk, which was covered with pictures of little children and dogs. He wore small horn rimmed glasses. "Who are you?" he asked, horrified.

Marlena got out her gun. "We're looking for the holding cells," she said.

"And the pregnant girls," I said. Palomino was here too somewhere.

"Pregnant girls?" Marlena asked.

"My brother's girlfriend is here. They have some place where they keep teenage mothers. Then they take their babies away from them."

"They still have places like that?" Marlena said.

The man had put his arms in the air. "D-don't hurt me," he said. "I have a map of the castle here on my desk. You're welcome to look at it all you want."

"Thanks," said Marlena, sidling over to him. He shrank from her gun as she waved it in his face. With trembling hands, he gave her the map. "In the dungeon," she said. "Figures." She handed me the map.

The castle had six levels. The lowest level was labeled "Dungeon" and showed rows of small rooms. They looked like cells.

"Pregnant girls?" I asked the man.

He shook his head, his eyes wide. "I d-don't know anything ab-bout that. Really."

"Looks like there's an elevator at the end of this hallway," I said to Marlena. We'd go for Jason first. Once we had him, he could help us find Mina. That is, if they hadn't gotten to him yet. I gulped. How soon could a trial and execution take place, anyway? It had been about three days since Jason and I had been captured from Rome. They couldn't have done it already. Could they?

"Let's go," she said.

But as she opened the door to go back into the hall, a loud alarm went off. It was an annoying beeping sound.

We both turned on the man. "Did you do that?" I asked.

"No," he said. "No, no. I swear."

Another alarm started to go off as well. This one sounded

like a school bell.

The man slid off his chair and crawled under his desk. "It's like the end of the world," he sobbed.

Marlena and I glared at him. She opened the door a crack to look outside. "It's pandemonium out there," she said. "There are people running all over the place."

"Because of us?" I asked. I was confused.

"I don't know," said Marlena.

A loud recorded voice came over PA system. "Alert," it said. "Lock system disengaged. Manual lockdown procedures commencing. All personnel to designated areas." It repeated. And repeated.

"Lock system disengaged?" Marlena said, yelling over the sound of the alarms and the recorded voice.

"Jason," I said.

She flung open the door. We ran out into the hallway, which was filled with people in suits and men in black outfits, running in various directions. Marlena and I sprinted for the elevator at the end of the hall. Once inside, the door snapped closed on us. Marlena punched the button for the ground floor. The elevator whisked us down. When the door opened on the dungeon floor, I was astonished.

It really did look like a dungeon, complete with bars and chains. It was dank and dark and musty. All of the cell doors were open and empty. Marlena and I raced through the dungeon, but there was no one there.

Abruptly, the recorded voice changed. "Security breached," it said. "Powering down."

It didn't make much difference in the dungeon, but when we got back to the elevator, it wouldn't work.

"I think Jason shut down the electricity," I said.

"Great," she said. "Apparently, he didn't need us to rescue him."

"We've still got to find him," I said. "And Palomino."

"Stairs," said Marlena, pointing.

Inside the stairwell it was pitch black. We grasped the railing and went up them as fast as we could. Two flights up, we heard someone clambering down the stairs. Marlena put out her hand to stop me from moving and pulled us up against the wall. We flattened ourselves there.

"Hello?" said a voice.

Dammit. Whoever it was had heard us.

"Jason?" said the voice. Wait. I knew that voice. I was used to hearing it say things like, "You are forbidden to sleep in the same bed," but it was familiar all the same.

"Hallam?" I called.

"Azazel?"

"It's okay," I told Marlena. We started back up the steps until we met Hallam.

"Were you in the dungeon?" he asked.

"Yeah," I said. "It's empty."

"Great gods," said Hallam. "I don't know where Jason is. It's a bloodbath up there."

A bloodbath?

"What do you mean?" I asked.

"I mean," said Hallam, "that there are dead people

322

everywhere."

"You think it's Jason?"

"I don't know what to think. I came when I found out he was here. I was able to get in, because I know the protocol from when I worked for the Sons. I found him in the dungeon. I helped him dismantle the locks. I was supposed to meet him back in the dungeon. But then the lights went out."

"Oh God," I muttered. "You talked to him? How did he seem?"

"That's why I told him to meet me, Azazel. I've never seen him like this. Never. He seemed ..."

We both knew how he seemed. My grandmother's words came back to me as she was describing the curse she'd laid on Jason. *Soon, he won't even be human.* God. I had to find him. I had to get to him. I didn't know if my grandmother could actually really curse people, but she sure had done a number on Michaela Weem. It was possible, I guessed, in a world where men went nuts from a kiss and Jason could come back from the dead.

"Where do you think he went?" I said. "You think he went to Hoyt?"

"Could be," said Hallam. "Hoyt's office is on the top floor. It's where the Council Room is."

"I don't understand," said Marlena. "What's wrong with Jason?"

"Maybe nothing," I said. "Hopefully —"

I was cut off as a door below us opened. Gray light

streamed in and a woman toddled in, holding her protruding belly. "I can't make it down these steps!" she protested to the person who was coming in behind her. "It's dark."

A pregnant woman?

"Hello?" I yelled. "Are you guys from the pregnant teenagers wing?"

"Who is that?" called the pregnant woman.

"Do you know Palomino?" I asked.

"Yeah, we know Mina. Who are you?"

I turned to Marlena and Hallam. "Go with them," I said. "Find Palomino. Get her out of here. Get all of those girls out of here."

"Where are you going?" asked Marlena.

"To get Jason," I said, starting up the steps.

"I'm coming with you!" Marlena protested. "I don't even know this Mina person!"

Hallam caught her arm. "Let her go," he said. "When Jason's like this, she's really the only person who can do anything. Come on."

The stairs went on forever. At first I ran, but I started to sweat and gasp for breath. I slowed to a walk. I couldn't tell where I was. It was so dark. All I could do was take a step at a time and climb higher into the castle. Once I paused at one of the floors, so I could see where I was. I was on the fourth floor. The fourth floor was littered with about twenty bodies. Some of them had just been shot, but a few were worse. One man's entrails spilled out of his stomach, dragging out onto the floor. Another man's jaw hung loose from his body, torn away from his face. I slammed the door and kept going.

As I reached the sixth floor, I heard screams and gunshots. There's nothing like the sounds of men screaming. It's eerie, because it's high pitched but throaty. And, somehow, it's scarier. Maybe it's sexist, but you don't expect men to scream. At least, not like that, you don't.

I pushed open the door to the sixth floor. The same gray light greeted me. There was no light, so the only illumination came from small windows. I stepped over the bodies at the door, trying not to look at them. And I walked in the direction of the screams.

On this level, the castle didn't resemble an office. There was a plush carpet on the floor. The original stone walls were showing. Paintings of women and horses and strange mythological creatures decorated the walls. It reminded me of the ceiling in the library at the Sol Solis School. A man pushed by me, hobbling away. His leg had been shot, and there was blood smeared all over his suit. I kept moving forward, a feeling of dread knotting in my stomach.

I was going to find Jason, I told myself. I loved Jason. I tried not to remind myself of the time that Jason had cut off his own mother's finger and left it for his brother with a note. I tried not to remind myself of Jason stumbling into our apartment in Bradenton, covered in blood. I tried not to remind myself of the matter-of-fact way Jason had talked about killing Jude.

Soon, he won't even be human.

325

What would he be, then?

I rounded a corner, and there he was. He was standing in front of a closed door which had Ian Hoyt's name on it. There were two men lying on the floor near him, wearing suits. They weren't dead. They had shots in both of their legs, and they were trying to crawl away from him. Jason was standing over a third man, his foot on the man's hand. He was shooting the fingers on the man's hand. The man was screaming each time one of his fingers exploded into gore. There was huge, leering smile on Jason's face.

I shuddered. "Jason?" I said.

Jason didn't even look up. He just leveled his gun in the direction of my voice and pulled the trigger.

CHAPTER SIXTEEN

April 30, 1991

He was so small the first time I saw him. So little. And even though it had been an agonizing ten hours trying to push him out of my body, I didn't hate him. I know I should. I have seen in my visions what he will be capable of. I have seen him standing tall while the bodies lie around him dead. I have seen him turn on everything and everyone that ever loved him. But when I held him and looked into his tiny bright eyes and his arms batted at the air in front of me like he was trying to grab at something only he could see, I felt this burst of ...

Maybe it was love.

I can't do it. I can't kill him. He's just a baby.

I hit the floor. The bullet sailed over my head. "Jason, it's me!" I shrieked.

He did turn then. He looked at me. Sort of. His eyes were dull, the way they had been when he'd come back from doing whatever he'd done to Sutherland that night in Bradenton. They looked through me. Expressionless, he kicked the man he was torturing away from him. The man screamed again. Almost as an afterthought, Jason turned and put a bullet neatly in the man's head, right between his eyes. The screaming stopped.

Jason walked to me. He was still holding his gun. Aiming it at me.

I started to push myself to my feet, but Jason knelt down

in front of me. He put the gun to my forehead. I stopped breathing.

"Jason," I gasped. "It's *me*."

A flit of something went across his eyes. Recognition, maybe? I took the opportunity to grab the barrel of the gun. I tried to wrest it away from him, but he held onto it. I managed to twist it, so that it wasn't facing me anymore. I drew my own gun.

I was scared now. Jason didn't recognize me. He seemed to have gone completely and totally crazy. And I didn't know what he was doing to these men or what he planned to do to me. Michaela Weem's words echoed back to me, from months ago.

You will lie dead while he feasts on your guts.

Had I been wrong, all those months ago, when so many people had urged me to kill Jason? Was he really the monster they'd painted him to be?

Jason was tugging on his gun. He was stronger than me, and with one heave, he pulled it away from my grasp. I leveled my gun at him, struggling to my feet. We surveyed each other, guns trained on each other. Jason's finger tensed on his trigger.

"It's Azazel," I said again.

Jason cocked his head. The huge grin on his face was fading. "Azazel," he whispered.

His gun dropped to his side. He rubbed his face with his hand, squeezing his eyes shut, and when he opened them, he could see me. He looked around himself, at the bodies, at the men who were mangled by gunfire, and he *screamed*.

The gun fell out of his hand, landing softly on the carpet. Jason dropped to his knees, suddenly sobbing.

I went to him, kneeling next to him, gathering him in my arms. He took my hand, the one still holding a gun, and pulled it up to his face. He rested the barrel against his cheek. "She said," he whispered, "that you were the only one who could kill me. So you have to do it. You have to do it or God knows what else I'll do."

I dropped the gun like it burned me. It fell between us. I put my forehead against his, kissing his cheeks and his nose. "I would never do that," I said. "I could never do that."

"You don't understand," he said, pulling back. "I've been lying to you. All this time, I've been lying to you. I tried to tell you, that first night in Rome, but I couldn't. I tried again in the hotel, but I—I couldn't tell you. I thought I'd lose you, but you should have known."

"Jason, shh," I said. "Let's just get out of here."

And go where? I wondered. More running? After what we'd done here, the Sons would hunt us down like dogs. But I needed to get Jason away. I needed to—

"Listen," he said. "After the sorority house. They sent me on missions. Not with Hallam. Not always with Hallam. Sometimes by myself. I did things. Things like ..." He gestured around himself. "Things like this. I don't always remember all the details. They're fuzzy and ..." He sucked air in through his nose. "Your brothers. Those things they showed you. They were all true." And then he really started sobbing, like his heart was going to break.

That fucking bastard Edgar Weem. I would never forgive him for this. "It's not your fault, Jason."

This wasn't a curse. This wasn't my grandmother's twisted idea of revenge. This was a cold, calculated way of bringing up Jason to make damned sure he could do something like this.

He didn't look at me. "Because of prophecies or fate?" he asked. "Because I'm made of evil and I'm meant to destroy?"

"No," I said. "Because your father is an absolutely horrible man." I put my finger under his chin and turned him to look at me. "If it didn't bother you, I'd be scared. Then you'd be evil."

I was sure. Agnes had said that I need to trust myself. Well, I did. I knew this was right. I knew Jason better than anyone on earth. If there was evil in him, I'd know about it. "You were abused," I said. "And we've both been through a really hellish year. But since we've come this far, we might as well finish the job."

"The job?"

There was so much he didn't know. "The Sons are trying to blow up the world in 2012," I said. "So, we should probably go kill Ian Hoyt."

"No more," he said. "No more killing."

"Okay," I said. "I'll do it." I bent my face to his, which was wet with tears. And I brushed my lips gently against his.

And a crescendo of explosions underscored our kiss.

I pulled back. "What was that?" I said.

Jason shook his head. I got up. Ian Hoyt's office was right behind Jason. I tried the door, but it was locked. Picking up my gun, I put two bullets in the knob. The door swung open. There were about fifteen men crowded in Ian Hoyt's office, all wearing suits. They'd probably cowered in here when they'd discovered Jason was loose. That wasn't the strange thing, though. The strange thing was that they were all dead. They were all holding guns, and their head were slumped forward or to the side. It looked like they'd all just shot themselves. And from the smell of smoke in the room, they must have just done it.

You put that suggestion in those men's heads. You planted their insanity.

Oops. Had I just made a whole castle of men shoot themselves?

EPILOGUE

"Chance," yelled Mina from the top of the steps, "it's your turn to make up a bottle."

Chance and Jason were sitting in the living room of what used to be my grandmother's house playing *Call of Duty* on a huge widescreen TV. I was half-watching them, half-writing in the journal my therapist insisted I keep. Jason and I, as I had predicted, needed *lots* of therapy.

"Two seconds," Chance yelled back.

"Dude, it's cool," said Jason. "I'll pause it."

Marlena came in through the front door, her keys jingling. "Is Hallam back from work yet?" she asked, ducking her head into the living room.

"He's got a late class on Wednesdays," Chance reminded her as he got up to go into the kitchen to make a bottle.

I followed him. Sometimes Chance needed help with this kind of stuff.

"That's right," said Marlena. "I keep forgetting that."

The house was huge, and Chance and I had inherited it after Grandma Hoyt's death, which had been officially ruled an accident. So the six of us lived here. Hallam and Marlena had apparently struck up some kind of romance over all the dead bodies at the Sons' headquarters. I liked the fact they were here, and I liked them as a couple, even if it was only because I could now tease Hallam about "living in sin" on a regular basis.

All of the surviving members of the Sons had indeed

committed suicide, and it hadn't just been the ones in the castle. Apparently, members of the Sons all over the world had jumped out of windows and thrown themselves into traffic. No one really had any idea how or why they'd done that, and I wasn't talking. It was a freak thing, like Jason coming back from the dead, I said.

It wasn't that I wanted to hide the fact I might have some kind of crazy power. It was just that I didn't quite understand it yet, and it freaked me out. With the help of Agnes, who did indeed exist and live in an inn in Tuscany, I'd been able to contact some people stateside who worked with people with special talents. We were working on getting it under control, figuring out exactly how it worked.

"You want me to get the bottle?" I asked Chance as I entered the kitchen.

He shook his head. "It's my turn. I've got to figure out how to do this." He looked around the kitchen with a panicked expression. "Where's the formula?"

I pointed to the counter. "In front of your face," I said.

"Oh," he said, reaching for it. "Right."

I grinned at him, tousling his hair. He brushed me off.

The threat was really all gone. The Sons were all dead. The Satanists were all dead. There was no one left chasing Jason and me. Sometimes he still woke up in the middle of the night and sat straight up, searching the room for danger. Sometimes, I still had awful dreams. The one I hated the worst was the one where Jason didn't ever recognize me in that hallway in the castle and shot me anyway.

But Jason and I were talking. And Jason was talking to a therapist. He wasn't ever going to be normal. Neither was I. We both knew that. But we were doing the best we could. We'd enrolled in classes at the local community college. I was still undecided as to what I wanted to major in. I remembered that, sometime back in Bramford, I'd wanted to be a fashion designer. I didn't know why. I'd never sewed anything in my life. I was taking time to try to get to know who I was.

And I wasn't drinking anymore.

I didn't want to say anything as drastic as I was an alcoholic. Someday, I might be able to have a few drinks with dinner or something. But I wasn't even going to try that until I was legally of age.

I heard the screams of my niece Jenna before I actually saw either Palomino or the baby. I turned to the door, waiting for them to walk in.

Palomino blew wisps of her hair out of her face. "God," she said. "Can you take her, Azazel? You're the only one she'll get quiet for."

I held out my arms and Palomino placed baby Jenna in them. I smiled down at her, and she quieted immediately. Chance handed me the bottle, which I popped into Jenna's open mouth. I watched her suck contentedly. Maybe I was biased, but she was the most beautiful baby I'd ever seen.

I took Jenna back to the living room and sat on the couch next to Jason. He leaned over me to tickle her tummy, then smiled at me. "She sure does like you," he said, kissing me.

I smiled. "Yep. I'm good with babies, Jason." I winked at him.

He laughed. "Don't go getting any ideas," he teased. "We're barely eighteen."

I looked back down at little Jenna, so snug in my arms. Impressionable minds, indeed. It wasn't too hard to convince her to be quiet. And I didn't think of it as hypnotism at all.

Tortured for more?

The Stillness in the Air, Jason and Azazel: Apocalypse

Keep reading for a sneak peak at the first chapter.

Want freebies, information on new releases, discounts, and more? Visit my website to join my email list.

vjchambers.com

THE STILLNESS IN THE AIR

Before...

October 2012

I picked at a piece of lint on my sleeve, evading the question. "There was a guy," I said. "I haven't seen him in a few years."

The counselor nodded, leaning forward. "It didn't work out?" she asked.

I pushed my hair away from my forehead. She couldn't possibly understand how painful it was to talk about this. "We were teenagers, you know? It was that kind of crazy, silly sort of thing you think is love when you're seventeen. But..."

"It wasn't love?"

"He was violent," I said. "Not to me. He was always nice to me, but he'd get really angry sometimes, and he'd kind of go crazy." I paused. "Actually, that's not true. He wasn't always nice to me. There was this one time. One time, he almost killed me."

"So it was an abusive relationship?"

No! Well. "It was...it was just intense. I did things when I was with him. Things I didn't think I'd ever do. I still sometimes remember those things. Dream about them. I had a sort of problem with alcohol for a while. It was just better to get away from him. To get away from all of it. You know?"

"And there hasn't been anyone since?"

I shrugged, not looking up. "I've dated a couple guys. But...as screwed up as it sounds, being with them, it's like...it's boring. There's no spark, you know?"

"It's common for women who are abused to feel an excitement, to miss the adrenaline of the relationship, even though they know they were being hurt."

The counselor didn't know what she was talking about. And she was getting me off track. "Look, I didn't come here to talk to you about my relationships. I just heard that I could get prescriptions through the college for free. And that's all. I've been taking this pill for years. Will you give me the pills or not?"

"I just think it's possible, from what you've told me, that these pills are cutting you off from your emotions. Clearly, at the time they were prescribed, you were in a state where you weren't functioning. But it's clear that you don't have the same kind of trauma in your life. Maybe it's time to face yourself again."

"No," I said. "No, that's not it. Not at all." I needed the pills to stop me from being able to influence people with my mind. But if I told her that, she'd think I was nuts. "Never mind. You're obviously not going to help me."

"You have to talk about this to someone. If it's not me, then please tell me you have a friend or a family member — "

"Everyone in my family is dead," I bit out. "And no, this isn't something I ever want to talk about. Mostly, I just want to pretend it never happened."

Which wasn't easy. Things that Jason and I had done had pretty much permanently screwed up the world. When I'd used my powers to convince all of the Sons to commit suicide, I'd effectively killed off three quarters of the U. S. government. Now the government belonged to a bunch of Wiccan tree-worshippers — The

Order of the Fly. I'd given up hope that things would ever go back to the way they used to be. I got up out of the chair, ready to leave.

"I'll write you the prescription," said the counselor.

"You will?" I said. That was great. That was awesome. I sat back down. "Thanks."

"But I have to say that I wish you'd make some appointments with me. Maybe twice a month. To talk about this. I think you need to process what happened to you."

That was the last thing I needed. "I'll think about it," I told her. She smiled. "You do that."

I watched as she scribbled on her prescription pad, wondering why I hadn't just lied to her. I could have easily have just said, "No, I'm not in a relationship. No, I haven't had any serious issues with relationships. I just want to focus on school right now." Why had I opened up to her? I knew it was stupid to open up to psychiatrists. They never understood. They never really believed me.

I'd only come here for pills. Hallam and Marlena might be working for the government these days and since the government was overrun by the Order of the Fly, they might think it was practically criminal to suppress one's magical talents, but I didn't care.

The counselor ripped the prescription off of her pad and handed it to me.

"Thanks," I said. As long as I had the pills, I didn't have any powers. That was the way I liked it.

The lights in the office abruptly switched off, along with the hum of the fan overhead. The room went dark. I blinked, trying to force my eyes to adjust. I could barely make out the face of the counselor, who was frowning. "Was there a storm?" she muttered. "Maybe something just tripped a breaker."

I shrugged. We both stepped out of her office and into the hallway outside, which was just as dark. The college counselor's office was in the lower level of the freshman dormitory, and above me, I could hear whooping. Freshmen seemed to think anything at all was an excuse for impromptu parties. I'm sure they were all hoping the lights stayed out. It would probably mean cancelled classes.

I said my goodbyes to the counselor and made my way through the hallway to the lobby of the counselor's office. A student work study was on her cell phone behind the desk, babbling excitedly, "My laptop's got a battery, and I'm looking at it on the internet. The power's out all over the state. We're gonna be out of class for sure!"

I rolled my eyes. Predictable.

Outside, the sky was blue and clear. No storm. Not even a cloud. There were faint imprints of purple and pink dancing over the horizon. I squinted. What? Aurora borealis? In New Jersey? During the afternoon?

What was going on?

CHAPTER ONE

APRIL 2013

Kieran slammed the door of the beat-up Subaru we'd been driving. "So this Jason guy was like your high school sweetheart or something?"

I stepped out of the car myself, stretching. It had been a long car ride. I took a look around. We were standing in front of a church, which looked a little worse for wear. It had a high bell tower, which looked proper and picturesque, but the addition on the back of the building stuck out like tennis shoes on a prom queen. "Sort of," I said. "There wasn't much about it that was sweet, though."

The Kentucky air was warm, but we knew that since we'd been driving with the windows down the whole way. I peeled my shirt away from my back. It was stuck there with sweat. The car we had was equipped for air conditioning, but using the a/c was a complete waste of gas, and it wasn't like we had easy access to gasoline these days.

"Right." Kieran stepped over the trailer on the back of the Subaru and opened the trunk. We'd been dragging a motorboat with us all the way from Georgia. "He's psychotic or something."

Psychotic? That was putting it a little strongly.

Kieran handed me my bag. I didn't know why he was suddenly so talkative anyway. We'd barely said anything to each other on the eight-hour drive to Columbus, Kentucky. Things between Kieran and me were a little awkward.

I took my duffle and slung it over my shoulder. "He's not psychotic. Not exactly."

Kieran shoved his shoulder-length sandy hair behind his ears and grinned. "He tried to kill you, didn't he?"

Only once. And he hadn't exactly been himself during that moment. Of course, I guess Jason's sense of self was a lot different than what I'd originally thought it was. Especially these days. I shrugged. Was there any point fighting about it? "He's kind of psychotic, I guess."

Kieran lifted his own duffle out of the trunk. He half-grinned.

Damn it. Why did he have to be so freaking gorgeous? It would be a lot easier if he weren't. Of course, if he weren't beautiful, things wouldn't be awkward, because I never would have—

"Azazel!"

I looked up, looking for the person who was yelling my name. Marlena was at the door to the church, just under the tower. She was grinning.

I hiked my bag up on my shoulder and strode toward her. "Marlena, it's so good to see you."

She met me three steps away from the door and enfolded me in a tight hug. "I know," she said into my shoulder. "It's been too long." Marlena was black and British. I loved the lilting sound of her accent. And she was the closest thing I had to an older sister or a mother figure. I'd missed her.

She released me, and I stepped back to present Kieran. "This is Kieran."

"Your bodyguard?"

"Her partner," said Kieran, offering her his hand.

She shook it, raising an eyebrow. "Partner?" She smiled at me, mischief dancing in her eyes.

Kieran winked at me.

I cringed. "Not like that," I said. It had only been once. And I'd been drunk. And… I wanted to change the subject. "Where's your husband, the man in charge?"

"Hallam's inside. He's fiddling with the radio. It's down again." Marlena motioned us inside.

Inside the church, it was darker, despite the fact that the windows, originally stained glass, were all busted out. The air was much warmer, even though a breeze fluttered through the broken glass. I tried to remember what air conditioning felt like, or what electric lights looked like. It had been over six months since I'd experienced either.

"We got the transmission that you were coming," Marlena continued, walking us into the sanctuary, "but it went down the next day, and we haven't been able to get it back up." The sanctuary still looked like a church. There were plush pews lining the rectangular room. Most of them were covered with sheets, blankets, and pillows. Apparently, people were sleeping in here. The front of the room no longer contained a pulpit, however. A few drums containing gasoline were stacked against the wall and several pallets of bottled water. I knew the look of the provisions well. They came straight from the Order of the Fly emergency shipments.

Marlena walked through the aisle between the pews, heading straight back through the church. We followed.

"Has the situation changed?" Kieran asked. "Anything we should know about that headquarters couldn't tell us?"

"No," said Marlena. "He's still here. He still wants to see you." She paused and looked over her shoulder at me.

I cringed again. I'd been dreading this ever since Georgia. I didn't want to see Jason. I didn't want to see him at all. "That's not the only reason I came," I said. "You told headquarters something about the Key of Asher."

We stepped up onto the platform that used to contain the pulpit.

"Sure," said Marlena, "and you can talk to Lily about that after you see him." She stopped at a door at the back of the platform, her hand on the knob. She looked at me, and then she cast her eyes down on the floor. "He's different."

"We haven't seen him in years," I said. What did she expect? Or did she think I'd kicked him out of the house for no reason? He wasn't different, anyway. He'd always been that way. He'd just gotten worse at hiding it.

Marlena turned the knob and opened the door. "Well, if anyone can get through to him, it's you." She smiled at me.

It was my turn to look away. Get through to him? Whatever.

We walked out of the sanctuary and into a dim hallway. A little bit of light streamed through two open doors on either side of the hall. Inside one, I could see rows and rows of stockpiled ammunition. Guns were hanging on the walls.

Inside the other, a group of people were crowded around a radio.

"So that's still the plan, then?" Kieran asked. "We want to recruit him? We want Azazel to convince him to join us?"

"Of course that's the plan," said Marlena. "What else would we want to do with him?" She waved into the room with the radio. "Hallam!"

Hallam's shaggy head looked up. When he saw me, his face lit up. "Azazel, you're here!" He broke away from the others, dusting off his hands. He looked older. His face had more lines. He'd grown a full beard and mustache. There was a streak of gray in his beard.

Still, I was glad to see him. Hallam had been lots of things over the years: a guy I was terrified was going to kill me, the overbearing father figure I'd never wanted, and overall, a good friend. He was British too. I also dug his accent. He hugged me even tighter than Marlena had, nearly crushing my ribs. I oomphed as he released me, trying to catch my breath to introduce Kieran again, but Hallam was already pumping his hand. "Kieran, I presume?"

Kieran smiled. "Azazel didn't tell me this was going to be like a family reunion." He grinned, looking annoyingly attractive again. "Actually, she hasn't been talking to me much lately at all."

I glared at him. "Should I see Jason now? Is there any reason to wait? Anything I should know?" The sooner I got this ridiculous mission out of the way, the sooner Kieran and I could get back to Georgia. Hopefully, I could get us reassigned to separate units, and I'd never have to see him again.

Hallam shoved his hands in his pockets. "You don't want to rest after your drive?"

"Rest?" I repeated. I laughed. I guess I sounded a little bitter. "I haven't really had a chance to rest in six months. I doubt that's going to change any time soon."

Hallam nodded. "He's been tied up in the back room for days. He and a bunch of the locals have been giving us problems ever since we arrived. After we captured him, and he saw me, he's been asking to see you."

"I didn't want to tie him up," Marlena said, pleading with me to understand.

"He and his little group injured a member of our party," Hallam said. "We had no choice."

"It doesn't bother me that he's tied up," I said. But it did, a little. Not because I cared if he was uncomfortable, but because it didn't make any sense. Jason had broken out of a maximum security holding cell in England. There was no reason for him to stay tied up in a church in Kentucky. No reason at all. I swallowed. "Take me to him."

Hallam sighed. "If you're sure."

"I'm sure."

Hallam pulled some keys out of his pocket. They jangled as he walked down to the end of the hall and opened up one of the rooms. All four of us went inside.

The room had a smashed piano in one corner, and stacks of bent folding chairs in another. There was one window, high up on the far wall. It was still intact. It was closed. The room was stifling.

Jason was against another wall, his arms tied above his head. The rope was secured against a coat rack that was bolted into the wall. He wore a ragged t-shirt that clung to his muscular chest and a pair of cut-off jeans. He was sweating and his dark hair was pasted against his forehead. His eyes were closed.

Marlena reached for my hand and squeezed it. I let her, but the scene didn't bother me. Well, okay, it did. But not because I felt bad for Jason. I didn't give a flying fuck what happened to Jason anymore. It only bothered me because I was seeing him, and I really didn't want to have to look at him again. I pulled my hand away.

"Hi babe," said Jason without opening his eyes.

Oooh. So I was supposed to be impressed that he knew I was here without actually seeing me? Big deal. I crossed my arms over my chest.

Jason opened his eyes. He caught my eyes with his own. I clenched my teeth. He looked the same. "Didn't you miss me? I missed you," he said.

"Somehow, I've soldiered on without you," I said. I wanted to leave. I wanted to run out of the room and never look at him again. But they wanted me to try to get him on "our side." So I'd try.

"I want to talk to Azazel alone," said Jason, stretching his arms as best he could.

"Jason," said Marlena, her voice cracking. Jason and Marlena had known each other since they were kids. I'd heard him once refer to Marlena as the big sister he'd never had. It was killing her to see him like this. "We just want to help you."

"Just Azazel," Jason repeated.

"No can do," said Kieran, from behind me. He stepped forward, touching me on the shoulder. "They sent me here to protect you."

I stepped away from Kieran, shying away from his touch.

"They sent *you* to protect her from *me*?" Jason laughed. "They really underestimate me, don't they?"

Kieran's eyes darkened. "I'm not leaving her alone with you."

"What is he? Your idea of a rebound?" Jason grinned. His skin crinkled a little around his eyes. It never used to do that. It looked good on him.

I shook myself. Don't find Jason attractive, I told myself. Think of Jason in that car garage that night, with the body just a few feet away from him. Think of Jason telling you it was an accident, as if that made it all better. "It's been years, Jason. I'm past the rebound stage. Kieran and I work together. That is all."

"Yeah? Well, he doesn't look at you like a co-worker," Jason smirked. He wriggled against the ropes that held him. I could see that they were a little loose. Damn it. He'd be out of them in two seconds. Hallam knew Jason. Hallam had trained Jason. How could Hallam be so stupid? "I only want to talk to Azazel."

I turned to Kieran. "It's okay. I can handle him."

Hallam nodded. "She can. She's talked him down from worse."

Kieran didn't look happy about it, but he nodded once curtly and headed out the door.

Hallam put a hand on my shoulder. "We'll be right outside if you need us."

I nodded, pulling my pistol out of its holster inside my shorts. "I've got a gun."

They left. Marlena looked like she might start sobbing. I shut the door after them. I didn't turn around right away. I just stood, facing the door, staring down at the gun in my hand. I thought about turning quickly, before he had a chance to see what I was doing, and squeezing the trigger three times in succession. My aim wouldn't be good the first time, because I was turning, so I might miss. He'd have a chance to get free of the ropes. He'd go for the window, maybe, or the door. But he didn't have cover, and he wasn't armed. I could get him in the chest, I was sure. Maybe the head. And he deserved to die. He did. But…

I flashed on his arms around me while I was screaming, awakening from a nightmare. I thought of his deep voice, his gentle hands. I thought of how much he seemed to care about me then. I couldn't do it. Not all of him deserved to die. There was a part of Jason that was worth keeping alive. I just wasn't sure how deep he'd buried that part.

"You look beautiful." His voice was husky. "I had forgotten how beautiful you are."

I turned around, bringing up the gun. "Shut up," I growled.

He laughed. "Damn. You were always so sexy with a firearm. I'm getting all hot and bothered."

I reholstered the gun. "What gives, Jason? We both know you could be out of here in five minutes. Why the charade? Why stay tied up here?"

Jason laughed again. He slid his hands out of the ropes, easy as pie. Standing, he massaged his wrists. "I wanted to see you. You always hang up on me when I try to call."

He hadn't called in over a year. Part of that time, he couldn't, because no one really had phones anymore. Not on the east coast, anyway. For a few days after the blackout, the landlines had worked, until the generators in the stations went down or the people manning the phone companies had run screaming for home. Very few people even had landline phones anymore, though, anyway. At least half the cell phone service went out the instant the solar flare hit. It must have knocked out some satellites in space. Everyone else's cell phones stopped working as soon as they couldn't recharge them.

But before the lights went out, he did call me. Usually once every few months. It didn't matter if I changed my number. He always found me. "Well, I'm here now. What did you want to talk to me about?"

Jason crossed the distance between us in three steps. I started to take a step back from him, but before I could move, I was in his arms. He pulled me tight against him, one hand on the small of my back and the other tangling itself in my hair. I had forgotten what it felt like when he touched me. His caresses were white hot, searing into me. I didn't fight it. I was consumed by the sensation. His lips pressed against mine, and I opened my mouth to him, letting his tongue probe me. Fireworks exploded at the end of all my nerves. I melded my body against his, my arms going around him, exploring the sculpted perfection of his back, his shoulders. Ah, God. Jason.

And then I pushed him away.

He was startled, so I threw him off balance. He tried to step backwards to correct his loss of center, but he stumbled and thumped to the floor on his backside. I had my gun out again, trained on him.

He held up his hands in surrender.

"Don't ever do that again," I said.

"Right. Because I could tell how much you hated it."

I decided to ignore his sarcasm. I was angry. "You and a bunch of locals kept Hallam's group from getting west because you wanted to make out with me? Seriously?"

"No," said Jason. "I stayed tied up in this room, because I wanted to talk to you. I wasn't planning on trying to kiss you." He took a deep, labored breath and shifted his gaze to the ceiling. "Can I stand up?"

"I don't think so," I said.

"Are you going to shoot me?"

"I haven't decided yet."

He lowered his hands. His voice went low and intimate. "I don't think you'll shoot me."

"I might," I said. "I'm not seventeen years old anymore, Jason. You can't charm me that easily."

His eyes raked my body appraisingly, taking in every nuance. "Yeah. You're not seventeen."

I half-wanted to shoot him just for that. "*What* do you want?"

"I've only ever wanted you."

"That's not true. You used to want to be a normal guy. You used to want to have normal experiences, to live in a John Hughes movie."

"I'm not normal," he replied. "And in case you missed the memo, it's the freaking apocalypse. The lights went out. There is no normal."

"It's normal out west," I said, teeth clenched. My arms were starting to shake. I lowered my gun so Jason wouldn't see, but I didn't put it away. I hated it when he started talking about how he wasn't normal. It was his excuse for everything, and it wasn't enough. Not anymore. I was through forgiving him.

"If it's normal out west," Jason said, "then why haven't they sent any rescue teams to help us? Where's the freaking Red Cross?"

"The Red Cross' Administrative Headquarters was in D.C.," I said. But he was right. It didn't make sense. Even if the east coast had no power, and most companies were based there, why hadn't the rest of the entire United States responded to the crisis? Why hadn't other countries responded to the crisis? We couldn't communicate with anyone. We didn't know.

"There's no reason to go west," Jason said. "All I want is for your precious Order of the Fly to pack up and get the hell out of here."

"How can you say there's no reason to go west?" I asked. "We need help. People are dying. If you'd seen the things I've seen, you'd realize that."

Jason shrugged. "How can you be sure the people out west even want to help us? It's the freaking Bible belt. Face it, Azazel, when your precious Order of the Fly took over the government, all of the people out there hated it."

"Maybe they're trying to help. Maybe they can't. But whatever is happening, we know they had power. Right after the outage. We have to get across the river. And you and your little goons are blocking us."

Jason stood up. He walked over to the broken piano and began to plunk some of the keys. They didn't make any noise. "Here in Kentucky most people weren't crazy about the Order of the Fly either."

"Columbus was liberal," I said. "They got that Democratic candidate here—"

"Because it's a poor state, and they needed federal funding. Not because they agreed with the OF's agenda on religious freedom." He looked at me. "Understand, I don't care if they want to use magic, and they want to promote the rights of Wiccans and pagans. I never cared about that, you know that. But I'm not letting anyone go west."

He wasn't? Why did he care? "Why not?"

Jason crossed the room to me and took my hand. I pulled it away. He let his own hand dangle in the air for a few seconds and then he dropped it. "Things are good here. Now."

"What? Things are not good. There's no electricity. It's chaos."

"Yeah. There's no...there's no government. There's no authority. There aren't people with tons of power trying to throw their weight around and force people to do stuff they don't want to do. Everyone is free."

Was he insane? "There are mobs. There are gangs of people stealing food and gasoline, shooting innocent people. There are turf wars and starving babies. People are not *free*." I'd been travelling up and down the coast, trying to help the military keep order. I'd seen what the world had become.

"That will stop," said Jason. "Soon. I'm just not going to let the OF stick their noses into this and ruin everything. I will stop the OF. After I stop them, I can help everyone else. I can bring everyone back together, and we can all have freedom. We can live without anyone looking over our shoulders."

Kieran was right. He was psychotic. I took a step back, shaking my head.

"Can't you see it, Azazel? You and I were made for this. You wouldn't be working with the OF if they didn't recognize your talents were perfect for this situation. All our lives, people have prophesied that we would be important if something like this happened. We are the key players here. Why don't you help me? Leave the OF, and help me—"

"Help you what?" I said. "Rule the world?" I felt cold all over. Jason was mentioning things from our past, things that I thought I'd buried when I'd made every single one of the men chasing us kill himself.

"Help me help the world rule itself," said Jason. "With your powers, we could—"

"I'm not using any of my powers," I said. "Not anymore."

Jason looked shocked. "You're not?"

"You know what happens if I do!" He'd been there when we found out. He'd watched the tiny casket get lowered into the ground. He'd known that it was all my fault.

"Azazel, even Agnes told you that we were important to the future of the world. You and me. We're supposed to be part of this massive change that's overtaking everything. This power outage is the first step. And if you just run from who you are—"

"Who am I, Jason? Am I Kali? Am I the vessel? Your dark counterpart? The person who's supposed to save you? The person who's supposed to kill you? If this is the apocalypse, am I the messiah or am I the anti-christ?"

"We're both all of that," he said, his eyes burning. "But apart, we're nothing. You and I are made to be together. We are soul mates. You can't keep running from me. Not now. If you used your power, you'd—"

"No."

Jason must have heard something in my voice that told him I was serious, because he didn't say anything. He was close to me now. He reached out and stroked my cheek. I recoiled.

"Don't touch me." My voice was hoarse.

He was quiet for a little longer. When he did speak again, he was quiet. "You know that what happened was an accident. I didn't mean for him to get hurt. I wish you could forgive me."

"I wish it wasn't so easy for you to forgive yourself." I turned and walked to the door of the room. "They sent me here to try to convince you to join the OF and help us return order to the world. I guess that's a lost cause."

"I'll never join them. I don't deal well with people telling me what to do."

That was true, as far as it went. He'd never been particularly good with any kind of authority. I put my hand on the doorknob. "You might want to tie yourself back up again."

He rushed to me, grabbing both my hands. I tried to pull away, but he held me firm. "Azazel, is there any way you'll come with me? Please?"

He was just as exquisite as he'd always been. Dark, dark hair. Huge dark eyes like pools I could swim in. His heart-shaped face. I didn't know if I would ever look at him and not feel a stirring inside me. I'd always want him. But that was all.

"I love you," he said. "I'll always love you."

"I can't ever love you again." My voice was shaking. Was it from rage? Fear? Pain? I wrenched my hands away from his.

He looked wounded, like a little boy. Then he squared his shoulders. He laughed. "Tell Hallam, tell Marlena, tell the Order of the Fly to leave. Leave, or I will make you leave." His mouth twisted into a cruel, satisfied smile.

I crossed my arms over my chest. So it was going to be like that, was it?

"You know me," he said. "You know I can do it. They don't know what they're up against. Make them see that it's impossible to win against me."

"It's not impossible," I said. "If anyone's your match, it's me."

Jason chuckled. "I taught you everything you know."

I shook my head. "Not everything."

Jason turned the knob on the door.

My hand went to my gun. "You're not just going to walk out of here."

"Watch me."

I drew the pistol, flipping off the safety.

Jason's hand paused on the knob. He looked at me. "Are you fucking that Kieran guy?"

I was caught off guard. "What? No."

He moved too fast. His hand was on my wrist in a second, twisting. I let go of the gun. He caught it with his other hand.

Damn it. He had me. Jason pointed the barrel of the gun at my face. Fine, then. I could play dirty too. "Maybe once," I said. "He didn't need me to show him where my clit was."

Jason made a little growling sound in the back of his throat and seized my arm, twisting it. Good. I'd gotten to him. He yanked me against him, my back against his front. He put the gun against my temple. He breathed in my ear, "It's like our first date, babe."

Right. Me, Jason, Bramford, crazy Satanists, and Jason with a gun to my head. Except back then, I'd been sure Jason wasn't going to shoot me. Now, I didn't know.

Jason opened the door. He walked me into the hallway.

"Sorry," I said to the shocked faces of Hallam and Marlena. "He didn't go for it."